PRAISE FOR
KAPPA QUARTET

"Located somewhere between the shattered filmic worlds of David Lynch and Satoshi Kon's apocalyptic anime, Yam's narrative hypnotises us into questioning our reality in ways that are terrifying, revelatory and fundamentally profound."
— Cyril Wong, award-winning author of *Ten Things My Father Never Taught Me*

"Irreal and intricate, Daryl Yam's riveting debut teases the perimeters of what a Singaporean novel can be."
— Amanda Lee Koe, author of *Ministry of Moral Panic* (2014 Singapore Literature Prize, English Fiction)

"*Kappa Quartet* builds on the promise of Daryl Yam's short stories, and confirms that he is an author to watch. And read!"
— David Peace, *Granta* Best Young British Novelist and author of *Tokyo Year Zero*

KAPPA QUARTET

A NOVEL

DARYL QILIN YAM

EPIGRAM BOOKS
SINGAPORE · LONDON

Epigram Books UK
First published by Epigram Books Singapore in 2016
This edition published in Great Britain in May 2017 by Epigram Books UK

A CIP catalogue record for this book is available from the British Library.

ISBN
978-1-91-209872-9

Printed and bound in
Great Britain by Clays Ltd, St Ives plc

Epigram Books UK
55 Baker Street
London, W1U 7EU

10 9 8 7 6 5 4 3 2 1

www.epigrambooks.uk

To my family: John, Christine, Derek & Davyn

"Words, sounds, speech, men, memory, thoughts fears and emotions—time—all related... all made from one... all made in one."

—JOHN COLTRANE

CONTENTS

PART ONE

1

THE BOX

DECEMBER 2011

MR ALVIN

I met the kappa Mr Five, at an izakaya in Kichijoji two years ago. The most distinct thing I remember about the place was the laughter: there were bright peals of it, small, crystal clear eruptions of it, like the sound a can of beer makes when the tab is popped open. And yet no matter how often I looked over my shoulder that night I couldn't tell where it came from. The laughter came from everywhere and landed somewhere else, some other place other than myself, my heart the very thing that came too close to bursting.

I don't know how I ended up in Kichijoji that December evening. I don't recall having gone to that neighbourhood the last time I had been in Tokyo, and that was another five years back: my wife and I had come for our honeymoon, in 2006, and we'd spent a week and a half in the city. I'd booked us a suite at the Grand Hyatt, and we were there to see the cherry blossoms, it being the season in early April.

But there was nothing to see in December. There were no flowers: only the bright lamps of streetlights, and neon signboards clamouring for attention. I tried to recall the very last thing I did, just before I'd ended up there, but nothing came to mind.

Quickly I went into a nearby store and bought myself a thick winter jacket, with fur lined along the hood. It was cold, after all. I then made a list of my belongings: I had my wallet, the clothes on my person, and my Blackberry. Sitting inside my briefcase was my passport, and several documents from work. I had everything, that much I knew, but the signal on my Blackberry was dead. I looked around me, confused. Lost. For a moment, I wondered if this was all a dream.

It was a little past nine when I stepped into the izakaya.

It took a lot of wandering around, down a long and narrow alley right outside the Park Exit of the train station; it was crammed with restaurants and diners on either side, and there were many passers-by walking up and down the road, looking at signs and menus and storefronts. I realised I probably hadn't eaten at all that day, even though, for some reason, I found myself strangely devoid of an appetite. I was nevertheless aware that I needed to put something in my system, and thus persisted in my search. Eventually I found the place, towards the end of the alley—the entrance to the izakaya was very nondescript, just a wooden sliding door—but I managed to catch a glimpse of its interior as a customer took leave: dark panelled floors and beige papered panels, with ornate lamps wrought in a dark, greenish metal. I stepped inside.

There were customers everywhere, seated in booths tucked in incredible corners. I noticed this immediately. For a second I feared the place was too busy, but a waiter quickly made his approach, and directed me to take my shoes off at the front and deposit them at a locker. He then led me towards a seat by the counter, behind which a number of cooks were busy grilling and cooking up the orders. I watched, amazed, as great fumes rose from their stations, into the vents installed in the ceiling. I turned to the waiter and requested an English menu.

"I want this," I said later to the boy. "This please." I had my finger on a glass of beer, ¥460, and the waiter nodded and left. I removed my newly-bought jacket as I watched him go, and started to fan myself with the front of my shirt. The izakaya felt unusually warm and stuffy, but I was grateful for that. I then heard a man laugh beside me, seated on my left at the counter. I turned to see that he was laughing at me.

"It is a nice atmosphere, is it not?" the man said.

"You speak English?"

"I do," he said. "Quite well, in fact."

The man smiled. His face was covered in large boils, from the base of his jaw to the top of his hairline. They seemed especially huge, under the yellow light and oily fog, and each boil seemed to be about an inch wide. They looked like they might have overwhelmed his facial features, but his eyes, big and bulbous, remained full of expression. The man raised a tall glass of beer to his mouth and asked what my name was, and I told him I was Alvin, a Singaporean. He said that he was Mr Five.

"Mr Five?"

He nodded. He then held up a hand. "Five," the man said, "as in the level of ground motion Tokyo endured during the Tohoku earthquake." He extended that hand towards me. "It is nice to meet you."

I shook his hand. "It's nice to meet you too."

Mr Five drained the last of his beer as the waiter came back with mine. "Not having another one?" I asked. He shook his head. "I am driving tonight," he said to me. "One glass will do just fine."

I nodded. I took a sip from my glass and felt the cold beer run down my throat. Mr Five watched as I did so.

"You look lost," he said.

"Lost?"

"Like you came here by accident," he said. I told him that was mostly true. He then looked at my clothes: a blazer over a white linen shirt, complete with a tie in dark blue. He asked if I had business in Tokyo, in this particular part of town, and I told him I didn't.

"I wouldn't call it that," I said.

Mr Five watched as I took another drink. "Are you here on holiday, then?"

I thought about it. "I don't think so," I said. "I wouldn't call it that either."

He frowned. "So you are neither here for work, nor for vacation."

"That's right."

Mr Five leant back in his chair. "So what brings you to Tokyo, then? If you do not mind me asking."

I shrugged. "I don't know, actually. I can't even recall how I woke up this morning," I added.

He narrowed his gaze towards me. "When did you arrive in Tokyo, Mr Alvin?"

"I—I'm not sure."

"And is this your first time here?"

"No," I said. "This is my second time."

"Your second?"

"Yes. My second," I said. "The first time, I came with my wife. It was our honeymoon."

Mr Five turned in his seat. He grabbed the menu, and appeared to look at the food.

"And was it a good honeymoon, Mr Alvin?"

I blinked. "Yes," I said. "But there was a hiccup."

He looked towards me, a deeper frown etched across his face. The boils along his brows clustered tighter together.

"What do you mean?" he asked. "I do not quite understand."

I took another drink from my beer. I set the glass back down. Somehow the man seemed genuinely concerned.

"It was our eighth day in Tokyo," I began. "We were due to leave in two days, and we talked about how we should spend our last moments in Japan. We worked out a good plan, mapped out where we wanted to go. We then went straight to bed. The night couldn't have gone any smoother."

"But?"

"Well, my wife couldn't be found the next morning. I woke up and she wasn't there."

He asked me what I meant. I thought about it. I told him it was as though she had simply vanished. I said, "You could still make out where she had slept the night before, on her side of the bed. You could still smell her scent on the pillows. And her things, they were all still in our room. Her suitcase was still open beside the dresser, full of her things. But she was gone."

"All you had were remains," said Mr Five. "The remains of a person."

"Exactly," I said. "I panicked, of course. I didn't know where she had gone. I thought she might have gotten breakfast or something, but she was nowhere to be seen at the restaurants. I went to all the other facilities—to the pool and the gym and so on—but she wasn't in any of those places either. It was only much later, at around nine in the morning, when I found her seated at the reception."

"The reception?"

"Yeah," I said. "I remember hurrying towards her, sick with worry. I asked her where she had been."

"And what did she say?" asked Mr Five.

"She said, 'I took off last night. The feeling just came over me. I took off to some other place and wandered around on my own, looking at things. And now I'm back.'"

Mr Five ordered a plate of fried chicken, and another bottle of beer for me. The basket of chicken smelt good, and yet I didn't feel drawn to it for some reason.

"Are you sure you will not be eating, Mr Alvin?"

"I'm sure," I said to Mr Five. "I'm all right."

The waiter left. Mr Five turned back towards me.

"I do not wish to pry," he started to say. "But I wonder if your wife ever did this sort of thing before."

"You mean, before we got married?"

Mr Five nodded.

"Well, no," I said. "I don't think so." I then told him that we'd been in a relationship since we were seventeen.

"Oho!" went Mr Five. "That is amazing, Mr Alvin. How did it begin, if I may ask?"

I reached into my back pocket; I took out my wallet.

"I fell in love with her when we were in junior college. It's like high school, but only for two years. Yeah. It was the first day of class, and we all had to stand up and introduce ourselves. Say one interesting thing about yourself, the teacher said. When it was her turn, she stood up and told everyone that her father was a taxi driver, not by choice but by necessity. She said she learnt to live without means. I think it really made an impression on everyone at the time."

"Especially on you."

"Yeah," I said. I opened up my wallet: notes, cards, receipts. "There was another thing we had to say, something about our aspirations in life." I paused. "She said she had no idea what she wanted to do. She said she didn't think she'd have an idea any time soon. But Yong Su Lin wasn't going to let something like that scare her."

My second bottle of beer came. I set my wallet aside, and thanked the waiter. I tipped its contents into my glass, and watched it fill up again.

"Why do you love her, Mr Alvin?"

I looked at Mr Five. "I find her beautiful," I said. "That's the first thing. The second thing happened a bit later, but it's this: whenever I look at her, I feel compelled to give her everything. Everything that I have." I watched the foam sitting on top of my beer, fizzing out of sight. "She disappeared again, you know."

"When?"

"About a week after we came back from Tokyo," I said. "She disappeared for four days this time. When she came back, I asked her where she had been, and she didn't want to say."

I returned to my wallet, and pulled out the passport-sized photo of my wife. I showed it to Mr Five. In the picture, Su Lin had short hair, and gorgeous skin. Her lips were thin, her eyes strong and penetrating. But her most recognisable feature was her nose: straight and well defined. It nearly hurt to look at her.

"She said I should try disappearing one day."

"Did she really?"

I nodded.

"She said I should take off to another place, be a stranger all over again." I put the photo away and zipped my wallet back up. "I told her that what she did wasn't disappearing, though. That it was just running away."

Mr Five kept his eyes on me. He looked at me, unsure of what to make of the situation. I continued.

"Su Lin said it wasn't running away if she knew she was coming back. She said it wasn't running away if she didn't have a choice in the matter." I took hold of the glass, and drank the beer. "And then she left it at that."

I checked my watch. A quarter past ten. Staring at the hands of my watch, I wondered if I was oversharing, and that I might have intimidated Mr Five. But he seemed unfazed, somehow, by Su Lin's vanishing acts. Instead he ate through his fried chicken fairly quickly, and wiped his fingers clean on a napkin. He smiled.

"Tell me, Mr Alvin—do you know where you are sleeping tonight?"

I told him I had no idea. I hadn't even thought about it. Mr Five cleared his throat.

"It turns out that I am driving back to my hometown tonight," he said. "It is in Yamanashi prefecture. I can drop you off at a hotel I know, located on the shore of Lake Kawaguchi. I know the owner. All I have to do is make a call, and I can have a room set up for you straight away."

I considered his proposal. "How far away is this place?"

"Oh, quite far," he said. "It is near Mount Fuji, if you are interested in that sort of thing. But the ride will only take another two hours of your time."

I checked my watch again. Ten twenty. "Will the hotel still be open?" I asked.

"I could call," said Mr Five. "I could call my friend and everything would be sorted."

I took my glass and drank down half of it this time. "You'd do that for me?" I asked. He nodded.

"Out of all the people in the world right now," he said, "I would do it for you."

After we settled the bill, Mr Five led me to the parking lot. His car was a silver Lexus, a rather impressive and roomy sedan, the back of which was filled with an assortment of boxes: Tupperware, cardboard, big and small, you name it. It was such a sight. I tried counting them all, but quickly gave up. I asked him if he was moving back to his hometown.

"Oh, no," replied Mr Five. "It is simply a delivery I have to make."

I opened the door to the passenger seat. "Would you

mind if I ask what's inside all of these boxes, then?"

"Not at all," said Mr Five, getting into the driver's seat. He put his key into the ignition and started the engine. "There is nothing in them, actually."

"Nothing at all?" I said, disbelieving. I looked over my shoulder. There were probably up to ten of those boxes, twelve. "They all look so different from one another."

"That is true," said Mr Five. "And yet they are all essentially the same, wouldn't you say?"

They are all essentially the same, I repeated to myself. "What are you delivering empty boxes across the country for?" I asked, and Mr Five chuckled.

"There is a need for everything, Mr Alvin. Even boxes with nothing in them." He paused. "But not all of them are empty, to be perfectly honest."

I asked him to clarify. Mr Five frowned and crossed his arms, as he tried to think of an answer. Finally he said, "One of the boxes is filled with an unknown substance. Nobody knows what this substance really is, even though we encounter it all the time. It is a part of our world, most certainly, and yet it is as indescribable as it is inseparable from our existence. It is beyond all description, but it is most certainly incredibly heavy." He smiled at me. "That is why I have to make this delivery myself. I cannot trust a mover or a delivery man to do the job on my behalf."

I looked over my shoulder once again. The boxes shook, ever so slightly, as Mr Five began to drive.

"Whoever you're delivering this box for ought to be really grateful," I said.

Mr Five nodded. "You are right."

The radio wasn't on, but I didn't really care; I turned to ask if he could switch it on, but then quickly changed my mind. I was seated on his left, and discovered something else about Mr Five that I hadn't noticed before: there was a cavity in the side of his head, a perfectly circular crater in his skull, a few inches above the top of his left ear. Its diameter was probably no wider than two fingers. I stared at it, long and hard, before I turned and looked out of the window. He's a good person, I reminded myself: a good person in a strange body. Buildings came and went as Mr Five drove further west out of the city.

"Do you have any children?" he asked.

"A girl," I said. "Her name's Michelle. And you?"

"Me?"

"Yes," I said. "What about you?"

"I have no children," said Mr Five. "But I have a wife. We have been married for a long time."

"I see. You must share many memories together."

"Yes, I would say. We do." Mr Five smiled. "We make a pretty uneventful couple, however, compared to what you have been through."

I turned towards the window. I said nothing, for a while.

"Judging from your silence, Mr Alvin, I believe there is still one more part of the story that you have yet to tell."

I kept my eyes focused on the view.

"The third time she disappeared, she took off for two and a half weeks. It was the last time, though. The disappearing thing didn't happen anymore after that."

Mr Five didn't reply. In the window I could see his reflection, his arms holding on to the wheel. There was a turn he had to make, and he made it; and then there was a traffic light, and he had to stop. And then the light changed. He kept on driving.

It was half past midnight when we stopped at the hotel. We had driven along a huge lake: it stretched so far into the night, I couldn't see where it ended.

Hotel Koryu, it was called; a hot spring hotel. There weren't any lights on in the reception, save for one spotlight trained onto the front desk. Mr Five turned back to me after exchanging a few words with the lady manager.

"According to my friend, you have a room waiting for you on the second floor."

"Thank you," I said to him. I then bowed to the manager. "Thank you very much."

Mr Five smiled. "She also tells me that a particular acquaintance of mine is still here, in this very hotel."

"Oh, really?"

"Indeed," he said. "Like you, I offered him a chance to stay at this fine establishment. If you do not mind, I would like to have dinner with the both of you tomorrow evening, at the dining hall down the corridor. I think it will be worthwhile, having the two of you know one another."

"All right," I said. "I don't mind."

"Thank you," said Mr Five. "As a matter of fact, I believe this person might be Singaporean as well." His smile grew wider. "Imagine the odds."

A while later, the manager and I stood side by side on the porch as we watched Mr Five get into his silver Lexus. After he drove away, the manager led me to my room, and passed me a brochure of the hotel's facilities. "Onsen and dining hall, downstairs. Private onsen, this floor. Outdoor onsen, this floor also." The manager then pointed down to the far end of the corridor. "That way," she said. She then bowed. "Goodnight, Mr Alvin."

I went into my room. It had a simple layout, with a mattress on the floor and a small television on a wooden stand. I took my clothes off and slid beneath the sheets. I closed my eyes and a wave—the sudden rush of it—broke over my consciousness. I slept for the longest time that night: it was a long and restful sleep, full of dreams, none of which I could remember. I didn't fully wake till four in the afternoon, and I stumbled about my room, trying to regain my bearings. Japan, I reminded myself. I was in Japan. I found a note slipped through the crack beneath the door: *Mr Five will see you at 7pm.*

I went down to reception at six forty-five. The lounge was gorgeously lit, due to an artificial fireplace in the central wall. There were a few kids in the corner, banging on a couple of old arcade games plugged in behind the front desk. I went over to the sofas and sat across from a young man casually flipping through a magazine. He had remarkably pale skin, as well as a head of rich, dark hair. He wore a grey cashmere pullover. Everything about him was slim, from the bridge of his nose to the shape of his legs. I took a random magazine from the stands and began to browse its contents.

The hour came and went. Once in a while I looked up from my magazine, and checked to see if a silver Lexus might be driving up to the porch. I noticed how the light, spilling from the fireplace, grew like a puddle of water: it seeped across the floor and towards the front desk, without fully reaching the corners of the place. It became pretty clear that Mr Five was a no-show.

Eventually I caught sight of the manager coming towards the lounge. She had two slips of paper in her hands, one of which she gave me, and the other to the young man. The note said: *I'm afraid an urgent matter has come up, and I can't stay in Yamanashi any longer. Please have dinner without me.*

I looked up from the note. The manager was gone—and so was the young man. I was the only one left.

I walked over to where the kids were. The lot of them had gathered around one of the machines. Pac-Man, it was, and I laughed for a bit. I then headed back to my room; I still wasn't hungry at all.

•

It had been July, the third time she disappeared, and she told me so in advance. "I think I'll have to go away again, sometime next week." She used the words *go away* as though she were taking a vacation.

"Do you know when exactly you're going?" I asked. She told me she didn't.

"I don't have an exact date," she said.

I asked if I could come along somehow, on whatever trip she had planned in her mind. Su Lin shifted: she turned to look at me, straight in the eyes in the middle of the night. We were both in bed at the time.

"The kind of place I'm going," she said to me, "is the kind

of place where only I can go. Nobody else can come along. You should know this by now."

I thought about what she said. Every word felt like a weight, like a heavy kind of thing that settled in the depths of my lungs. "I'm sorry," I said in the end. "I don't know what you mean."

She turned over. She grew quiet for a few seconds. There was a green star, shining from the corner of the air-conditioning unit, and it was our only source of light in the room.

"Alvin," she said. "I need you to listen to me, all right? I want you to cast aside all the thoughts in your brain, and listen very carefully to what I have to say. Can you do that for me?"

"Yes," I said. "Of course I can."

My wife remained completely still. Lying on her side, she barely seemed to breathe. I did that sometimes, in the middle of the night, straining to hear her breathing sounds. For some reason, I was convinced that Su Lin was going to die: not in some distant future, but in the now, the today or the tomorrow, and it would have all been my fault.

Finally, she spoke. She said: "There is this world, and then there is another."

"Another?"

"Yes. Another. And there is only one way by which you can escape."

She paused again. Her words kept sinking within me, in a slow, free-falling kind of way. My chest grew heavier by the minute.

"Which way is that?" I asked, but she turned back over. She laid a hand on my chest, a perfectly cold and smooth hand; I could see the bare nape of her shoulders, and the perfect creases in her neck.

Su Lin said to me, "The way by which you came, baby."

I was a wreck by the time she came back. Her parents had called repeatedly over the sixteen days, wondering where their daughter had gone. Twice they came over to our flat, demanding to know what had happened, where had she gone, why hadn't anybody said anything. I told them I didn't know. We had to call the police.

It was the middle of the night. I don't know what time. Su Lin stood at the front door, without a suitcase or a single piece of luggage. She looked as though she had simply gone for a walk and returned in time for supper.

"Hey," I said, and really, what the hell, it was all I could manage to say. I nearly fell to pieces before her, wondering what was going on. The whole time I kept wondering if this was her messed-up way of saying she wanted to leave. *I don't know anything*, I wanted to say to her. *I don't know anything anymore.*

My wife took a step forward. She kissed me, at the front gate of our flat, before leading me to the bathroom. My feet followed after her feet, my hand dragged forward by her hand. She was in control—she always had been—but at that moment, I was nothing. I was nothing, and I was also anything she wanted me to be. She took her pants off. She took mine off as well. She pressed her back against the wall, and hooked her legs tightly around my waist. We kept at it for an hour—fucking, and then stopping, and then fucking some more. "Come in me," she then said—"come inside me." I will never fully understand what happened that night, the way in which things unfolded; but all that mattered was that she had come back home.

A thin barrier had formed around our flat, over the next several days. I wondered if this was how happiness worked: how temporary it was, and how fragile; how it demanded your greatest attention, lest any misstep caused it to break. When I finally asked Su Lin where she'd been during those sixteen days, she told me she didn't want to say. "I want to talk about something else," my wife said. For a minute, Su Lin and I stood in the kitchen, saying nothing to one another; already I could feel the barrier breaking down, one flaky piece at a time.

"You should go away sometime. One of these days," she said. "In fact, the first time you go, you should just take off and not tell anybody. Not even me. Forget you have any ties at all."

I locked eyes with her. "Wouldn't you want to know where I am?" I asked. She shook her head.

"When it's time for you to go, you won't even know it yourself."

I continued to look at her. "You knew the last time," I said. "You knew you were going somewhere."

A month later we found ourselves in the car, parked outside the neighbourhood clinic. She had to submit a blood sample; her period hadn't come when it was supposed to, and she had suspicions that she might be pregnant.

They took their time, her and the doctor; I could hear them both, laughing along with the nurse, as I waited in the reception. Su Lin was pregnant, of course, with Michelle, but I didn't really know what I was in for back then.

She settled herself into the passenger seat as I started the engine.

"There was a song, playing in the clinic," she said to me. "Do you know it?"

I looked at her, trying to think back. There had been a lot of songs playing in the clinic. Songs I didn't recognise. I told her I couldn't remember.

"It was 'People'," she said. "Shirley Bassey."

I asked her how she knew.

"The doctor told me, after I tried asking the nurse. He said it was something his mother had listened to when she had gone through chemotherapy. Since then he'd play her albums in his clinic."

"Is his mother all right now?" I asked. My wife shrugged.

"Our conversation kind of ground to a halt soon after."

"Why is that?"

Su Lin looked out of the window.

"He asked me what I did in my spare time," she said. "I told him I didn't know. I do nothing but time still goes by."

Neither of us spoke again until we were nearly home. Something was on her mind, but I couldn't figure out what. There were all kinds of things racing through my mind as well, but I couldn't focus on anything to settle on. All I could do was drive.

My wife laid a hand on mine as I pulled up the brake. Her voice was soft when she spoke.

"I have one more thing I need to tell you," she said. "Will you listen to what I have to say?"

I didn't say anything. I merely waited for her to continue. She spoke after a few seconds.

"You will experience a particular feeling when you reappear," she said. "You will only experience this feeling when you come back, from wherever you've been to. You might hate that feeling, or you might like it. You might even like it a little too much."

I killed the engine. "What are you saying?" I asked her. "What are you trying to tell me?"

All was quiet in the car. My wife spoke after a while.

"I'm saying: you can either let that feeling go, or you can hold on to it as tight as you can. Whatever you choose, I won't blame you. I'll just accept your decision."

Neither of us said anything more. And neither of us got out of the car. She had her hand on top of mine, after all. Finally I said, "You're holding on to it, aren't you. That feeling you just talked about."

Su Lin nodded, quickly. "Yes," she said. "I'm holding on to it." Her voice had turned to a whisper at that point.

Five years later, it was my turn to leave. And it was true, what my wife had said: when it's time for you to go, you won't even know it yourself.

●

It was a quarter to five in the afternoon when I sat up in bed. Nearly a day had passed since that time I sat in the lounge; I had simply lain on my mattress, drifting in and out of sleep, occasionally switching the television on. I checked my Blackberry—still no signal.

I got up. I walked over to the mirror stand, groggy with

sleep. I couldn't focus. Some people have said my nose is similar to my wife's. Others have commented that my eyes are my plainest features, while my wife's are her best. As I continued to stare at myself, lethargic, I realised I hadn't eaten a bite of anything since I'd arrived in Japan. I slapped my hands all over my body, just to wake myself up—I hit myself, repeatedly, until my skin turned pink. Had I lost any weight? It certainly didn't seem that way.

Hoping a good shower might wake me up, I browsed through the hotel brochure, and took note of the outdoor onsen that the manager had mentioned. It was conveniently situated down the corridor, just like she said. In the end, I decided that it didn't matter if it was cold outside; I'd rather be alone than bump into the other bathers downstairs. I stumbled around my room, and searched for a towel.

The sun had fully set by the time I left my room. The length of the corridor, lit by ambient lights in the ceiling, was utterly empty as I made my way towards the bath. There was no sound either, save for the faint hum of the boiler, and the gurgling of water travelling down the pipes. There was a wide window at the end of the corridor, located just beside the entrance; I could barely make anything out as I looked through the glass. It was completely dark outside.

I went through the Male entrance and began taking off my clothes. I had never been in an onsen before, but I had gone to a jjimjilbang in Seoul, so I figured the same rules applied. I placed my belongings into a tray and shelved them into a locker. I then noticed a second set of belongings, pigeonholed in a far corner, in which I saw a grey-coloured pullover. The young man at the reception, I thought to myself.

I tried to peek. I could see him through the partition, seated in the middle of the outdoor bath. He was submerged up to his neck, gazing out at the view beyond. But there was nothing much to see, beyond the wooden trellis: from where I stood, I could barely distinguish the lake from the surrounding low mountains. Spanning the lake was a bridge, an expressway, with red and yellow points in the night.

I first warmed myself with a brief shower before sliding the partition open. The young man looked over his shoulder. I felt his eyes scan me from head to toe as I stood before him in the nude, with nothing but a small white towel clutched before my crotch.

"Cold?" said the young man.

It was four degrees Celsius. "Y-you think?"

He smiled. "Come in," he said, moving to the side. The water lapped over the edge of the bath. I tested the temperature with a foot, and then with a leg, followed quickly by the rest of my body. I let out a deep sigh as I settled into the water, and allowed the cold to leave my bones. I closed my eyes.

"It's nice," the young man said. "Especially before dinner."

I opened my eyes. I didn't expect him to keep talking. "I wouldn't know," I said. "I haven't eaten at all."

"I noticed," the young man said. "You're not hungry?"

"No," I replied. The young man didn't say anything more for nearly half a minute.

"I'm hungry all the time," he said.

"Really?"

He nodded.

"You're Singaporean, aren't you?" I asked.

He nodded again.

"That's right," he said. "I'm Kevin."

"Alvin," I said. I paused. "Mr Five brought you here, didn't he?"

"He did, yes," said Kevin. His pale face looked almost golden under the warm lighting. "I didn't expect him to bring a second person," he added.

"Hmm," I said. "He brought you here from Tokyo?"

Kevin nodded. "I was looking for a bookstore. In Nakameguro."

"I'm sorry," I said. "I don't know where that is."

"That's all right. What about you?" he asked.

I tried recalling the name of the place. "Kichijoji," I said. "Park Exit. You been?"

Kevin shook his head. We didn't say anything more. This time the silence lasted for about a minute or two, until he let out a snigger. I looked at him, surprised by the sudden laugh. He looked at me as though he felt guilty.

"It's a bit pervy, isn't it?" he said. "When it's just two men in a tub."

"You're a joker," I said. "But this bath is outdoors as well, so it's got that kinky element."

Kevin shook his head, and rubbed at the corner of his eye. "Are you having naughty thoughts about me, Mr Alvin?"

I let out a laugh. "No, unfortunately. No."

Kevin made a face. The young man looked almost discouraged. "That's too bad," he said. He turned back to the view beyond the trellis. "I'd make a good lover, I think. Or, at least, I imagine myself to be so. Except I wouldn't know for sure."

"So you're gay," I said. He nodded. "Virgin?" He nodded

once more. I said to him, "You'll find somebody eventually."
I then asked him how old he was.

"I'll turn twenty-two soon. And you?"

"I'm thirty-one," I said. "No, thirty-two. That's not too old,
is it?"

Kevin shrugged. He then took a handful of water and
splashed it over the top of his head. I watched as the water
streamed down Kevin's face, in thin, branching rivulets. He
had his eyes closed, and seemed to savour the moment.

"Can I ask you a question?" he said.

"Sure."

He opened his eyes, and looked towards me. "You're
married, aren't you? You have a wife and kids and everything."

I was surprised. "You can tell?" I smiled. "Just one kid,
though. Michelle. She's four and a half."

He asked if I was planning for a second child. I told him
I didn't know. I told him my wife and I didn't even plan for
the first. Michelle just happened—a heat of the moment sort
of thing. Kevin kept quiet, and continued staring into the
distance. He then asked if marriage was easy. I told him I
didn't know.

"Is it hard?" he asked.

"I don't know either."

A pause.

"Does it make you happy?"

I tried not to flinch. "Yes," I said to him. "I'm the happiest
man I know."

I looked down towards the water. I then followed what
he did: I took a handful of water, and splashed it on my face.
I could feel the same rivulets of water, finding paths of least

resistance across my face. But none of the heat entered my head. Kevin leant back against the side of the bath, and rested his head on the edge.

"It's strange," he said. I asked him what was. He said, "I don't know why Mr Five would want us both to meet." He rolled his head to the side and looked at me. "We're such different people, you and me."

I didn't know how to respond to that. "Are we really?" I asked. Kevin leant forward again.

"Let me ask you another thing." He looked into my eyes, as intently as he could muster. "What do you see, when you look into the mirror?"

I tried to imagine. I tried to recall the last time I had consciously looked into one, and thought back to that time in my room, when I had wondered if I'd lost weight or not. "I don't know," I said to him. "I never really think about this kind of thing."

"Not at all?"

"More or less. If I were to look in the mirror—and I mean like, really, really look—I wouldn't know what I'd see, to be honest."

Kevin paused for a few seconds. "That sounds worrying," he said. "Sounds like the onset of a mid-life crisis, Mr Alvin. Then again, thirty-two's a bit young for that." He gave me a smile. "You've still got time."

"Thanks," I said. "Whatever that means." I took a second look at myself in the bathwater. I watched the bottom half of myself shimmy and turn in all sorts of directions. "What do you see, Kevin? When you look in the mirror?"

"You want to know?"

"Yes," I said. "I want to know."

His smile grew tight over his face. "I try not to look in them," he said to me.

"Why not?"

The young man didn't answer for a while. I waited. Finally, he said, "Whenever I look into the mirror, I see a lot of people. Lots and lots of people. And they are all trying to squeeze into that same frame of glass, and that makes me sick." He then paused for a few more seconds, before looking towards the lake beyond. "What do you see?" he asked. "Out there?"

I strained my eyes. I had been looking this whole time, but not really looking. "Not much, really. Just darkness, I suppose."

"Lots of it?"

"Definitely," I said. "Lots and lots of it."

"That's nice," said Kevin. I looked at him again. His eyes felt especially far away now; they were fixed onto something else, something beyond reach for either of us. Eventually he spoke again, and softer this time.

"Sometimes I feel so empty, Mr Alvin."

I turned away from him. I then rested my head on the edge of the bath. I could see why Kevin had earlier assumed that position. I could feel my entire body stretch across the onsen, the current of water lapping itself between my thighs. I could feel my body floating.

"Do you feel empty? Really?"

Kevin didn't move. "Yes," he said. "I do."

I smiled.

"That's nice."

I returned to Singapore the following day. At the front desk I left a note for Mr Five, expressing my thanks for his help. I took a train back to Tokyo, and then another to Narita. When I touched down at Changi Airport, I took a taxi straight home. It was raining.

My Blackberry buzzed repeatedly during the ride. Work e-mails, I saw. I watched as my inbox grew bigger and bigger, the messages stacking on top of one another. I ignored them and set the Blackberry aside.

Back home, I took out my keys. I unlocked the front gate, followed by the front door. I stepped inside. It was dark both outdoors and indoors: it was night, and yet all of the lights were still off. My hand groped along the wall, fumbling for the switch. *No one's home*, I thought to myself, until I heard a faint sound coming from the bedroom. I walked in.

It was my wife. She was on her knees, seated before the stereo. Her eyes were closed. Music was playing: "People" by Shirley Bassey. I could tell now. "Do you know Barbara Streisand first recorded this song?" my wife said to me. "The song was originally hers. There was a musical called *Funny Girl*, made ages ago. But Shirley Bassey sings it much better, I think. She did a much better job."

I knelt beside her on the floor. I told her I was glad she felt that way. We were so very close. A part of me wondered where Michelle was, but another part of me didn't care. She let out a gasp—*oh*—as I felt my way into her panties. Su Lin was so wet I couldn't believe it, and I slid a finger inside. I got hard in no time at all.

"You know that feeling you talked about? The feeling that you said was so strange?"

Oh. Oh. "Of course I remember." Oh.

I put a second finger inside her. Su Lin grabbed my wrist and forced my hand even deeper between her thighs.

"I'm letting go now," I said to her. "I'm letting that feeling go."

"You're letting it go," she said.

I nuzzled her neck. "I'm letting it go."

The next morning, I got out of bed and went straight to the office. It was a Sunday, and so nobody was in. I packed my things in a box and typed a quick e-mail, detailing my resignation. I then left the office and dumped the box in a trash bin outside.

Everything had been cleared out by the time I got back home. There was nothing left: nothing in the kitchen, the living room, the bedroom. Even Michelle's things were gone. Everything I had touched, she took away from me. It's not that she'd disappeared again, nor do I think she ran away. But I knew she wasn't coming back.

●

We headed down to the public baths, because that's where the vending machines were. They were lined up in one long row, in the resting area on the first floor. It was a lounge much bigger than the one in the reception: there were sofas and armchairs and coffee tables; plenty of people walking about in robes, stretching their arms and legs out after their long baths.

Along the wall were several television sets, airing whatever

channel was on: on one of the screens there was Bill Murray
in one shot and Scarlett Johansson in the next. She was
wearing a pink wig over her hair. They were singing karaoke,
the two of them; Japanese subtitles flashed across the bottom
of the screen as they gave one another fleeting, meaningful
looks. Behind them stood the city of Tokyo, shrouded in
bokeh. Kevin took a seat beside me with a bottle of milk in
his hand. For a while, we said nothing but watched what was
on TV.

"I have a dream sometimes," he said.

"A dream?"

He nodded.

"It's this one particular dream, and it recurs from time to
time. I don't exactly know why. I dream I am in the middle of
a pool, and there's no one around me. Nobody whatsoever.
It's just me in the middle of a pool, and I am floating on the
surface, half in and half out of the water like I'm supposed
to. I can feel the water in my ears, hear it block out all the
sound—and all I can hear is that fine line, you know? The
line that's supposed to be pure silence, but isn't." He took a
sip of milk. "That's the kind of dream I have."

2

THE ANUS IS THE CENTRE OF THE SOUL

MAY 2012

Haruhito Daisuke

"A taxi burst into flames that morning," the young man said. "It burst into flames in the middle of a tunnel."

I didn't say a word. I just looked into his eyes and nodded twice. As he paused, I stole a glance at the fish tank, standing in the corner of his bedroom. It was a fairly large one, about a metre long and half a metre wide, and in it swam a single catfish. Its skin was of the pearly white variety, but its fins and whiskers appeared to be dotted by flecks of black ink. It lay motionless at the bottom of the tank, gazing out of the glass. I had wanted one of my own once, but my daughter Kawako objected to the idea. *Think of the space*, she'd said.

The young man continued. "It was a terrible accident. But it was kind of awesome, you know?"

I crossed and recrossed my legs, and clicked on my ballpoint pen. I flipped open my memo pad, turned to a fresh page, and wrote down the young man's name.

"What morning is this again?" I asked.

"On the twenty-fourth of April," he replied.

A month ago, I noted to myself, as I wrote down the date on my pad: *24 April 2012*.

"Thank you," I said to him. "You appear to be very good with dates, Mr Lim."

"Am I?"

I nodded again. "Whenever I ask my clients to recollect the precise date of events, they usually can't recall as quickly as you have demonstrated. Most of the time they end up scrolling through the calendars on their phones."

"I guess that can be quite troublesome," the young man remarked.

"Occasionally," I said. "Do taxis burst into flames very often?"

"What," the young man said, "in Singapore?"

I didn't say a word.

"Well, no," said the young man. "Nah. That's the first time such a thing has ever happened." He then leant forward on his chair. "Why do you ask? Do you think it might have something to do with…"

I looked up from my memo pad. "With?"

"You know," he said. "My *condition*."

I gave him a smile. "It might, or it might not. As of now I'm not entirely sure. But if you promise to tell me everything that happened to you on the twenty-fourth of April, from start to finish, I might just be able to give you an answer."

The young man nodded. "Okay," he said. He then looked down towards his feet. "I guess you must see a lot of people like me."

I shifted in my seat. "To tell you the truth, Mr Lim: quite rarely."

●

There are not many names for the kind of people in my line of work. Over the past thirty years or so, I'd been referred to as many things: an investigator, a private eye, some say a therapist; a relative of mine once called me "the fortune-teller" during a family gathering, which I found to be a far cry from anything that I actually did. I didn't even pretend to tell fortunes. I would stress that I am an ordinary man with no extraordinary talents; I merely have a keen eye for detail, and a penchant for the English language. If I were thus compelled to give a title to my profession—anything along the lines of *doctor*, *banker*, or *lawyer* for example—I would call myself a specialist. People in my line of work tend to refer to one another as such.

On the night I was informed of Mr Lim's situation, my daughter was paying me a visit in the Tokyo office. Her name, Kawako, means "a child of the river". In many senses I find it appropriate. She seems to spill, continually, towards the sea, while her worries stem from an unknown point, from a place beyond what I can detect. She brought me dinner that evening, and watched as I opened my bento box. She often reminded me of her mother, especially with her long, curly hair. But her height, her lankiness and the pointedness of her ears—all of those came from me.

Kawako smiled as I picked up a radish with my chopsticks.

"I don't know how I ended up like this," she said to me.

I chewed on my food. I swallowed.

"Like what?" I asked.

She shook her head. "Like I have nothing to say anymore."

I didn't know how to respond. And then the call came—from a fellow specialist based in Singapore. My secretary said that it was an urgent matter. I looked at Kawako.

"Go on," she said. "Take it."

I picked up the call. The specialist at the other end of the line was a woman named Ms Neo. She had a friend of a friend whose son was suffering from a particular problem.

"What kind of problem?" I asked in English.

"It's very hard to explain," she said to me. "I don't exactly know how to put it."

"In the simplest of words, then," I said to her.

She laughed. "Sure," she said. Ms Neo then said nothing else over the next several seconds. On my end, I watched as Kawako turned her head, first towards the ceiling, and then towards a wall.

"You must understand that this is an unusual situation—it's a case I've never seen or heard of before," began Ms Neo. "I spoke to another colleague about it; his name is Ahab, and he confessed to being unable to help at all. He then recommended I speak directly to you, Mr Haruhito."

"I see," I said in reply. I knew the name: Ahab. "I must say you've made me very curious."

Ms Neo laughed again. "Thank goodness, then," she said, although I could sense the tone in her voice beginning to harden. "I believe this young man—this son of a friend of a friend—might have lost something very important to him. Something so important, so crucial to his very nature, that he didn't even sense its loss."

"What do you mean?" I asked. "What exactly did this man lose?"

I imagined her shaking her head, rubbing a finger along her temple. "I think he might have lost his soul," she said.

I couldn't believe it. "His soul, you say? That's something nobody should be losing." Kawako remained blank, unmoving. "How did you arrive at this conclusion, Ms Neo? Did you personally see this young man?"

"I did," came the voice from the receiver, as Kawako got up from her chair. I kept my eye on her. "The thing is, the young man is completely fine. He acts as though nothing in his life is out of place, one hundred per cent functional." Kawako walked towards the centre of my office, slowly, her arms raised above her head—I didn't know what she was doing. "I asked him the other day, how he felt about the piece of news, and he told me he was okay." Kawako moved her hips. She snapped her head to the side. She moved her hips again. "But he's not, Mr Haruhito: if you know where to look, and if you look at that spot hard enough, you can see it for yourself." Kawako was dancing, I realised; she danced as though she were in pain. "The young man has lost his soul."

●

Mr Lim lived along Sixth Avenue in Singapore, in a small two-storey terrace house off the main road. His bedroom was located on the second floor. The air-conditioning unit hummed softly as it blew a soft breeze around the room, and cooled the parquet tiles beneath my feet.

His room seemed ordinary enough: a queen-sized bed in one corner, and a few movie posters along the wall. There was a study desk, placed below the window; a sliding-door wardrobe, just across from the bed; a tall bookshelf, sparsely littered with books and DVDs. Aside from the door that led to the corridor, there was one that led to an en-suite bathroom, and another to a balcony. And then there was the fish tank, and its quiet, scaleless inhabitant. The whiskers of the catfish probed the walls of the tank, like the feelers of a large insect.

In another sheet on my memo pad, I jotted down all the other details concerning Mr Lim that his mother could supply. His first name was Kevin, and his Chinese name was Wenlong; an only child, he was born on 16 January 1990 in KK Women's Hospital. His was a natural birth, but the doctor had to extract him via vacuum, because his mother had become too tired to push in her fourth hour of labour. For the next three months, while his skull was still soft, his father would put a hand over Mr Lim's head and rub it in a circular motion, just to coax the shape of his skull back into a perfect, round shape.

His father passed away from late-stage colon cancer in 2009, when Kevin was repeating his second year at Hwa Chong Junior College. He and his mother had visited the man many times at the hospital, adjusting their schedules around his visiting hours. It was on his father's deathbed that Kevin confessed to his parents that he was a homosexual;

they felt glad and relieved, to a point: like most parents, it was something they had always known. From 2010 to 2011, Mr Lim fulfilled his National Service, and moved on to an internship at Singapore Press Holdings, as a journalist for one of their local dailies.

"Is he currently in a relationship?" I'd asked his mother.

"Not to my knowledge," she replied.

"Did he have any in the past?"

"None that I know of."

I looked up from my pad. "Why do you say so?" I asked. "Do you think he might be hiding them from you?"

His mother shrugged. Madam Lim was a senior financial planner in her late forties, and she possessed a natural poise and demeanour, a refinement that arose from a life of class. Her hair was long, straight, and well-maintained. Under the afternoon light streaming in from the veranda, I identified a rather prominent mole in the space between her neck and right shoulder, which I particularly admired. But Madam Lim was under a significant amount of stress; that alone seemed obvious enough.

"Kevin has no reason to hide them from me," she replied. "It's been three years since he came out to me and my late husband, and I've never had any issues with it. He of all people should know that."

"I see," I said in reply. With my ballpoint pen I wrote down the words *single* and *virgin (?)*. "What does your son want, most of all?"

She seemed perturbed.

"Is that a serious question, Mr Haruhito?"

I nodded.

She closed her eyes. "I think he wants to be loved."

I noted it down. "I see," I said again. "Has your son ever gone on any trips? Excursions? Has he ever travelled abroad?"

She cleared her throat. "The both of us try to go on holiday once a year. After his father passed away, we went to Kunming, the province in China where his father's family came from. Before his enlistment in 2010, we went to Rome and Venice, followed by Paris. During his block leave in 2011, we went to California."

"Is that all?" I asked.

"No," she said. "Soon after his National Service ended, he and his platoon mates went to Japan."

My interested was piqued. "Japan?" I said.

"In December, yes," said Madam Lim. "It was the month between his ORD and his internship. There were seven of them, and they had all decided to go on a tour to celebrate their release from the army."

"Which parts of Japan did he go to?"

"I'm not exactly sure. I know he went to Tokyo. Osaka? I'm not quite clear on that. Somewhere in between they stopped by Mount Fuji, I believe."

"So you're saying they went to Yamanashi prefecture?"

She shook her head. "I'm not sure," she said again. "Admittedly I'm not too familiar with Japan."

I smiled. "I don't blame you," I said to her. "My father is from Tokyo, but my mother was from Saga prefecture. I'm sure you've never heard of it. It's near the very end of the country, within the southwest region. The prefecture is particularly famous for its ceramics."

"Is that so?" said Madam Lim. "That's nice."

I sensed she didn't appreciate the detour in our conversation, and so went back to the matter at hand. I asked her when she first noticed any changes in her son.

"About a fortnight ago, I suppose—towards the middle of the month," she said. "It was a Saturday, around four thirty in the afternoon. I had a faint feeling that something was amiss since the start of the week, but I didn't fully come to realise it till the weekend."

"Why?" I asked. "What did you realise?"

She took in a deep breath, and exhaled through her nose. "It was something about the air in the house," she said. "Something lighter. It reminded me of the time the both of us had gone to Kunming. It was springtime, then, and I remember how light the air had felt, and yet how heavy it was with pollen, the scent of nature. It was like being in a florist's."

"How peculiar," I commented.

She shrugged again. "Maybe it's part of being Singaporean. Things like humidity, especially—we sense very keenly those kinds of things."

"I see." By then there were already a number of new words scrawled across my pad: *Yamanashi, Saturday, 4.30, before Saturday, spring, Kunming. The air.* "What else did you notice?" I asked.

"I realised the same feeling had applied to him."

"To your son?"

She nodded. "He felt like the air in the house: heavy, and yet light somehow. As though he was and wasn't there. Call it a mother's instinct, or a woman's intuition, but I knew that something was wrong. And so I called a friend, and then that friend referred me to, um—"

"A specialist?"

"Yes, yes. Ms Neo. She came round to the house, a few days after my friend had made the call. Just before Ms Neo left, however, she said that there was nothing she could do about the situation. I asked her to help me think of a solution nevertheless. And so she resorted to calling you."

"Yes," I said. "And so she called me."

Madam Lim gave me a smile. "As an atheist, I was rather grateful when Ms Neo said her work had no religious affiliations whatsoever. Is that the same for you?"

"Yes," I said. "We only deal with living things, Madam Lim. I suppose that's the most anybody can ever do."

"Right," she said. "And I understand you are a specialist as well? From Tokyo?"

"Yes," I said. "In Japanese, the word for specialist is 'senmon-ka'."

Her lips moved: *senmon-ka*.

I looked down at my notes. "Tokyo is a remarkably strange city, Madam Lim. It is stranger than most. But even then, it's been a while since I've seen a case like your son's."

"Well," she said. "You sound very experienced, Mr Haruhito. You must be a very busy man."

"I wasn't, actually. Not really." I gave her a smile in return, in the hope it might comfort her. "I am now," I said.

Her own smile faltered, by just a little.

I made a move to pack up my things. It had been a fruitful interview, I thought, but I felt that there was something more I needed to know. After I was done packing, I turned to Madam Lim and shook her hand.

"Can I ask you one final question before I go?" I asked.

"What do you want the most, Madam Lim? If you could have anything in the world."

She looked at me, uncertainly. She began running a finger down her collarbone. It seemed she was trying to gauge how serious I was again, and how honest she should be in turn. Eventually she said to me: "The life that I had before."

"Before what?" I asked. Madam Lim cast her gaze downwards.

"Before everything, Mr Haruhito. Before any of this ever happened." She paused. "That is what I want the most."

●

Nothing really remarkable had happened on the morning of the twenty-fourth of April. Mr Lim assumed it was the same as every other morning, because he didn't really remember much of it. He had gotten up at eight, taken a shower and dressed for work. He took his breakfast, and then rode the subway to Braddell MRT station. He arrived at his office a few minutes past ten. He had just arrived at his desk when his editor quickly informed him of the situation: a taxi had caught fire on the CTE.

"CTE?" I asked.

"The Central Expressway," said Mr Lim. "On the way to the AYE. It caught fire in the Kampong Java tunnel."

I shook my head. "My apologies."

"No worries," he said. He then spelt it out for me: *Ayer Rajah*, *Kampong Java*. The tunnel so happened to be rather close to his home, added Mr Lim; it was approximately ten minutes away by car. As I scribbled down the details, he then asked if I had to make a note on everything he said.

"As much as possible," I replied. "It's not up to me to decide if every detail counts."

Mr Lim nodded. "I get that."

After a quick debrief by the editor, it was decided that the photographer assigned to the story would drive them both to the site of the accident. The photographer went by the name of Rahul, and drove a Nissan saloon in a bright shade of yellow. In spite of its loud exterior, however, Mr Lim had noticed that there was nothing in the car except for a small water bottle, tossed onto the backseat. A tripod lay across the car floor.

Elton John's "Rocket Man" played loudly from the speakers as they made their way towards Cairnhill. There they parked the car, gathered their essentials, and trekked their way towards one of the smaller exits of the tunnel. According to Rahul, they had to enter the tunnel via one of the exits, which entailed climbing down a grass-covered incline. It was a pretty steep incline, and the grass was fairly shorn but thick. It normally would have been dangerous, thought Mr Lim, if either of them had lost their footing and tumbled down the slope, straight into passing traffic. But the roads were completely empty that day; not a single vehicle had driven along those lanes.

"They really closed off the entire tunnel," Mr Lim had remarked. The combination of heat and nervousness made him sweat rather profusely at this point. If he'd known better, he wouldn't have worn loafers to work that day.

"Yeah," said Rahul, his sideburns slick with perspiration. "They really did." Mr Lim saw he already had his camera at the ready, his right index finger positioned and steady on the shutter button. The only thing he had was his pen and paper, tossed into his satchel. Mr Lim refocused his attention, and concentrated on climbing down the rest of the slope.

The two of them got onto the road. Mr Lim looked at Rahul, observing the scene before them. He then looked at the Kampong Java tunnel and its ceiling looming over their heads.

"Walk to the side," came Rahul's voice from behind. "You're in the middle of my shot."

The exit they had walked through was Exit 5. Mr Lim had to calm the inexplicable pounding of his heart, as he situated his self within the vastness of the space. If it had been any other day, they would have been facing oncoming traffic, travelling at thirty-five kilometres per hour—but all they were met with that morning was the constant buffeting of a hot and sticky wind. It pressed itself against their bodies, causing their shirts to flap wildly like flags in the wind. How many lanes did the tunnel have? Was it four, or five? And how high was the ceiling? The facts seemed to have escaped him as the wind volleyed down the walls of the concrete chamber, filling his ears with a deep, sonorous groan. In reality the tunnel was only seven hundred metres long, and yet it felt as though they had walked for much longer.

Eventually Rahul had spotted a small white motorcycle, parked by the side of the lanes. "We're nearing the scene," he said. And then they found the taxi, or what was left of it, about twenty metres or so from the entrance of the tunnel.

"It was a total heap," said Mr Lim to me. "A complete wreck. I could just about make out the structure of the taxi itself: the hood, the bumper, and the wheels. You could still tell where the seats were, although that wasn't very clear either. The frame was charred and black and ruined, but it was also coated with this grey-white substance. It was a taxi by all means, but it had become so utterly reduced to, to—to whatever it had become. It was a taxi without being a taxi. Do you know what I mean?" he asked.

I took down everything he had said. "Were you reminded of anything in particular, Mr Lim? Any memories or recollections of past events?"

"Not really," he said.

"And did you linger long, Mr Lim?"

"We couldn't. There were the police, the fire department, the ambulances. LTA officials as well. They were all wearing these vests, you see—but either way they spotted us coming from quite a distance. It was a tunnel, after all, so you couldn't not see us. By the time we got close enough to take pictures, they told us to go. I left them with my details so they could give me their official statements later."

"And then?"

"And then we left," said Mr Lim. He shrugged. "We walked back out of the tunnel, climbed up the grassy slope. We returned to our car and drove back to the office. This time, however, Rahul took the CTE, and you could see this incredibly long traffic jam, stretching on for ages on the other side of the road, while it was completely clear on ours. It looked like one of those scenes in a movie—when the world is ending and everybody's trying to leave the country—but really, no one's getting anywhere."

No one's getting anywhere, I wrote. "What did you do at the office?"

He scratched his head. "I spent the rest of the day conducting interviews from my phone and typing up the article."

"Nothing else?"

"Nothing else."

"I see," I said. "Around what time did you get back home, Mr Lim?"

"Around nine thirty, possibly ten."

"And what did you do then?"

"I took a shit, had a shower and went straight to bed."

Shit, shower, bed. "What about dinner?" I asked.

"We had pizza sent to the office. It happens from time to time." He sighed. "It was very uneventful, after the whole thing in the tunnel. I can't say anything particularly special happened after that. All I did was sit on a chair, conduct a few interviews over the phone. And then I took the train back home."

"I see." *Chair, calls, the train.* "And yet somehow you managed to lose your soul, somewhere in between all of these events."

"Apparently I did," he said. "What else is new?"

I looked up from my pad. I clicked my ballpoint pen and set it aside.

"Do you not believe you've lost your soul, Mr Lim?" I asked.

He looked at me, with an unreadable look in his eyes. "I don't even know if it was ever there to begin with, Mr Haruhito," he said. "But something in me says I might have lost it on that day."

"As opposed to any other day?"

He nodded. He stuck out his lower lip as he did so. "As opposed to any other day."

●

It was towards the end of May when I next saw Madam Lim. It was a couple of days after I had conducted my interview with her son, a pre-arranged meeting to be held at Guthrie House on Fifth Avenue, during which I was to update her on any progress I might have made in my investigations. It was also agreed that Ms Neo should join us during this meeting, to provide a third opinion on my findings, if necessary.

I suppose the main question on my mind since the start of the case was why it had been referred to me. I was by all means an ordinary man of no extraordinary talent. There was nothing very particular about me, aside from the admittedly peculiar nature of my work—but this is something I shared with my esteemed colleagues from around the world, Ms Neo included. So why, then, did Ms Neo's colleague recommend my services to her? And why, then, did Ms Neo agree that my help was necessary in a situation like this? It was something I resolved to find out from Ms Neo herself by the end of our meeting.

We met at six thirty on a Wednesday evening, in one of the bakeries located on the ground floor of Guthrie House. It was a rather homey yet posh setting, with white tables and chairs laid out around a counter, beside long shelves of artisanal bread. I was the first to arrive at the bakery, followed shortly by Madam Lim and Ms Neo. My first thought upon seeing them was that they couldn't have dressed more differently. Madam Lim was suited in a tailored blazer and skirt, in bold, fashionable colours, while Ms Neo wore a plaid shirt and faded denim jeans. And yet from a distance, they managed to look like two sisters, leading two very different lives of their own.

They promptly sat on the other side of the table. In order to get the conversation started, I asked Madam Lim how her son had been faring over the past few days. When she answered, I noticed that her voice sounded considerably wearier than before. There were also these dark circles beneath her eyes that her light layer of foundation couldn't hide.

"To be perfectly honest," said Madam Lim, "I don't know."

She paused. I leant back in my chair and waited for her to continue. Ms Neo rested her left shoulder against the wall and looked at the corner of the table.

"It's the nature of his job, I suppose."

"As an intern?" I asked.

"As a journalist," she said. "There's not much difference between being an intern and a full-timer over there. An intern gets low pay and more slack for his mistakes. That's all. Other than that, an intern has to work just as hard. He works the same shifts and stays for the same number of hours."

"What kind of hours are we talking about?" I asked.

"On a good day, ten to six. On a really 'good day', he might not leave the office till ten o' clock, or even after midnight. That means he has a story to file."

I took out my memo pad and began taking note of the details. "Has he had a lot of stories to file lately?"

"I don't know," said Madam Lim. She pinched the bridge of her nose. "Unfortunately I don't read the paper he works for."

"I see," I said. "What you do know, however, is that he's not been home much."

She nodded. "That's right. I barely see him, let alone

bump into him in the house. I leave home at seven in the morning, and come back around six in the evening; he leaves at eight forty-five and comes back after I do. He even had to work over the past weekend. The only time I saw him was an hour after I had my dinner, about two nights ago."

"How was he?"

"Pale, sickly," she said. "I asked him if he was fine, and he told me he was. He acted the way he always did—lively, a bit snarky—but the complexion of his skin really worried me."

"I understand," I said. "Any other updates, Madam Lim?"

"No. That's all from me. And you, Mr Haruhito?"

I snapped my memo pad shut, and tucked it back into the pocket of my suit.

"I've made some progress, Madam Lim. But unfortunately I still don't have any answers for you, or for your son."

"I see," she said. "Nevertheless, Mr Haruhito—I'd still like to hear about what you've been up to, so far."

"By all means," I said. I thought back to the first step I took after Mr Lim's interview. Like opening a drawer full of folders, I ran over my memories until, finally, I came upon the right one. "The first thing I did, Madam Lim, was to investigate why the taxi had caught fire on the twenty-fourth of April."

Ms Neo leant forward on her chair at this point. "The taxi?" she asked. "Are you talking about the incident on the CTE?"

"Yes," I replied. "When I asked Mr Lim when he thought he might have lost his soul, he didn't know how to answer at first, which, of course, is a most natural response. Nobody immediately knows the answer to that question. But when I pushed him to provide me a date, any date that first came to mind, he told me about the taxi that caught fire that day: on the twenty-fourth of April."

"And you trust him?"

"Of course," I told Ms Neo. "There's no better source to trust than the source itself. That is my belief."

"So did you find out anything about the taxi?"

"Not much, in truth," I said. "Mr Lim showed me his notes on the story, as well as the statement he had received from the company that managed the taxi. They said it was a fuel leak, exacerbated by the heat of the morning."

"Who was in the taxi at the time?" asked Madam Lim.

"No passengers," I said. "Just the driver, a Mr Yong. I managed to make a few calls and obtain his details, his home address included."

"What for?" asked Ms Neo. "Did you pay him a visit?"

I nodded. "Yes I did, Ms Neo."

Her eyebrows were raised. "But why, Mr Haruhito? Do you actually think the driver might have something to do with Mr Lim?"

I shifted in my seat.

"No, to be honest. I did not. By the time Mr Lim entered the tunnel that day and saw the taxi with his own two eyes, the driver, of course, was long gone. If anything, the connection between Mr Lim and Mr Yong was a tenuous one. But it was a connection I still had to establish and enquire into.

"According to the driver's details, he lives in a public housing estate situated along Sengkang East Way, about a hundred metres or so from the nearest train station. His apartment is located on the ninth floor. When I went there

I found him and his son-in-law hoisting a brand new flat-screen television through the door.

"I asked the middle-aged man if he was Mr Yong. He said that he was. He then asked me in turn who I was, and what business I wanted with him, and I told him I was there to investigate how his taxi had caught fire. His son-in-law then asked if I was a representative from the taxi company. I told him I wasn't; I was a private consultant, hired by both the management and the taxi manufacturers to get to the bottom of the case, so that no incidents of this nature might occur again. I then showed them my card.

"'Your name,' said Mr Yong. 'Haruhito Daisuke. So you're Japanese?' I then bowed, and told him that I was. Mr Yong then rushed his son-in-law into the apartment and told me to follow him inside. I did.

"At first glance, Mr Yong's apartment didn't seem to possess anything particularly remarkable—that is, until he led me to a modest-looking piano, where a number of framed photographs had been arranged across the top in a neat row. He said to me, 'Come, come, Mr Haruhito. I need to show you something. There,' he explained, 'are pictures of my hiking trip last year. Eighteenth of November.'

"'I see,' I said to him. A closer look told me that the hiking trip seemed to have taken place in a rainforest of some sort, and that he wasn't the only one involved in the trip. Among the faces, I discovered, was the face of his son-in-law, who at the time was busy unplugging the television that was to be replaced. I asked Mr Yong why he felt compelled to show me these pictures.

"'Because,' Mr Yong explained, 'we were in the very middle

of MacRitchie Reservoir Park, in search of a lost shrine.' A shrine? I asked him, and he told me that it wasn't any old shrine: it was a shrine built by the Japanese in 1942, during their occupation in the Second World War. The Japanese demolished it in 1945, following their surrender to the British forces, but its remains still stand in the middle of the reservoir. The name of the shrine was Syonan Jinja." I turned to Ms Neo. "Have you ever heard of this shrine, Ms Neo?"

She didn't answer for a while. "Yes, Mr Haruhito," she said. "I have. Unfortunately the place is now in ruins. There remains nothing special about the shrine."

"I see. And you, Madam Lim?" I asked. "Have you heard of this shrine before?"

"No," said Madam Lim, shaking her head. "This is the first time I've ever heard of such a thing. Frankly I'm surprised the government hasn't turned it into a tourist spot or something."

"Hmm." I had ordered iced lemon tea for the three of us, and took a quick sip from my glass. "It appears that Mr Yong agreed with Ms Neo's sentiment. In spite of the sensationalism that might surround the existence of a 'lost shrine', it was nothing but a few steps on a stairway, terraced into the side of a small hill, leading up to the foundation of what had once been the shrine itself. He then showed me photos of what used to be a wide bridge, spanning a river, and how they had to circumnavigate it in order to access the ruins. There was another photo of Mr Yong's son-in-law, washing his face in the pool of a small bath by the side of the shrine. The only remarkable thing about the place was how moss had covered everything, and how, in spite of the mosquitoes, there was a freshness to the air he could never quite breathe outside of the reservoir. 'It's the trees,' said Mr Yong: 'Nature's lungs.' But that is all there was to the shrine."

Madam Lim blinked. "Nothing more?"

"Nothing more," I replied. "Nothing but a blank slate, where a building used to stand."

She turned to Ms Neo. "Do you sense that there could be more to this shrine thing?"

Ms Neo shook her head. "I doubt it. Even the connection between Mr Yong and the shrine is, to use your word, *tenuous*. If he had gone there in the third week of November, that would mean there was, what, five months between the shrine visit and the explosion?"

"It wasn't an *explosion*, Ms Neo. The taxi merely caught fire," I said.

"Well, it certainly was dramatic, Mr Haruhito," said Ms Neo. "I've seen a video of it. There was black smoke everywhere; nobody could see a thing from inside their cars. Did you ask the driver how he felt about the accident?"

"I did," I said. "Till this day, Mr Yong still doesn't fully understand how it happened. One moment he was driving, the next he realised that the hood was on fire."

"Was he frightened?"

"At first. On hindsight, however, he felt relieved. He felt very glad it happened."

Madam Lim frowned. "Why?"

"He said that compared to his hiking adventures, driving a taxi was horrible. There was no life in it whatsoever. All he did was go through the motions; day in and day out, driving down the same roads in the hope that somebody might flag him down for a trip to who-knows-where. Whenever he was stuck in a jam he'd look at the cars beside him, and see that their drivers were just as numb and bored and witless as he was. And whenever he drove down a tunnel in an expressway, he felt as though he had lost all control over himself, all sense of his limbs and his motions and his actions."

"Why's that?" asked Madam Lim.

"Do you drive?" I asked her.

"I do," she said. "As a single parent, I have no choice."

"What do you do when you drive through a tunnel, Madam Lim?"

She blinked. "You just—drive."

"And what can you not do?"

A look of realisation came over her face. "You can't stop."

I nodded. "Every time Mr Yong drives into a tunnel, he imagines the tunnel as something that never stops, as though the tunnel is longer than it actually is. Every time he comes out of a tunnel he feels a sense of release."

"Are those his exact words?" Ms Neo asked.

"More or less," I said.

For the next minute or so, the conversation came to a halt. I had nothing more to say. I took a sip from my glass of iced tea, which seemed to prompt a sigh from Madam Lim. She was pinching the bridge of her nose once more when she asked what my next step was.

"My next step, Madam Lim? I might have to conduct a second interview with your son."

"That's fine," she said. "I'll let him know when I get back home." She stood up from her chair, and slung her leather handbag over her shoulder. "I have to be home for dinner anyway; Kevin texted me during the afternoon to say he had a half-day off." She turned to her companion. "Would you like me to drive you to the nearest station?"

"It's fine," said Ms Neo. She gave me a look. "I'd like to have a few more words with Mr Haruhito, if you don't mind."

"All right then," said Madam Lim. She placed two ten-dollar notes on the table. "Thanks for the meeting. And for everything you've done, as well." Madam Lim then turned and left the bakery.

I took another sip of iced lemon tea and placed the glass back down. Now that it was just me and Ms Neo, I felt more inclined to express what I really thought about the case of Mr Lim's soul. But I also felt it was important, especially in cases like these, *not* to utter the first word. I interlaced my fingers on my lap and merely waited for Ms Neo to say something. Ms Neo, in return, got up from her seat and sat in Madam Lim's chair.

We were now seated directly opposite one another. One person's gaze became inevitably locked into the other's. In an exceptionally calm and even voice, she said, "I suppose the most interesting thing about the cab driver is the parallel he drew between the reservoir and the tunnel. Wouldn't you agree, Mr Haruhito?"

I couldn't help but smile. "It is a rather subtle link, Ms Neo."

There was a brief pause of a few seconds. She then said to me, "You know that Mr Lim couldn't possibly have lost his soul on the twenty-fourth of April."

"No, he could not," I said in return. "To my knowledge, it's possible to have your soul stolen, extracted, even disposed of. It's impossible, however, to *lose* it. No loss of autonomy or self-control will ever be enough to lose something so precious."

"But you know his soul couldn't have been stolen or extracted either," said Ms Neo. "Disposal is possible, yes—but theft, no. Petty crimes of that sort don't happen in Singapore, Mr Haruhito."

"So why would you say, Ms Neo, that Mr Lim had lost his soul? Was it to appease the mother?"

"Yes," she replied.

"And what about me, Ms Neo? Why lie?"

"I wasn't sure of the truth."

I raised an eyebrow. "And yet a part of me believes you are certain of what has happened to this young man. The only thing holding you back right now is fear."

She looked away. She shifted her gaze to a corner of the table. "It is my belief," said Ms Neo, "that he never had a soul in the first place."

"Indeed." I reached for my glass. With my straw, I quickly tipped an ice cube into my mouth, and began to crush it between my teeth. I leant back in my chair. After I was done with the ice, I told her I was fifty-eight years old, and went on to ask Ms Neo how old she was this year. "Twenty-seven," came her reply.

"And how long have you been in the profession?"

"Three years."

"Three years!" I said. "You've learnt more in three than I have in ten, Ms Neo. And you're merely a year younger than my own daughter."

A small smile played on her lips. "Thank you, Mr Haruhito."

I leant my body forward. "You must understand that this is a very *Singaporean* situation," I said to Ms Neo. "Where I come from, people don't last very long after they have had their souls stolen or extracted. What begins is a process of decay, and whether it takes a day, a month, or even a year depends entirely on the person's constitution. The same goes for suicide: in some cases, the disposal of one's soul causes instantaneous death, while in others the body never goes away completely— but even then, the damage to one's soul is permanent. But tell me, Ms Neo: what happens when a person is born *without* a soul? What would you call that person?"

"There's no name for that kind of person," Ms Neo replied. "Such persons tend to result in stillbirths, or miscarriages."

"Alas," I said. "And yet in Singapore, it appears that if one is born without a soul, one manages to live, nevertheless. One continues to live in spite of its absence."

"Hmm. That certainly seems to be the case, Mr Haruhito." She then redirected her gaze to my eyes. I looked back into hers and did not waver. "You probably think I shouldn't have had to enlist the help of a Japanese specialist," she said. "But I believe you already know the reason why."

I merely maintained my smile. "I do, Ms Neo. It appears that Mr Lim might have caught something during his recent trip to Japan last December. Something only a person without a soul could catch."

Ms Neo tilted her head to the side. "What did he catch?" she asked.

"The seed of a desire," I replied. "Do you know what a shirikodama is, Ms Neo?"

"I think so," she said.

"It is said to contain the essence of one's soul. It is also said to resemble a small bead, nestled deep in one's anus. *This*," I stressed to her, "is a particular belief held amongst a subset of Japanese people: that the anus is the centre of the soul."

"And thus the taxi."

"Yes," I said. "It is possible, Ms Neo, that when Mr Lim saw the burnt remains of Mr Yong's taxi inside the Kampong Java tunnel, a part of his subconscious flared into being, like an animal approaching a surface of water, encountering its own reflection for the first time. A part of him thus became self-aware, allowing that seed he had caught in Japan to take root and grow. And now he is on a hunt."

"For a soul?" she asked.

"Not now," I said, "not necessarily. But eventually."

Ms Neo nodded. She looked away again. At that point I felt a deep sense of satisfaction, as though my work here was more or less done; there were no solutions, but at least there was an understanding. I reached over to my glass of iced tea in one final attempt to drain it down. Ms Neo let out a sigh.

"Mr Haruhito," she said. "Would you like to grab a drink with me? I believe the both of us could do with a break."

I set my glass down and smiled. "It would be my honour, Ms Neo."

She took me to Holland Village, where we each ordered a beer at a bar. There were many other bars there, crowded along a single street, but the atmosphere was nice. It reminded me of the Shinsen area, but bigger. Ms Neo and I shared a single table on the sidewalk, and we sat on upholstered wooden stools. In the middle of a table was an ashtray full of cigarette butts.

"So," said Ms Neo, her voice raised over the volume of the bar's music. "You said something about a daughter?"

I nodded. "Her name is Kawako," I said, keeping my voice low.

"And how is she? How is she doing?"

I smiled. "I don't know, Ms Neo. I honestly don't know. She perplexes me, sometimes."

Ms Neo frowned. "Why's that?"

I shook my head. I thought it would take me a lot longer to reply to Ms Neo's question, but the truth was that I'd had my answer ready for a while now. "All of us are bound to go down our own separate paths," I said. "It took too long for me to realise that my daughter and I were never on the same one to begin with. She strayed away from me a long time ago."

Ms Neo grimaced. "I'm sorry," she said. "I shouldn't have asked."

"It's fine," I replied. "She lost her mother when she was very young; they barely even got to know each other. Since then, I've realised that her mother was always the better parent."

Ms Neo asked how old she was. I said, "Kawako, or her mother?" and Ms Neo shrugged. "Both?"

I rubbed my hands together. "Her mother was twenty-nine when she passed away. Kawako was around three or four at the time."

Ms Neo took a drink from her beer. She asked me what had happened, and I continued staring at my hands.

"Her mother had something very precious, embedded

deep inside her being. It was a very rare thing—it was terribly, terribly bright—and someone came and took it away."

Ms Neo looked confused. "'Someone'?"

I nodded. "You know of kappas, don't you?"

She nodded back.

"Then I have nothing more to add," I said. I then decided to switch the topic. "Tell me about yourself, please."

She smiled. It was a sad kind of smile.

"Me?" she asked.

"Yes," I said. "You."

"I'm sorry, Mr Haruhito," she said. "But there's nothing special about me."

I didn't dare to believe her. "Are you sure, Ms Neo? Everybody has a story."

She shook her head. Ms Neo had a pained look in her eyes; it was the same look Kawako had given me, during that visit to my office. She said to me, "My story was over a long time ago, Mr Haruhito. Somewhere there is a book, and in it I am a character. A few pages later I am nowhere to be seen."

●

It was half past one in the morning when I received a call from Madam Lim. "Kevin's gone," she said. I asked her to tell me what had happened—but all she said was that he'd disappeared. "All of his things are still in his room—even his keys, his wallet, his phone. But he's gone, Mr Haruhito. Completely."

Madam Lim picked us up at Holland Village, and drove under our directions. Ms Neo knew the quickest way to the

Kampong Java tunnel, and got Madam Lim to pull over to the side. It was just like what her son had described to me: the vastness of space, the empty roads, as well as the sheer incredulity of the situation. I couldn't help but sway on the balls of my feet as the hot wind buffeted around us, whipping us about. I held on to Madam Lim, and she held on to me.

We didn't exactly know what we were searching for. All we could do was keep walking, keeping our eyes peeled for the smallest of details. Eventually we came upon a door, carved into the tunnel wall; it seemed to be designed for emergency purposes, like a fire access of sorts, although none of us knew where the door really led. Was it a storage shed? Power control? It was perfectly camouflaged, coated in the same yellow-grey colour of the concrete. We would never have found it, if it hadn't been left ever so slightly ajar. We prised the door open.

The young man was seated on a chair, in what seemed to be a perfectly empty room. A single light bulb hung over his figure. A desk might have been here before, even shelves. All I could see were the traces of things that could have been, furniture that might have once existed. Now the only thing left in the room was Mr Lim, his eyes staring straight ahead. There was just a slight flicker in his eyes as he registered the three of us, standing uncertainly before him.

To say that he was different would be an understatement. It would be more accurate to say that he had transformed into something else altogether. He was still noticeably Mr Lim, with his slight figure and shaggy dark hair—but his skin was now perfectly white and flecked, very curiously, by spots of black. A number of things began to connect in my mind as I spotted a pair of gills, flapping at the sides of his neck, as well as a small set of whiskers, hanging from his cheeks. As his mother stepped forward, not quite believing what was seated before her eyes, I caught a slight twitch in his lips. I realised that the strange clicking sound in the room was, in fact, a quiet, sucking noise.

"Kevin?" said Madam Lim.

The figure cocked its head to the side. It blinked once, twice, at the woman's steady approach. Its gills flapped, revealing a layer of soft, pink flesh.

"I can call Ahab," said Ms Neo.

I pointed towards the door. "Take her and go."

"What?"

"Leave," I said. "Now." I kept my eyes fixed on Mr Lim as I heard Ms Neo grab Madam Lim, and force her out of the room. And then the door slammed shut.

I took a moment to assess my surroundings. It was a nothing sort of room, and here I was, confronted with the creature Mr Lim had become. I suddenly became aware of how alone I was in this world, and how that loneliness had been a result of the things I had done to myself. And now here I was, after years of work and neglect. Here was my devil.

The figure twitched again. I thought of many things at that moment. I thought of Madam Lim, outside with Ms Neo. I thought of Kawako. I thought of her mother—my late wife. For a second, I allowed myself to question everything I knew, everything I had believed in: maybe there really wasn't a bead inside any of us, worthy of taking in the first place. Perhaps all this was mere superstition. I wouldn't know what I'd see, anyway, if somebody had taken that bead and broken it. I held on to this particular thought as the figure on the chair stopped moving—and then leapt forward.

3

THE WOMAN ACROSS
THE RIVER

JULY 2012

CHIBA MARI

I

The café was warm and bright, as it had been throughout
the rainy season.

This was a place I had frequented several times over the
past week; three times, in fact, and each time with a different
person. The first time I came, I was drawn, quite rightly, by the
dark blue awning that hung from the eaves of the storefront,
the name of the café printed on it in large, white characters.
Here the river was narrower: a large and deep canal. A muddy
odour rose from its waters.

There was a great sense of calm to the place, even when
it was at its busiest. Frames of pressed flowers and dried
twigs decorated the beige-coloured walls, as leafy potted

ferns hung unassumingly from the ceiling. And I grew to admire the café's assortment of cakes and baked goods, neatly displayed in a glass case. Bags of coffee beans and tea leaves for sale were artfully arranged to the side.

Only a handful of people were in the café today, scattered across the dozen tables or so. It was a small space, made intimate by the friendliness of its staff. An old couple sat in a corner while a high school student occupied another, plugged into his music player as he read a book. A man with dreadlocks leant back against his chair as he read the paper. There was no music in this café, no soundtrack: only the sound of cups laid down on their saucers, as well as the surprising hiss of the steamer, located behind the cash register. The flap of the newspaper, as the man with dreadlocks flipped a page. Once in a while I could hear a murmur or two, coming from the kitchen, as members of the staff passed messages to one another. The old couple raised their voices for a brief moment, complaining about taxes.

I took a seat beside the storefront window, with a view of the cherry trees and the dark green bushes, planted beside the railings that ran along the river. Outside, a gentle rain poured over this seemingly remote part of the city. I looked at my watch and noted the hour.

One forty-seven, I said to myself.

I still had time.

•

This whole thing was my agent's idea. The plan was to seat myself at the designated table beside the storefront window, and wait for a person to arrive at an appointed time. The person would then come and sit opposite me, and proceed to tell me a tale. Whether the tale was true or not was none of my concern: all I had to do, my agent said to me, was listen.

This unique arrangement had been brought about by rather unfortunate circumstances. I have been a novelist for nearly fifteen years now, and a recent winner of one of Japan's top literary prizes. Needless to say, it's not just my livelihood that depends on my ability to write: a core team of editors and publishers have worked tirelessly to support me, to whom I feel bound by obligation to do my part. Lately, however, I've developed an issue with my writing: for the past year or so, I found myself unable to produce a single sentence worthy of a new novel.

It wasn't self-doubt, nor was it fatigue—I just found myself completely devoid of inspiration. I was like a well with no water left to draw, and after a year of struggling, I couldn't shy away from the problem any longer. My agent, Mr Shimao, naturally became concerned, and thus came up with this rather unusual plan. I asked him point-blank over the phone if he had ever done this for his other writers before, and he said that he had. "You're not the only client of mine who has run into a bad case of writer's block," he said. "This thing happens to everyone. But not everybody will admit to it."

I then asked if he was sure his plan would work. "You seem pretty confident about it," I said.

"I am confident, yes. It always seems to do the trick. I guess it's got something to do with the people, or maybe it's got to do with the café. Either way, it works."

"And these people," I said. "How do you find them, exactly?"

"I just do," he replied. "I am more than just a literary agent, Ms Chiba."

I asked him what else he did then, if not merely being an agent. He said he was also a specialist.

"I see," I said, taking note of the term. "And I'm supposed to get inspiration from the stories these people will tell me?"

"That is the plan, yes. But like I said—how exactly you'll gain inspiration is something neither one of us will ever know."

I remained doubtful. "But what if I don't like what I hear?"

"Just drop me a message," my agent said. "I'll arrange for another person to come by."

I was nervous, the first time I went to the café. I sat at the designated table and waited for my person to arrive. It was a teenager, I discovered to my surprise: she was dressed in her high school uniform as she walked into the café, established eye contact with me, and sat on the opposite side of my table. She began her tale with a dream she had one week ago—a dream that had haunted her since.

"I dreamt I was in class, busy making arrangements of some sort. Our teacher told us that we could leave whenever we were ready, although I wasn't sure what it was that we had to be ready for. And then I learnt that there was a game of survival, apparently, happening right outside our classroom. A life-or-death kind of situation. The moment we were done getting ready, we were to step outside and participate in this game, after which the winner would be the last one remaining."

"That sounds scary," I said.

She remained rather still. "Armed with this new piece of information, I realised then why we were all so busy, packing our bags and checking all of our items. None of us wanted to step outside of the classroom and be killed, just because we were unprepared. Suddenly, however, the lights in our classroom went off."

"They did?"

She nodded. "Everybody screamed. We screamed twice. The first scream was timed at precisely three seconds: we screamed out of fear, it was so dark. Nobody knew why the lights had gone off. The second time we screamed, however, was out of realisation. This one lasted four seconds."

I asked her what all of her classmates had "realised". She looked down at the table.

"We realised that the game had already begun—that whatever our teacher had told us was a lie. The game waited for no one; it wasn't going to start when we stepped outside. The game was going to happen right in the middle of our classroom. Next thing I knew, I felt a hand grab my wrist and a voice whisper in my ear: *This I can do.*"

"'This I can do'?" I repeated. The girl in her high school uniform nodded her head once more.

"Even now I still wonder what that was supposed to mean," she said.

After the girl left the café I called my agent, and told him that she wasn't the right fit for me. There was a brief pause over the phone. "I see," he said. "It's disappointing news, but I'm not going to ask why. I'll fix you up with somebody else."

•

A grating sound came from a corner of the café: the old couple had risen from their chairs. They moved, slowly, towards the cash register. They paid for their food and the service.

"It was lovely as usual," the couple said, to the staff manning the counter, who thanked them and wished to see them again. A waiter then retrieved their umbrella from the stands, and opened it for the couple just before they left. A bell, hanging by the entrance, jingled as the door swung open.

The man with the dreadlocks raised his hand. "Could I have water, please?" he said quietly. The high school student, still reading his book, bobbed his head to an unknown beat.

A waitress approached me.

"Excuse me," she said. She seemed embarrassed. "Are you Chiba Mari, by any chance?"

She had a very pleasant smile, I noticed. The tag on her front said *Lisa*. I told her that I was.

"Ah!" said the waitress, holding her hands together. "You have been here so often the past week, I kept wondering if it was really you or not. My younger brother is a big fan of yours."

"Oh, thank you," I said. "Please tell your brother I am grateful for his support."

The waitress nodded and asked if there was anything I'd like to order. "I've noticed that you prefer tea instead of coffee. Would you like to try a pot of our barley tea?"

"That would be nice," I said. "And maybe a pot of chrysanthemum tea as well. I'm currently expecting a friend, you see, who should be here any time soon."

"Most certainly," the waitress said, and bowed. "I'll come

back with your order in just a moment."

Lisa walked back to the counter. Just then, a lady in her late forties entered the café: she was impeccably attired, dressed in a white blouse and a pair of knee-length culottes, dyed blood orange. She held a small collapsible umbrella in one hand and an expensive-looking handbag in the other. Her hair, tied into a tight ponytail, fell down her back in a single, straight line.

"Hello," she said in English. "One iced Americano, please. To go."

The staff looked confused. "To go?" they repeated among themselves. Eventually they figured it out, and handed the lady her takeaway cup of iced coffee. The lady then thanked them and walked out of the café. On the bench outside, beneath the shelter of the blue awning, she sat with her back pressed against the glass of the window, the only thing separating her from my table. I checked my watch once more.

"I still have time," I told myself; it was five minutes to two.

She came in ten minutes later, around five past the hour. This young woman was my fourth this week, after I had informed my agent that I was losing faith in his plan. "Don't worry," Mr Shimao had told me over lunch one day. "You will like the next one."

The young woman's name was Kurosawa Akiko. She had shoulder-length brown hair, and a set of full but delicate lips. Her face was long and cut like a European's, complemented further by earnest, deep-set eyes and a row of small, nicely arranged teeth. She was attractive, most certainly, but in a chiselled sort of way. I wondered, briefly, if a person such as her could tell me a story worth hearing. Akiko introduced herself as a salarywoman in her late twenties, and a fairly new resident of the area. The lady seated outside appeared to be blocking Akiko's view of her own apartment; apparently she lived right across the river.

"If you look over her shoulder," said Akiko, "you can more or less find it."

I asked if she lived alone, or if she lived with her family.

"I live with my best friend now. Kawako. I've known her since my first year at university. I moved in after her father passed away."

I leant back in my chair. Lisa, the waitress, came back with our pots of tea.

"I saw the summer come once," Akiko said, pouring out the chrysanthemum tea. "I won't ever forget it. It was the fourth of June, a rather dry and sunny day, during which one could hear the first cries of the cicadas. I remember reading the weather report that afternoon: nothing but rain for the rest of the week. It was such a pity, I thought—that we'd only get one real day of sunshine."

She set her pot down.

"The wake for Kawako's father was to be held that day, at a small temple nearby. His name was Haruhito Daisuke. Apparently he caught something fatal while he was on a business trip to Singapore last month. Kawako, of course, urged her father to return as quickly as possible. Just forty minutes before the plane was due to land, however, he was found dead in his seat."

I poured some tea for myself. "What killed him, exactly?"

I asked. Akiko raised her cup to her lips, and took a quick sip.

"It was organ failure, according to the coroner's report. It began in the colon, before spreading to the rest of his organs: his kidneys, the liver, the heart. It was a lot like cancer in its later stages, spreading upwards like a poison. As to what brought this condition about, the coroner had not a clue."

I set my pot down. "That's really hard to believe," I said. "To have no clue whatsoever? Over something so deadly?"

Akiko almost seemed to laugh. "I posed the same question to Kawako, and all she said to me was, 'It was a little strange, I guess, from the way you put it.'" She shook her head. "I told her it didn't make sense—nothing did. 'Doesn't everything happen for a reason?' I said to her."

"And what did she say to that?" I asked.

"She said to me, 'Perhaps. I like to think so too.'"

A lot of things came together for Akiko that day, on the fourth of June. More than a hundred or so people had attended the wake, even though it was meant to be a relatively simple affair. There were friends of Mr Haruhito's, his extended family, and even his former clients. The whole lot of them came in a steady stream, crowding the main chamber of the temple.

"There was a large azalea tree, planted in the middle of the courtyard," Akiko told me. After taking note of the wide shadow it had cast, she elected to sit out of the main chamber's proceedings and stand beneath the shade of the tree, where she could be on her own for a while. It was not long, however, until she saw a man step out of the chamber. He joined her at the tree.

"It was Nobuo, I realised: an old friend whom I hadn't

seen in six years." Akiko shook her head. "'It's been a long time,' he said to me, and I could not believe it. I said to him, 'It has, hasn't it?'"

"When was the last you had seen him?"

"It would have to be our graduation ceremony, at the end of our fourth year at Waseda. We promised to keep in touch afterwards, although that never happened in the end. We were too swept up in our new jobs to make any sort of effort. The most I ever saw of him since was his name in the paper, where he wrote articles that covered the local crime beat. And then there he was, standing beside me in a black suit and a skinny tie, at a wake for his uncle."

"His uncle?"

Akiko nodded. "Nobuo is Kawako's cousin," she explained. "The second child of Haruhito Daisuke's older sister."

I drank from my cup of tea. "And I'm assuming Kawako went to Waseda as well?"

She nodded once more. "The three of us—Kawako, Nobuo and myself—all studied at Waseda at the same time. Each of us had different majors, but we were all freshmen at the same university, and had formed a trio of sorts. But our trio eventually fell apart, just before the start of our second year, so that the next time I saw him was during our graduation, when we were bound to part again." She smiled. "All this happened a long time ago."

"I see," I said. I was aware, in a sense, that we were deviating somewhat from the present narrative, and I wanted to refocus her attention. "So you and Nobuo were standing beneath the tree, yes?"

"Yes," said Akiko. "Beneath the tree, in the courtyard."

"Was it awkward, starting a conversation with him? Or did the both of you talk as if you were old friends?"

Akiko shook her head. "It was the former situation, unfortunately. After a brief exchange we lapsed into a long, uncomfortable silence. I remember feeling the heat at the time, prickling at the edges of my scalp." She scratched at her hairline. "The afternoon was so still and windless, I could hear the final strains of the monk's sutra. His voice was distant, like the tolling of a bell."

I ran the sentence over in my brain. "That's a very poetic thing to say," I remarked.

Akiko looked at me. For such a cute and harmless-looking girl, her eyes almost seemed to harden at the compliment. She thanked me, regardless, and continued with her story.

"Kawako appeared, of course, dressed in a simple black dress and black leather pumps. She hadn't tied her hair up that day, so it fell down her back, all the way down to her bum. It was all curly and wild, the way it had always been.

"She found me and Nobuo, standing beneath the azalea tree. She came up to us and said that it'd been a long time. Kawako couldn't recall when the three of us had last stood together like that, and neither could I, to be honest. I don't think Nobuo could either."

"And then?"

"And then Kawako began to tell us about a dream she'd had the night before," Akiko replied. "I asked her what kind of dream it was, and she said that she had been in the air, watching a swimming pool from above, like a bird coasting on the wind. In the middle of this pool was a young man, floating on his back, completely naked."

I asked if this was a man Kawako had known before. Akiko said it wasn't.

"As Kawako hung in the air, wondering who this young man might be, it suddenly occurred to her that she might be in the middle of his dream instead—that she might have intruded on this stranger's mind somehow, or at the very least stolen that dream away from him."

"That's a peculiar thing to consider," I said. Akiko agreed. Akiko said she had told Kawako just as much, and Kawako had replied saying she didn't know how the thought had occurred in her brain. It just did. Nobuo then asked what had happened to the rest of her dream, and Kawako closed her eyes.

"She found that her dream had started to change," Akiko said to me. "She realised that the young man's body had overturned, and that she could no longer see his face. 'He was floating on his front, with his face in the water,' said Kawako. 'The man was dead.'"

It was the following day, after the funeral procession and the cremation were over, when Kawako asked Akiko if she would move into her apartment. *I have a free room now*, Kawako had said, *and am in need of a roommate*. Akiko looked at her, seated in the middle of what used to be her father's bedroom, sorting out the last of his things. She noticed that Kawako was leaving nothing behind: all of it was to go straight to recycling.

I'll think about it, Akiko had said to Kawako. *I'll do it for you, at the very least.*

Kawako stopped. *Don't think of me*, she said; *think of yourself.*

After they were done with the last of her father's things, Kawako went into the living room, where she had left her purse behind. She opened it up and took out a business card.

It's Nobuo's number and e-mail address, she'd explained, handing it to Akiko. She said he had passed it to her that morning, before the funeral procession began. He wanted Akiko to have it.

What for? Akiko had asked. *We haven't spoken in years.*

Kawako set her purse aside. *For old time's sake, I suppose.*

I drank the last of my tea, and poured myself a second cup. Akiko, now at a pause in her story, was busy looking out of the window, through the space above the lady's shoulder. The lady was still seated outside, halfway through her iced Americano. The rain, though light, continued to fall.

"Were you close to Haruhito Daisuke?"

She turned. "I beg your pardon?"

"Were you close to Kawako's father?" I repeated myself. Akiko shook her head.

"Kawako and I have been friends for nearly ten years now, and I've only met her father once," Akiko said. "Is that hard to believe?"

"I'm not sure," I said. "What kind of a man was Haruhito Daisuke?"

Akiko thought about it for a while. "A perfectly normal man in a strange profession," she said. "Nobody ever really knew what he did for a living. I think I remember Kawako saying once that he was a specialist."

I blinked. "A specialist?"

"Yes," said Akiko. "A specialist."

They met at a birthday party Nobuo's parents had thrown for Kawako. This was during the spring holiday, at the end of their first year at Waseda, when the three of them were still together as friends. Everybody had been gathered in the living room that evening when the power went out. The entire block had lost its electrical supply, and Nobuo's father had gone out to investigate. The conversation soon resumed, however, with people amused and joking in the dark. Phones were taken out, casting blue light over sections of the room.

Akiko could barely see anything. But she did notice Mr Haruhito, standing beside her and doing nothing in particular. He was neither in the middle of a conversation, nor was he busy attending to the food on his plate. He was doing nothing at all. This was the first and only time Akiko had ever met the man in the flesh, and it struck her as a little odd how she had not noticed his presence in the room before, what with his imposing height and skinny frame. She asked if he was indeed Kawako's father, and he said that he was. Akiko introduced herself.

I believe I've heard about you before, Ms Kurosawa, Mr Haruhito had said; *my daughter talks about you all the time. I hear you live in Akishima city?*

Akiko said that she did. Mr Haruhito remarked how long her journeys must have been, in order to commute to and from Waseda. Each ride on the train must have taken an hour at least. Akiko said that was true.

"Before I came to live here, I lived in an apartment a few streets north of Nakagami station," Akiko explained to me. "I've lived there all my life, with my parents, my grandparents and my two older sisters." Needless to say, there were times when Akiko felt an immense sense of claustrophobia: she felt it weigh like a bag of wet dirt in her chest. She constantly struggled for air.

Haruhito Daisuke had listened to Akiko with great attention. *You must have often felt the need to break free, Ms Kurosawa,* he'd said to her. Akiko said that she did, and going on long walks around the neighbourhood didn't do much to comfort her either. Mr Haruhito asked her why. She'd said: *Akishima city is a commuter town. It has nothing but residential blocks and health clinics and industrial complexes. Every summer, the residents either stay out of town or stay in their homes, to seek shelter from the heat. And then the entire neighbourhood would become too empty and quiet for me to bear.*

Does it give you nightmares? he'd asked.

Yes, said Akiko. *Every summer I dream of ghosts, of towns full of ghosts. And nothing the ghosts ever do in those towns would have any impact on reality.* She then paused, before adding: *I'm very glad I got to meet Kawako, Mr Haruhito. She's the first real friend I ever made outside Akishima.*

And Nobuo?

The second, came her reply; *it was Kawako's idea, actually, that the three of us form a group amongst ourselves. Kawako and Nobuo were close as cousins, and it was becoming evident that I was her best friend at university. It only seemed natural that I got to know Nobuo as well,* she'd said.

That's true, responded Mr Haruhito; *that's true.* He then paused for a while. *Can I ask you a personal question, Ms Kurosawa?* he said. Akiko said she didn't mind. He then asked

Akiko what had drawn her to his daughter. Akiko responded by saying it was her generosity, and her gentleness. She'd always feel at ease whenever she was around her.

What about Nobuo? asked Mr Haruhito.

He's honest, Akiko replied; *he is always searching for the truth. And for that I know I can always speak my mind.*

Mr Haruhito had chuckled. *Thank you for thinking so highly of them, Ms Kurosawa*, he said. He then paused again, before remarking: *It's a wonder why the lights have gone out.*

Akiko hadn't been sure either. *Maybe someone stole the light*, she said. She then sensed Mr Haruhito smiling in the dark. He said to her: *You remind me of a certain woman, Ms Kurosawa, a woman whom I came to know a long time ago, back when I was still a young man. I'd spot her from across the river that runs along my neighbourhood, just down the foot of my block. It was hard not to see her—almost impossible, in fact, to avoid the sight of her.*

Akiko had asked if she was a beautiful woman. Mr Haruhito chuckled once more.

She was, Ms Kurosawa, but it wasn't that. It was her soul, he said; *you can find it, if you know where to look—and hers was terribly, terribly bright. Too bright to have caught a direct glimpse of.*

Akiko tried to imagine it: the soul of a human being, glowing like the end of a firefly, or a lone satellite in the night. She knew, in the back of her mind, that she would never have a way of catching one. She asked if he had ever dared to approach her, this woman across the river, and he paused again, for the third time, before he said that he hadn't. She was on one side of the river, and there he was, alone on the other.

I wasn't brave, then, he'd said to her. *I wasn't brave enough to change my life.*

Akiko took hold of her pot, and poured herself a third cup of tea. I was on my third as well, and close to the end of my supply. I glanced quickly at the lady seated outside, and saw that she had finished her Americano. She was now busy checking something on her phone, running her fingers through the end of her ponytail.

"I wonder how that encounter must have affected you," I said to Akiko. Akiko pursed her lips.

"I thought about what he said, for the rest of the night. Even after the party was over," she said. "I remember walking home from Nakagami station and feeling a wind pick up around me, pushing me from behind. Next thing I knew I found myself standing right at my doorstep, not knowing how I had gotten there. I wondered if this was what Kawako's father had meant—to let life continue, to let it go on the way it always has. To just follow wherever it takes you without any complaint whatsoever, in whichever direction it chooses to pull you. I thought about the amount of courage it would require, just to affect any sort of change in one's destiny. But don't take my word for it, Ms Chiba. I might be wrong about what he meant."

I nodded. I took a sip of tea. "I can't help but also wonder how the three of you fell apart," I said to her. "If the birthday party had happened during the spring holidays, and the three of you stopped being a trio before sophomore year began, something drastic must have happened in between. That interval couldn't have been very long either."

Akiko shook her head, and kept on drumming her fingers on the table. "I wouldn't call it drastic," she said to me. "But it did change everything."

"What happened?" I asked. Akiko's fingers stopped.

"Nobuo asked me out for lunch, two days after the party. Over lunch he said he was in love with me."

"Oh," I said. "A confession."

"Yes." She paused. "Nobuo asked if I could remember that time when we had gone drinking on Valentine's Day— the three of us, at a karaoke joint in Shibuya, downing pints of Asahi as our other friends made fools of themselves. He asked if I remembered what I had said to him."

"What did you say, exactly?"

Akiko tilted her head to the side. "On that night in Shibuya?"

"Yes."

"I said that I had never willingly fallen in love before," Akiko replied. "I said that the only way I could ever fall in love was if somebody fell in love with me first." She looked out of the window again. "Instead I told Nobuo that I didn't remember. I told him I'd been dead drunk. I said there was no way I could recall something like that."

I kept my gaze focused on Akiko. "Why did you lie to him?"

She looked back towards me. "We lie to protect ourselves, Ms Chiba. And I was young, then, just nineteen. All I wanted was to keep our group together, and I didn't want something like that tearing us apart. But it did, in the end. Kawako found out from Nobuo, and wanted to meet me that night."

"That night?"

She nodded.

"Kawako called me and said that she needed to talk, and wondered if I was free. I told her I was. She then told me to meet at Kichijoji station, which was more or less a midpoint for us. She said she would meet me at the Chuo Line platform. I told her I could be there in forty-five minutes."

Akiko remembered getting off the train and seeing Kawako that night, dressed in a floral green dress and a nice, white cardigan. She was seated on a bench on the platform, and had stood up when she saw Akiko. They sat together as Akiko's train rolled away, and the commuting crowd gathered and moved towards the escalators. Kawako didn't say anything for a long time; a while passed before the din had quietened down, and she told Akiko that she was in love with Nobuo.

I blinked. "Kawako was in love with her cousin?"

Akiko nodded again.

Kawako's feelings for Nobuo, Akiko explained to me, began when Kawako was in elementary school. They were rather active as children, and would often play all kinds of make-believe games during family gatherings.

"Once, in a game of cops, Nobuo had pinned her down as the main suspect in a case, and screamed questions at her until she confessed to her crime. It was then she felt a strange stirring within her body, in both her chest and in her groin." Akiko paused. "It felt like a part of her had locked together, to use her words; the world had suddenly made sense to her. She felt a tight knot of feeling in her chest that she was determined to hold on to."

Was it infatuation? Was it love? Kawako didn't know. As

his cousin, it was easy for her to be close to him whenever she wanted, but the connection itself made it paramount that she should maintain a distance. As Kawako went through middle school and high school, she realised that it was becoming harder and harder to put his body out of her mind, the body that had pinned itself on top of hers. She saw Nobuo everywhere—running circles around the school field, sitting next to her in class, bumping into him in the corridors—even though they went to different schools. Whenever she saw Nobuo in the flesh at family gatherings, she'd find herself wet, so very wet—she craved for the press of his sex against hers.

"Kawako had a boyfriend once, but that relationship didn't last very long," Akiko said to me. "I'd seen a picture of him before. He was the vice-captain of the basketball team: tall, handsome, muscular. He was the kind of guy who looked even better in glasses, which is rare. When they broke up, he told her that she always seemed to be somewhere else, even when they were in the midst of sex. She didn't deny any of his accusations. She let him go."

When her first term at Waseda began, Kawako knew, of course, that Nobuo had chosen to enrol at the same university. Though glad he was studying for a different major, she realised that they both had many classes in the same faculty building; they would bump into one another, run into one another, just like how they would in her high school fantasies. Kawako found that she needed some way to be around Nobuo without being too close at the same time, and she figured that the best way to do this was to introduce a third party into their equation—a friend she could both trust and confide in, to serve as a link to the young man and a barrier against him.

That's where you come in, Kawako had explained to Akiko, as a second train came and left. *You were very kind, and very friendly towards me*, she'd said. *You made a friend out of Nobuo as well, just as I had predicted. For a long while you gave me a reason to be around him, Akiko, and I appreciate that. But now I have to step away.*

Akiko didn't know what Kawako had meant at first. Kawako remained as still as a statue, and stared at the tracks before her.

Who else knows? asked Akiko.

Only you.

Not even your father?

Kawako shook her head. *This is my secret*, she said; *it is mine to keep*. She shook her head again. *I'm a monster*, she'd added, softly under her breath.

It was then Akiko had noticed a train, coming in from the other side of the platform. The lights were small at first, like pinpoints in the distance, before growing larger and larger within seconds. Akiko felt a sudden kick in her chest—a sudden impulse, springing to life within her, as the wind picked up around the platform. She took hold of Kawako's hands, and held them tight in her lap. She told Kawako that she was her best friend: she was the key to her new life. She wouldn't know what to do without her in it.

But what about Nobuo? Kawako had asked. Akiko told her not to worry. *Just forget about him*, she'd said; *we'll forget about him.*

Back in the café, Akiko rested her hand on her cheek,

and looked out of the window: the lady outside, stranger as she was, was still seated with her back against the window, as though she too were a part of our conversation, of our special arrangement. The ice in her cup had now melted into a murky layer of liquid.

"Looking back, it is hard not to see how cruel we both were, in our own separate ways," Akiko said to me. "I was as much a monster as she was."

The lady with the ponytail finally made a move: she got up and left, and walked out of sight. It was still raining, gentle over the river, and there was a small ring of water left where the base of her cup had been.

"I moved into Kawako's apartment on the eighth of June," Akiko said to me. "It was the Friday following her father's wake, and I had anticipated that I would need the whole weekend, just to move my belongings from my old place to the new. It wasn't till Sunday, after I had brought back the last of my things, when I decided to give Nobuo a call."

"I'm surprised you didn't call him sooner," I said.

"I was busy," said Akiko. "I needed time."

Kawako's apartment, located in the 1-chome of the Aobadai district, was a cosy two-bedroom setting. "The kitchen bleeds into the living room, with the dining table caught in between. There's a small balcony at the living room, big enough to fit two people. Surrounding the balcony is a simple metal grille that leads up to the waist." She placed a finger on the glass of the window. "As you can see."

I leant towards the glass.

"According to Kawako, her father had lived there his entire

life," said Akiko. "His sister, Nobuo's mother, was the one who'd had to move out." She removed her finger from the glass. "I remember walking over to the balcony and catching sight of this café, its name boldly printed across a deep blue awning, like foam on the sea. There was a pavement sign near the entrance, proudly displaying its name."

I finished the last of my tea. "Do you think this is where Haruhito Daisuke might have seen this particular woman of his?"

Akiko didn't respond immediately. "I thought of that," she said. "But I wouldn't know."

Akiko had dialled Nobuo's number in the end, that Sunday on the tenth of June. He picked up the call on the fifth ring and cut straight to the chase: he asked her if she would like to meet up for coffee sometime, and Akiko said yes. She added that she had a place in mind.

"What place was this?" I asked Akiko. Akiko kept her gaze directed out of the window.

"It was this same café, Ms Chiba. And we sat at this very same table as well."

"Oh, is that so?" I said. I felt taken aback. "And what did you both talk about?"

Akiko gave me a smile. She then took out her phone, and appeared to be sending a message to someone. Her phone then buzzed, a few seconds later, to indicate that she'd received a reply.

"Your agent Mr Shimao would like to ask if you'd be willing to meet Nobuo," Akiko said. "Two days from now, to hear his side of the story." Akiko then tilted her head to the side. "What do you say, Ms Chiba?"

I leant back in my chair. "Sure," I said. "Tell him I'd like to."

Akiko typed into her phone once more. Another buzz came as quick as the last one. Akiko then put her phone away, and rose from her chair. "He says he couldn't be happier."

II

It was a minute to two when Takahata Nobuo showed up. He stepped through the door and found where I was, and sat facing me across the table. He was a tall man, and cut a rather trim figure; there was something about his build that suggested he ran quite regularly, was constantly on the move. He had the sort of figure that made me conscious of the weight I was putting on. Nobuo asked if I had waited long, and I told him that I hadn't.

"I was fifteen minutes early," I said to him. "I should have timed myself better. But I ended up feeling a little nervous and impatient, just waiting around at home."

"You were nervous?" Nobuo asked.

"I was, admittedly."

Nobuo smiled. It was disarming, his smile; it was the kind that caused his eyes to disappear. "You know, I was a bit shocked when I was told to meet you here. I didn't know this café was so well known."

I crossed my legs. "Were you shocked as well when Akiko told you to meet her at the café?"

"Not at first," he said. "But eventually. When I found the address I realised it was right next to where she and my uncle lived. And then Akiko told me that she had moved into Kawako's apartment. I was a bit surprised at first—everything's happened so quickly—and then it all just, I don't know. It made sense."

I nodded. I asked him what he made of that: of Akiko living with Kawako. Nobuo looked blank for a few seconds, before he said it was fitting, actually. I asked him how so.

"Well, the two of them have been best friends since freshman year. It's only natural that they both ended up living together. Especially since neither of them seems to be the marrying type."

"You really think so?"

"I know so," he said.

"What do you mean?"

He pouted slightly as he thought. "Well, neither of them has had a boyfriend since college. That's how I know so." He then smiled again. "Shall we order?" he asked, before motioning for the waitress. Lisa wasn't on shift that day, so it was a different girl this time. After a quick look at the menu, Nobuo ordered a plain black coffee for himself, as well as a slice of lemon tart for the both of us. I ordered a pot of barley tea again, just like the time before. After the waitress walked away, Nobuo leant over the table.

"You should really try the lemon tart," he said. "It's amazing."

I fixed him with a level gaze. "You're a pretty confident man, aren't you?"

He thought about it for a second. "You could say that," he said. "There's no point in being a reporter if you're not confident."

"That's true," I replied. "How has the job been treating you so far?"

"Well, I just got a promotion," Nobuo said. "I got it the day before I learnt my uncle had passed away, which is strange. Anyway. Now, instead of constantly being assigned jobs by the editor, I get to chase after my own stories and use my own contacts. It also means I get to manage my own time, and do whatever I want with it, as long as I submit a certain number of articles per week."

"That's nice, isn't it?"

"It is," he replied. "I guess you could say this transition suits my personality better."

I nodded. "It does seem that way, Mr Takahata. Congratulations are in order, then. I know we've just met, but I feel happy for you."

He smiled again. "Thank you, Ms Chiba." After the waitress came back, placing our ordered items on the table, he asked if the current demands of his work bore any similarities to my own. "Like, do you often find yourself with a lot of free time in your hands? Does it scare you, almost, how you can spend a whole day without doing anything?"

I felt amused, and poured myself a cup of tea. "Has that happened to you before?"

"Well, once. That was a horrible day. I sat around in the Supreme Court hoping to find a good story, but nothing exciting happened. There were no murders, no fraud, no tax evasion stories. Nothing. My editor told me that just happens sometimes."

"In that case, I operate very differently from you, Mr Takahata." I took a sip of my tea. "First of all, I always keep to a strict work schedule. Every evening, without fail, I sit down at my desk at eight o' clock and write till eleven thirty.

The next morning, I spend my time between breakfast and lunch editing whatever I wrote the night before. It's a very exact schedule."

"You do this every day?" Nobuo asked.

"When I'm committed to a novel, yes."

"So, hmm, how do you find inspiration for a novel? How do you know when it's time to commit to one?"

"That's the second thing," I said to him. "I'm not the kind of writer who goes out and talks to strangers and travels to a remote part of the country to get inspired. I've found that whenever I write, I find sources of inspiration within myself. My previous four novels have come from some part of myself that already existed within me."

"Oh, really?" said Nobuo. "I couldn't tell. And I've read three of them."

"You have?" I said. "Thank you. And it's true—the point is, I take what begins as a memory, or an aspect of my own life, and constantly mould and refine it until it has taken that step into fiction. It always starts from within, this process."

Nobuo nodded. He cut a portion of the lemon tart with his fork, and appeared to dwell on a thought as he chewed. "Have you ever feared that you would run out of memories or personal experiences to use?"

Yes, I said; I told him it was already happening. "I guess you could say this is my biggest weakness. In order for my work to succeed I have to rely on the life that I have lived so far. I have to constantly draw from within, sometimes to the point of near emptiness, for I believe there is a moment in a writer's career when they have done more writing than any actual living. And now here I am talking to you."

Nobuo looked at me for a long time, as though unsure of what to feel about the situation. "According to Mr Shimao, you'd like to have an account of what was discussed between me and Akiko, when we met here on the fifteenth of June."

"If possible, yes."

"Well, you must understand, Ms Chiba—I don't have the kind of memory Akiko has. I can't recreate entire conversations, unfortunately. I don't possess that kind of talent, and if I did it would make my job a lot easier." He then reached into his sling bag and brought out two items: a notebook and a compact voice recorder. "This is what I need in order to do my job."

"I see," I said, as Nobuo put them away. "You don't have to worry, Mr Takahata. I don't expect anything anybody says to be one hundred per cent accurate, anyway."

He nodded. "Thank you, Ms Chiba. For understanding."

I leant back in my chair. I held my cup of tea, and told him to give me the gist of it anyway.

"Well," said Nobuo. "I do recall Akiko asking if I was still in love with her."

I nearly laughed. "You must have been caught off-guard."

He nodded again. "I told her I wasn't sure."

"You're not sure?" I repeated.

"I have a girlfriend, at the moment. That's what I said to Akiko. Akiko then asked how many girlfriends I have had before this one. I told her five, which makes the current one my sixth." Nobuo paused. "At the beginning, I didn't know how to handle a relationship, so the first few ones didn't last long at all. Whenever I chased after girls, I'd forget to use my head. But as I got older, I got wiser too. My current girlfriend and I have been together for nearly ten months now."

"That's nice," I said. "Congratulations, once again."

He smiled. He almost seemed relieved. "Thank you, Ms Chiba."

For a while, neither of us spoke. He finished the rest of his lemon tart and drank his coffee, while I continued to sip on my tea. There were people outside, taking advantage of the sunny weather; they walked down the river in droves. Nobuo leant over the table once more.

"Can I ask you something, Ms Chiba?"

I nodded, slowly. "Ask away."

"You're a novelist, right? You must be looking at the three of us like characters in a story."

I smiled. "I'm not sure what you're getting at, Mr Takahata." He smiled back.

"I'm wondering if you think we're broken," said Nobuo. "The three of us. And I'm wondering who you thought has done the breaking."

"Hmm," I said. "I don't profess to know the answer, Mr Takahata. But I believe you know it already."

This is the part he remembers best.

After Nobuo and Akiko were done with their food that day, they left the café, and walked up the river towards Nakameguro station. He was going to take the Hibiya Line, followed by the Marunouchi Line, back to his office in Otemachi that afternoon. It had been raining rather heavily that afternoon; even though they both had their own umbrellas, they elected to walk under Akiko's, with Nobuo holding it up over their heads. How close they had been, walking together like that.

Nobuo told Akiko about a tropical storm that might be headed towards Japan. *It was reported two days ago, in fact. The Japan Meteorological Agency has yet to call it a typhoon, but we'll have to see. It's too far to tell at the moment.*

Akiko said she knew, of course. *It's called Guchol, isn't it?* Apparently he'd mentioned it earlier.

That's right, said Nobuo; *I'd forgotten.*

They had met again two days later, on the seventeenth of June. It was Nobuo's idea. It had been a particularly warm Sunday, hot and humid, although the sun was nowhere to be seen, and the sky remained overcast.

Nobuo and Akiko sat at a different table, that afternoon; the one by the window had already been taken. Nobuo ordered a cup of coffee, while Akiko had a glass of iced tea. It was a busy afternoon in the café, and they were aware of the people around them, chatting away, seemingly happy. It was strange, thought Nobuo, that he should feel so unhappy in contrast. He hadn't properly realised how unhappy he'd been, and for how long a time. It hadn't occurred to him till then how damaged he was.

Akiko was the first to speak. *I had lunch with Kawako today. Before I came to see you.*

How is she? Nobuo asked.

She's fine, said Akiko, *although she did appear a little troubled; a little too quiet.*

By what? asked Nobuo.

By us, I believe. The fact of us reconnecting, after all these years, said Akiko.

Nobuo looked at his coffee. *What makes you say that?* he

asked. Akiko replied: *She asked about our time together, right before I left the apartment.*

Ah. And what did you say?

I told her you had a girlfriend. I told her you'd been seeing her for ten months. I had a feeling Kawako wouldn't know.

Nobuo nodded. Of course Kawako wouldn't know. They were still cousins, sure—but they weren't friends anymore. He asked how Kawako had reacted to that, and Akiko said: *Kawako told me she hasn't seen your family since the funeral. Is that true?*

Nobuo nodded again.

She said she hasn't spoken to or seen any of her extended family since that day, said Akiko. *Every time she thinks she should make the journey to your house, she just loses all of her motivation. She then said it was a lot like her dream at the pool.*

You mean, the naked man? asked Nobuo.

Yes, said Akiko. *To Kawako, the man is just lying there, without any desire to move anywhere else*, she said; *he's perfectly content with staying where he is.* Akiko then paused, as though she were recounting the dream to herself. *At least that's what she said to me, anyway.*

Nobuo thought about what she had just said. *Has she had the dream again recently?* he asked Akiko, and Akiko shrugged her shoulders. She said she wouldn't know.

Nobuo wondered if this was what it all meant, for the three of them in particular: to live in the after; to mourn an ending.

After Akiko was done talking about Kawako, Nobuo told her that he couldn't stay long. *I have to meet my girlfriend in an hour*, he'd explained to her. *At Denenchofu.*

Akiko had looked confused. *But there's nothing to do at Denenchofu.*

Well, she likes to look at houses, you know? said Nobuo. *And it's where she wants to live in the future, when the time comes for her to settle down.*

Akiko in turn asked Nobuo how many of these walks he has had with her. Nobuo thought about it. *Eleven times, twelve?* He wasn't sure about the number.

I see, said Akiko. She then asked if he would propose to her in Denenchofu, when the time came for him to do so. *That would be quite romantic*, she said, *fulfilling all of her dreams.*

Nobuo shook his head. He asked Akiko to stop teasing him. They fell silent for a while. Akiko asked Nobuo if his girlfriend knew about their time together—about the fact that they were in a café just twenty metres away from her own apartment.

My girlfriend knows nothing, he said.

A tense silence followed his confession. Nobuo didn't know what to do, although a burning feeling in his face informed him that he might be crying. Akiko stared at his two hands on the table, clasped tightly onto one another. It was only when Akiko placed her hands on his that he realised he was also shaking.

I'm sorry, Akiko had said to him. *I've become such a bitch.*

Nobuo nodded. She let out a quiet laugh.

I wish things could have gone differently between us, said Akiko. *There are days when I look back and ask myself how I could have better handled things. But the truth is that no matter how many ways I try to look at it, the Kurosawa Akiko that existed back then would not have acted otherwise. There was no doubt who that girl needed to be with more.*

Nobuo said he understood. Akiko tightened her grip on his hands.

I'm sorry, she said again. *There is a cruel streak within me. I didn't know it then, but I see it now. I see it all the time.*

Nobuo turned towards the window. There, situated between two cherry trees, was where she lived now: in that apartment with Kawako. It was funny how much smaller it looked, from deep inside the café.

Do you know why I was in love with you? he asked. Akiko shook her head.

You never actually said why, she said.

He kept his eye on the apartment block.

You were holding on so tightly to the two of us, he'd said to Akiko. *It took a while for me to realise that you were doing it for yourself. Not for me, or for Kawako. You held on to us because you had to.*

Nobuo then told Akiko that he'd once considered dropping out of Waseda. I raised an eyebrow at this point of the story.

"You did?" I asked.

"That, or I kept wishing Kawako would transfer to another university," said Nobuo. "I wanted some way for the three of us to break up and go our separate ways, so I could ask Akiko out again and not feel guilty about it." He paused. "In the end, about a month after I realised the truth about Kawako, I began to find and make other friends of my own. Or rather, people finally were beginning to see that I'd had my heart broken, really, by two girls whom I'd considered to be my closest friends. And then things just became easier. Eventually I stopped feeling so attached to the two of them, and managed to move on."

Akiko had taken all of that in. She absorbed everything that he had said to her.

So you know about Kawako? About why she suddenly left your side? she'd asked him.

I was confused at first, he said in reply; *so many things were happening in the span of one day.*

Akiko bit her lip.

So you know, *then,* she said, *that your cousin was in love with you. That she has probably always been in love with you.*

He nodded. *The moment that possibility came to my mind, everything else just fell into place. Everything made sense.*

Akiko then asked him what had happened that day, after he had confessed to her over lunch. Nobuo said that he had gone straight home. He couldn't really remember how he'd gotten there in one piece, when he'd found himself constantly on the brink of tears. *I love you,* he kept thinking on the bus. *I love you. Why isn't that enough for you?*

He opened the front door. *I'm home,* he said. He then found Kawako, seated in his living room. She was wearing a floral green dress, with a white cardigan slung over her arm. Kawako had seemed like she was about to say something, but Nobuo had taken her by the arm instead. He dragged her into his bedroom. Kawako, too bewildered by what was going on, kept quiet and waited for him to speak. But he didn't.

"What did you do?" I asked.

Nobuo shrugged, as though it were no big deal. He began to play with the crumbs on his plate.

"I cried," he said to me. "I turned my back towards her and cried. I couldn't face her at all. I told her I was in love with Akiko, and that it was the bravest thing I had ever done. I then told her how Akiko had done the most cowardly thing. I told her how she said she didn't remember."

"About what she said on Valentine's?"

Nobuo looked up from his plate. "Akiko told you about that?"

"Yes," I said. "About that night in Shibuya."

Nobuo shook his head. He nearly seemed to laugh. And then he dropped his fork: he let it fall, with a clatter, as he held on to his hand. "I'm shaking," he said, holding it close to his chest. "Look at that, Ms Chiba. I'm shaking again."

•

I was back in the café, two days later; I was about to sit down, at my usual spot by the window, when the door swung open with a jingle of the bell. I checked my watch—one forty-five, it read—and looked up.

It was the lady again. Her hair was done in the same style, tied back into a ponytail; she also wore the same white blouse as the last time, and carried the same black leather handbag. But she wore a blue pencil skirt instead of her blood orange culottes, and stepped out of the café after she had received her takeaway Americano. My eyes followed her every move as the lady resumed her position at the bench outside, and like time repeating itself, the same waitress, the one with the younger brother, walked smiling towards my table. Lisa, her name was.

"Good afternoon, Ms Chiba," she said. "It's really nice to see you again."

"Yes," I said. "I've grown reliant on this place. Do you have any new recommendations for me?"

"Perhaps the peach tea?" she said. "We serve it with ice."

"I'll have that then," I said. "Thank you, Lisa."

Akiko came in at five past two, dressed in a raincoat and a pair of wellingtons. "If you are interested in the final piece of the story, you'll have to meet up with Ms Kurosawa again," my agent had informed me. "There's one last development that only she can tell."

The final chapter, or so Akiko put it, had taken place on the Wednesday when Typhoon Guchol was scheduled to pass over Tokyo. Both Akiko and Kawako had decided to stay at home that day, after office memos about the weather had advised all employees to do so. It was the twentieth of June, and Guchol had already battered its way into the southern region the day before. Akiko and Kawako both sat on the couch in the living room, watching the weather worsen from their view of the balcony. They made sure to use as few electrical appliances as possible, and lit a couple of candles for light.

"I was seated in my pyjamas, and had a light blanket wrapped around my body," Akiko said to me. "I remember taking note of the expression on my friend's face as she kept her eyes fixed on the world outside our apartment. I then walked over to the kitchen, poured myself a glass of water, and asked if she'd like one as well. She said that she would."

Say, Kawako, Akiko had said to her. *Can I ask you something hypothetical?*

Sure, Kawako replied.

Akiko handed her a glass of water. She then asked Kawako what would she do, if Nobuo had suddenly chosen to confess at that moment that he'd always loved her back this whole time?

Kawako seemed unfazed by the question. *Why?* she asked Akiko. Had Nobuo said something to her?

No, no, came her reply. *He didn't. It was just a thought.*

Kawako simply nodded, and Akiko pressed her to give an answer. *Well?* she asked; *what would you say?*

Kawako had remained mum, for several more seconds. She then answered, rather plainly, that she would reject him.

You would? said Akiko.

Yes, said Kawako. *I would reject him. Even though I still love him.*

Even now?

Kawako nodded again. *It's my curse, I think.*

Akiko set her glass of water down. Outside, the windowpane on the balcony door shuddered as the winds grew stronger. The bright green leaves of the cherry trees thrashed about, wildly, like small hands trying to reach and catch something in the air. (Always the poetic inclination, I thought to myself.)

It's crazy isn't it? said Kawako. *The way everything is blown about.*

Yeah, said Akiko.

You know that café you went to with Nobuo? The one you

can see from the balcony? She pointed. *It used to be a bookstore*, said Kawako; *before the café opened last winter. The bookstore stood in its place, for as long as I can remember. It's always been there, even when my father was a little boy.*

She turned back to Akiko.

It was his favourite place in the whole world. He even said that the bookstore had the knack to provide you with any book that you might need.

Really? said Akiko. *Any book?*

Kawako nodded. *Even books that you didn't think you needed before*, she'd explained. *Apparently the old couple that ran it had the gift of picking books they thought were truly meant for you.*

Akiko felt intrigued. She asked Kawako if she had ever gone into this bookstore, and Kawako said that she hadn't. She said that over the years, the bookstore had developed a bad feeling about it. It always looked as though it was steeped in shadows. From the balcony, all she could ever see of the bookstore was probably the side of the cash register, or maybe even a few bookshelves or two. But nothing else. That, and she never really liked books, anyway.

That's true, said Akiko; Kawako used to complain about her reading assignments, back when they were at Waseda. And then a thought occurred to her, just as she looked at the café now standing on the opposite side of the river.

Hey Kawako, she'd said.

Yes?

Has your father ever told you about this particular woman he saw before? Standing on the other side of the river?

Kawako shook her head. *What woman was this?*

Someone whom he saw when he was younger, she replied.
*Someone very beautiful, apparently. He also said she had a very
bright soul.*

Kawako frowned. She failed to recall a story of that sort.
She asked Akiko when her father had told it to her, and Akiko
said that it happened during her nineteenth birthday, when
the power had gone out. She said, *That was the only time I
ever met your father, actually. The both of us so happened to be
standing next to each other, right there in Nobuo's living room.*

And this woman had a bright soul, he said?

Yes, said Akiko: *a terribly, terribly bright soul. He told me
about this woman because he said that I reminded him of her.*

Really?

Yeah.

Kawako fell silent. After a spell, she said: *My father always
had a tendency to tell people the strangest things. All my life I
never had the faintest clue as to what he did for a living. But a
part of me thinks it's probably best I don't know. I feel like only
people with problems of a certain nature would come to him for
advice, and those who are perfectly fine and normal would not
even know that somebody like him existed.*

Kawako then finished her water, and sat the glass down
next to Akiko's. Akiko hadn't even drunk from hers yet. She
then realised that for the past half-minute, Kawako had been
looking directly into her eyes.

Hey Akiko, she said; *do you feel like your life doesn't belong
to you sometimes? That nothing you do, no matter how hard you
try, will have any real consequences at all? Do you ever feel like
there's no point to anything?*

Neither of them said anything for a while. Akiko then

looked away again, her gaze returning to the view from the balcony. The café swam in and out of view, between the leaves of the cherry trees. And then the rain started to fall.

Lisa the waitress came by again, after Akiko had taken her leave. She asked if she could clear the empty glasses from the table, and I said that she could. She then asked if I had enjoyed the peach tea.

"Yes," I said. "We both did."

The young waitress smiled. "I'm glad you found it to your taste," she said. Just before she could turn, however, I laid a hand on her arm. "Can I ask you something?" I said.

"Of course, Ms Chiba."

"Do you know anything about the lady seated outside?" I gestured towards her back. The lady with the ponytail, unaware of the fact that we were talking about her, held her iced Americano in her two, slim hands.

"Oh," the waitress said. "We know that she's a foreigner, and that she can only speak English. She always orders a cup of Americano, and sits outside for a long time. Sometimes she sits there for more than an hour, long after her coffee is finished."

"Why, though?" I asked.

"I don't have a clue," the waitress said.

"You never had the courage to ask?"

"Oh, I wouldn't dare," she said. "I can barely speak English at all. I've forgot most of it since high school."

I remained silent for a while. If I were Nobuo, I thought, I wouldn't have any qualms about approaching her at all. He was the kind of guy who would never let a girl slip by, just because he felt embarrassed or shy. The waitress then clapped her hands.

"Oh, Ms Chiba—there's one thing that I do remember about her."

"What is it?" I asked.

"The first time she came to our café, she asked if this place used to be a bookstore."

"Did she?"

The waitress nodded. "She apparently came to our café under the impression that it was supposed to be one. We then told her that we'd never heard of this bookstore before, and confirmed to her that she had gotten the right address. We told her that the bookstore must have closed down at the start of the year, before this café took over the premises. After that, for some reason, she's been here ever since."

"I see," I said. "Actually, could I order a cup of iced tea to go, please?"

"Sure thing," said the waitress, with a curious look on her face. "I'll be right back with your order."

I stepped through the door. I had my umbrella in one hand; I could feel the rain on the pavement, splashing onto the open toes of my sandals. I then quickly went under the shelter of the awning, and took a seat beside the lady on the bench. The lady took notice of me, and shifted a little to the side. She placed her handbag on her lap. Both of us remained quiet for a while, as we observed the rain falling onto the trees and the bushes and the river, swelling up high in the canal. I thought of a way to break the silence: I began by talking about the weather.

She seemed pleasantly surprised. "You can speak English?"

she said. Upon a closer look, I could see that I had been right: she was in her late forties, after all, but she had a small, youthful-looking face, marked by fine lines at the corner of her eyes. And her voice, I couldn't help but note, was deep and assured.

"Just a little," I said. "I went to an international high school in Hawaii. I then majored in American literature at university. I read a lot of Willa Cather, F. Scott Fitzgerald, William Faulkner."

"All in English, I suppose."

"Yes."

"That's wonderful," the lady said. "I've never read those writers myself. In fact, I hardly read at all."

"Oh?" I said. It was a surprising thing for her to say. Why would someone uninterested in reading be in search of an old bookstore in Tokyo? I couldn't figure it out. "Is this your first time in Japan?" I asked.

"Yes," said the lady. "My very first time."

"And where are you from?"

She pursed her lips, and tilted her head to the side. "I'm from somewhere else," she said. "Somewhere not too far away." She looked out onto the view. "This is the Meguro River, isn't it?"

I told her it was. She smiled.

"It's nice," she said. "I wish there were more rivers like these back home. Big, wide canals. Sitting here, I can't help but look at the cherry trees as well. Imagine how they must look like during the spring."

"They are very pretty," I said. "White blossoms everywhere."

"That's nice," she said again. "I've only ever seen the spring once, and I'll never forget it."

"Once?"

She nodded. "I was with my son, Kevin. We were on holiday in Kunming, which is a fairly small city in China." She looked at me. "You know China, yes? What about Kunming?" She chuckled. "Kunming is in the southwest region, I think. We were in a park, where there were hundreds of cherry trees, all in bloom." She waved her hand before her, as though tracing out a rainbow. "It was the most beautiful thing I'd ever seen."

A slight pause. "You have a son?" I asked.

"Yes," she said. "Just one. I'm here because of him, actually."

"You are?"

She nodded again. "The last time he was in Japan, he said he got to see so many wonderful things, and that he went to so many wonderful places. I guess I'm here so that I can understand him better."

I asked if he had come here before, pointing to the café behind us.

"He did," the lady said, "except this used to be a bookstore." She looked over her shoulder. "My son was here on a trip last December, and when he got to travel around Tokyo, he asked the tour guide if he could excuse himself, just so he could pay a visit to this place. And that's what he did." She then opened up her handbag. She handed me a notebook from inside it.

"Take a look," she said.

I opened the notebook. It was slim, probably only fifty pages thick, with an unadorned black cover. There was barely anything written inside, save for the first couple of pages, in which her son had made a few notes about the places he'd been to in Japan. At the corner of a page I saw a tiny illustration of Mount Fuji, next to a date in December. At another corner I saw a name: *Mr Alvin*.

"Apparently there was a rumour going around that the bookstore could grant you any book that you would need," the lady explained. "An urban legend, he said. All you had to do was step inside, and ask the owner for a recommendation. Whatever book you got would be the only book you needed for the rest of your life."

I asked her if an old couple had been running the place.

"I don't think so," the lady replied. "I think he said it was just an old woman, tending the cash register. Nobody else."

"I see," I said. I then asked her what book her son had gotten from the owner. She smiled.

"It was this very notebook," she said. "The one you're holding in your hands."

"But," I said, feeling a little shocked. I flipped through the rest of the notebook, to see if there was anything more in it. "There's nothing here," I said.

Her smile faltered, by just a little. "Exactly," said the lady.

4

PERDIDO

OCTOBER 2012

LISA

It was a quarter to eight when the phone rang. I had just come home from work and my stepbrother Junpei was in the living room, sitting by the kotatsu reading Chiba Mari's manuscript. Judging from the scene, he must have spent the entire day in the same spot, reading up to what seemed like three quarters of the draft. "I have a feeling it's for you," Junpei said, without lifting his eyes off the page. I walked over to the phone and picked up the receiver.

"Yo," the voice said. "Have you had dinner?"

"No, not yet. I just came home, actually."

Junpei's posture stiffened.

"Is that Takao?" asked Junpei. Before I could reply to him I heard Takao again, his Kagoshima accent clear through the speaker.

"Was that voice Jun?" he said.

I told him it was.

"Has he had dinner?" he asked.

I turned towards Junpei, and asked if he had. He told me he hadn't, as I expected. "I was waiting for you to return, actually. I'm sorry." I turned back to the phone and asked Takao if he'd heard all that.

"You bet I did." He sounded excited. "Why don't the two of you join me for dinner, then? I know of a great place by Nishiarai station. Friend's recommendation. I think the both of you will like it."

I caught Junpei flipping a page of the manuscript. "Does Takao want us to eat with him?" he asked.

I nodded. "You up for it?"

Junpei narrowed his eyes. "Is it nabe again?"

"I would think so," I said. "If it's Takao, it's definitely nabe." I let my hand go from the receiver. "It's nabe, isn't it?"

"It is, kiddo."

"It's nabe," I said to Junpei. Junpei kept up his stare for about three seconds before he shrugged his shoulders.

"Why not," he said.

I told Takao that Junpei was in, and he relayed instructions for us to meet at Horikiri station in half an hour. "I'm starving," he added. I told him we'd meet him soon.

I waited by the front door as Junpei got changed in his room upstairs. He came down in a blue cardigan worn over a yellow shirt, and a pair of oversized jeans with the cuffs rolled up. It was the second day of October, and everyone in the city could feel the autumn chill returning whenever it got dark. Junpei asked if it was cold outside; he'd lost all sense of the weather that day, staying cooped up in the house, and I told him that what he wore was enough.

"I don't know what's so good about nabe," Junpei said, as we wound down the alleyway towards the station. "Doesn't Takao ever get sick of it?"

"I don't think so," I said. We walked past a large three-storey house, from which you could hear the notes of somebody practicing on the piano. "How long have we known Takao already?"

"Around one and a half years?" he said.

"And have we ever seen Takao getting sick of nabe?"

"I don't think so," said Junpei.

"Well there you go," I said. "History has all the answers. Just think of it as a hobby of his, like how some guys are obsessed with trains and blow-up dolls and stuff like that."

"But instead of trains and blow-up dolls, Takao's obsessed with nabe."

"That's right. Although 'obsessed' might be too strong a word for it. It's a lot like you and reading, actually," I said. "You just can't get enough, can you? And you're always on the lookout for the next big thing."

"That's true," said Junpei, nodding along. We were walking past another big house this time, except this one was a bit run-down, with vines cascading down the front. From it came the screams and laughter of an evening variety programme. "Don't you ever get sick of it?" he asked.

"Of nabe?"

"Yeah."

"I don't think so," I said. "I think it'd break Takao's heart if I ever got to that point."

Junpei rolled his eyes. "Stop it," he said. "Just stop."

Takao was there as he said he would be: standing outside the main entrance to the station, leaning against a vending machine. Like us, he too was dressed rather casually, decked in a baseball jacket one size too small for his frame. I couldn't tell which team it was, but its colours were red and white with the number five stitched on its back. We caught his eye and he waved at us, gesturing towards the ticket barriers.

"Let's go, kids," he said.

The train picked up speed as the three of us settled into a row of seats. The neighbourhood rolled past our windows, all low-lying suburbia and the occasional large building. The scenery looked almost alien, especially at night, as I rarely travelled north on the Tobu Skytree Line. Junpei asked Takao if he had waited long at the station.

"Not really," he said. "I had *A Love Supreme* playing, from the start of the first movement, and the third had just come to an end. That much I know."

Junpei asked Takao how many movements there were. Takao said there were four.

"The first part is 'Acknowledgement'. The second 'Resolution', and the third 'Pursuance'."

"And the fourth?"

"'Psalm'," answered Takao.

Junpei grew silent. He had a small frown on his forehead. "Were you at the park by the river again?"

"As usual," he replied. Takao had chanced upon it a week ago, located on the east side of the Horikiri station; the park was a small section of a larger one that ran down the coast of the Arakawa River. As a kappa in his late thirties, he considered himself more than lucky to be in such proximity to a body of water. He loved the feeling of its sharp breeze, cutting across the top of his head, and he loved the indescribable warmth it gave him, at a time of the year when it was getting cold again. He'd go there whenever he was free, just to spend some time alone.

The train stopped at Kitasenju station.

"Did you spend a lot of time there?" Junpei asked. "Or was it just for a while?"

"Around thirty minutes," said Takao. "I had to leave because I was hungry."

The train moved on. It left the neighbourhood behind, all the lights and the activity of the city centre, as it ran across a bridge spanning the breadth of the Arakawa. The three of us fell silent as we turned around in our seats, and watched for those few seconds as the passage of water stretched before our eyes, dark yet alive in the night.

"A penny for your thoughts?" asked Takao.

I looked at him. I mustered a smile.

"I was just thinking about how long this day has been."

He smiled in return. "Did anything in particular happen at the café today?"

I shook my head. "Not really," I said. "It was just really busy, even though in reality nothing happened at all. I feel like I've been running on a treadmill all day, and my body is still buzzing, even after getting off the machine."

Takao laid a hand on my shoulder, and squeezed it. "Remember how enthusiastic you used to be," he said. "Talking endlessly about the food, or that writer friend of yours."

I kept my gaze on the passing view. "It's just one of those

days, Takao. I'm sure you understand."

Eventually we arrived at Nishiarai. The three of us stepped outside. Takao told us that the restaurant was located on the west side of the station, somewhere in the vicinity of a hospital and an elementary school. According to his friend, we should be able to find it once we catch sight of both places.

"Are you saying you don't have an address, Takao?"

Takao smiled at Junpei. "That's right, kiddo."

"No way," he said. He looked really unimpressed. "You're lying, Takao. Look at this place! It's just full of houses. There's no way we can find a restaurant, not here in the dark."

"Kiddo," said Takao. "Calm down, okay? We are not in the dark, you hear me?" He then pointed at a streetlamp. "This is the light," he said. "Learn how to follow it."

Junpei stared at his back as Takao walked onwards ahead of us. He then tugged at my arm. "Hey, hey, older sis. Do something about him."

I patted his hand. "Just roll with it," I whispered to him. "You've got me at least."

We walked past a house. I could hear the sounds of somebody washing dishes in the sink, the sharp clatter of plates being arranged on a rack. A child calling for its mother. They were sounds of an inner life, a world shut away from prying eyes, and I wondered, for just a moment, if a restaurant of any sort could exist in this neighbourhood at all. And yet there was a small road sign, planted at the corner of an intersection: it pointed the way to Kurihara Elementary School. We followed the arrow on the sign, with only a small, tingling sense of where we were going.

•

My mother came to date a man six years her junior in the summer of 2009. I was still a second-year student at university back then, and my mother was a kitchen assistant in an upscale bakery, located in the basement of a department store in Ginza. The man, on the other hand, was a corporate salesman for a multinational corporation, whose headquarters in Japan was based in Tokyo. This man was Junpei's father.

According to my mother, Junpei's father would drop by the bakery every Monday at one thirty, and every Thursday at two thirty, which so happened to coincide with her shifts. Every time he visited the bakery, he would always order a box of egg tarts or strawberry shortcake—goods that he felt he might placate his clients with. It didn't take long, apparently, for my mother to catch the eye of this particular man. The bakery had an open concept kitchen, the kind with windows through which the customers could observe the bakers hard at work, and my mother, well approaching her fifties, possessed an inexplicable charm and beauty.

On the day he asked her out for coffee, Junpei's father informed my mother that although his company was based in Tokyo, his bosses had singled him out to oversee operations in their Sapporo branch. The branch hadn't been performing very well over the past year or so, and his bosses had decided that a shake-up in the management there was necessary. Although Junpei's father was excited by the prospect of taking on a more managerial role, he found it a little too lonely: he knew nobody in Hokkaido, having grown up in

Tokyo all his life, and he wondered if my mother would like to accompany him there.

My mother, having never gone on a plane her entire life, was flattered that a younger man like him would ask her for such a favour. She said yes. After three weeks in Hokkaido, my mother came back home a seemingly younger woman, refreshed and rejuvenated by the experience. "I was so happy and in love I almost couldn't recognise myself," she said to me. "Everything in Hokkaido looked unreal. It was as though a new life—a life wholly different to the one I've always had—awaited me there in Hokkaido. I couldn't believe it."

Not long after their second trip to Hokkaido, my mother announced that she would be getting married to Junpei's father, and we moved into his house in Adachi city that fall. But it soon became apparent that my stepfather's job demanded more and more of his time in Hokkaido, and he was far from happy with the idea of leaving his wife alone in the city. And thus, both of our parents would travel up north for months at a time: it was an extended honeymoon of sorts, a long vacation that left me and Junpei to our own devices.

It helped that us kids were easy-going types, quick to adapt to any situation, although at first I had assumed that Junpei had a rather hard, inflexible personality. Still in his second year at middle school, he was convinced that reading and writing fiction was his life's calling, and refused to consider doing anything else as a hobby. In time, I realised that it was because Junpei was so set in his ways, so firm he was in his beliefs and in the things he wanted from life, that he had no fear of ever changing no matter what life threw at him. He was like a perfectly smooth stone at the bottom of a river, and for that I envied him greatly.

Once in a while, I'd receive a call from my mother, telling me how wonderful her life was in Sapporo, going to all sorts of parks and sampling all kinds of cuisine. She even picked up skiing fairly quickly, a sport she had always wanted to try. "It was such a fantasy," she once said to me, "going down the face of a mountain and then riding back up in a cable car. As though I were in a dream." During these calls I'd find it hard to break the news that I had dropped out of university, and talked about Junpei's life instead.

"He's now in his final year at middle school, and he's doing really well," I said. "He's become more and more serious about fiction these days, dabbling in a couple of short stories for me to read." I then told her about an inter-school competition that he'd participated in, just a few weeks ago. One of his submissions had earned him the first prize.

"Ah, that's amazing!" my mother said. "Your father and I have been visiting a number of bookstores in the area, trying to find something Junpei has never read before. We think we may have a couple of titles he might enjoy. Does Junpei have a favourite author?"

The answer was easy. "Chiba Mari," I told her. "Have you heard of her?"

"Hmm, I might have. Isn't she the novelist who did nothing but write the moment she graduated from university? The one who wrote *Dining Is West*?"

"That's right," I said. "He really respects her. It's his wish to meet her one day."

"That's nice," said my mother. She then seemed to pause rather thoughtfully. "Say, Lisa. Do me a favour, all right? I want you to ask Junpei something on my behalf."

"What is it?"

"Well, I want to know what kind of writer he is. And I'm not talking about the kind of fiction he wants to write—I'm talking about his practice, his habits, his routine. More specifically, I want to ask: does he need music as a stimulant? Or does he need total silence in order to concentrate? That's what I've been wondering lately."

Later that evening, I found Junpei in the living room, with his feet under the kotatsu, even though it was the middle of August. In front of him was his laptop, an e-book open across the screen. I asked him if he preferred music or silence whenever he wrote, and he took a while to find an answer to that question.

"I'm not sure," he said in reply. "I don't even think perfect silence is achievable, in any case. But I guess I'll go with that for now."

I got to know Takao two years later, in the summer of 2011. He was a clean-shaven guy, with bags under his eyes and hair that reached down his neck. He had a particularly tall frame, and was built rather burly as well, which made him appear rather impressive from afar. For clothes, Takao didn't stick to any particular style, but during the cooler months he'd wear a baseball jacket over a plain white tee. Whenever I asked him about the team on his jacket, he'd say that he had no idea. "I'm not a sports guy at all," he once explained to me. "I just like the material."

The first time I heard Takao practice on his saxophone was on a Saturday afternoon, when Junpei and I were both seated in the living room of our house. It was the middle of

July. I was casually flipping through the pages of a television guide as Junpei wrestled with a paragraph. It then came as a surprise when the two of us heard that clear, unmistakable sound. It was something I had never heard before, here in Adachi city: the sound of scales and arpeggios, played on a sax.

Junpei, seated in front of his laptop, stopped writing altogether. "That's a saxophone, isn't it?" His gaze was fixed onto the open window, as though he could somehow observe the notes in the air. At the time I had no idea where they might be coming from, or from whom.

"It is," I said. "Without a doubt."

"Didn't you play the sax yourself?" he asked, turning around.

"Yeah," I said. "A long time ago." I was part of the concert band, back in high school. "I played the baritone sax for a while, but that got too heavy for me, so I switched to the tenor."

"What's the difference?"

"The baritone's really big, and it's used to produce the bass. The tenor's more mid-sized, and is used to provide the harmony. Quite like a supporting role."

"And is that a tenor?" Junpei asked, referring to the sound of the sax, coming from outside. We listened as the musician went through his drills. I told him that it was.

Eventually word got around that the sax player lived in a house just two streets away from ours, according to one of my older neighbours. The guy was a member of a renowned wind orchestra as well. This older neighbour of mine then claimed she had bumped into him two days ago, leaving the supermarket with his instrument case in one hand, a bag of groceries in the other and a hole in the crown of his head, no larger than a five-hundred yen coin. "There's no mistaking it," my neighbour said, making a circular gesture over the top of her head. "That man's a kappa." She shook her head. "He has a pretty distinct accent as well, so my guess is that he isn't from Tokyo either."

"So you're saying he's from somewhere else?"

She nodded and waved her hand. "Somewhere far away."

I met him by chance a few days later, when I went to have dinner with a couple of old friends from high school. It was at a small restaurant within the 1-chome of Yanagihara, famous for its beef bowls, and several of my friends who had moved out of town wanted nothing more than to relive the taste of that beef and onion stir fry. Just before I left, however, I caught sight of a kappa, seated at the corner of the restaurant, an electric hot pot boiling on the table before him. It was a strange sight, especially during the summer—and in a manner of seconds I decided to take a chance, and approached his table. I had nothing to lose, in the final analysis. All I had was a gut feeling: this was the sax player everybody in my neighbourhood had been talking about.

"Hi there," I said, seating myself across from him. The hot pot continued to puff and emit steam as it boiled between the two of us. "I noticed you've been eating nabe all by yourself."

The kappa looked up from his bowl and stared at me.

"Is that supposed to be bad?" he said, in that strange accent of his. A year and a half ago, I didn't know enough about his particular accent to know where he might have come from.

"Just a little," I said. He sighed.

"Well, I'm a kappa, if that's any excuse." He placed his

chopsticks aside. "We tend to be solitary creatures." He then lowered his head: there was a hole in his scalp, a perfectly smooth, hairless depression where his crown should have been. The hole had been visible enough before, but now I could see it in its entirety. It was indeed no bigger than the size of a five-hundred yen coin.

"But is it true, though?" I asked. "That kappas prefer to be alone?"

"You could say that. It's not entirely false. And it's not that we can't form groups or cliques, or operate in teams—we get along with humans just as well as humans get along with one another. Kappas are just bad at forming groups with other kappas. You'll hardly ever find a group of people solely comprised of them."

"But why is that?" I asked.

Takao shrugged. "We've been conditioned, I think. To view our true nature as something we ought to suppress. And so, whenever a kappa comes across another kappa, all the kappa can see is his hidden self, openly reflected in the other person."

I crossed my arms over the tabletop. "And do you feel that way as well?"

Takao made a face, and picked up his chopsticks. "What's your name, by the way?"

"Lisa."

"I take it that's your first name, Lisa?"

"That's right," I said.

"My name is Takao," he said in return. "And how old are you?"

"Twenty, nearing twenty-one."

He whistled. "That's pretty damn young, kid." He then took hold of a ladle, and scooped out a large serving of food. He poured it into a spare bowl and handed it to me. "You like nabe, Lisa?"

"Not so much in the summer," I said. "You don't think it's too hot, or humid?"

He chuckled, and handed me a pair of chopsticks and a wooden spoon. "That's perfect for a kappa, kiddo."

"I see," I said. I then decided to go on a limb. "Do you play the tenor sax, by any chance?"

A look of surprise came over his face. "You live near Horikiri station?"

"Right next to the hospital," I said. "My brother and I hear you practice all the time."

He let out a laugh. "And here I was, thinking you were a total stranger." His accent sounded more distinct than ever. "We come from the same place, you and I."

•

Junpei said we were lost, and I had to agree. The three of us were lost. "What do you mean?" said Takao. "We're no more lost than when we first stepped foot in this neighbourhood. We'll find our way eventually."

We stopped in front of the main gates to the elementary school, and began to search for signs to the hospital. According to Takao's friend, finding the restaurant was a matter of finding both places. But neither of us had ever been here before, and in the dark, where the edges of things were least defined, all of the surrounding buildings only seemed to grow in size.

"Does the restaurant have a name?" I asked. "Maybe Junpei could look it up on his phone."

Takao scratched the back of his head, fingering the edge around the hole in his skull. "Perdido," he answered.

"What language is that?" Junpei asked.

"Spanish."

"And why would a nabe restaurant have a Spanish name?"

"I have no idea," said Takao, shrugging his shoulders. "But it's also the title of a great jazz number. The composer's Juan Tizol, a Puerto Rican trombonist. My friend plays jazz as well, so he naturally got drawn to the name."

"And your friend didn't think to give you a more specific address?"

Takao shook his head. "He tried to, kiddo."

"What went wrong?"

"After he left, he tried to find his way back. He wanted to see if he could obtain an address or a business card of some sort. He'd found it by accident, after all. But it was nearing midnight, and his girlfriend was getting afraid of the dark. Like us, it was their first time in a distant neighbourhood, and so they weren't familiar with the area at all. That's why all he had were the school and the hospital as reference points."

"Did he pay the restaurant a second visit?" I asked.

Takao shook his head. "He only ate there quite recently, about two weeks ago," he said. "He's not that keen on nabe either."

Junpei sighed and took out his smartphone from the pocket of his jeans. "Fine then," he said. "I'll bring up a map of the neighbourhood and we'll see."

He led us straight to the hospital, about thirty seconds

away from the school. Junpei continued to look at the screen of his smartphone.

"There's no restaurant listed on the map. But I'm sure if we just look around…"

I turned. There was a small, traditional-looking house, with a tiled rooftop and several cars parked along the front. The house stood conspicuously between two larger buildings, as though it knew it didn't belong in the scene. Faintly I could hear the sounds of music playing, as well as of cutlery, clattering on table surfaces. People laughed and talked in loud voices.

"Could that be the place?" I said.

Takao took a closer look. Hanging outside the door was a white T-shirt. The word Perdido was written on it, scrawled with a black marker. A look of satisfaction spread across Takao's face.

"This is it, kids," he said. "Let's go in."

We slid open the door. The restaurant turned out to be a fairly packed establishment, its size twice as big as the café where I worked. The air was thick and heavy with the smell of nabe and beer—the mood was nothing short of riotous. Seated around the tables were families both big and small, dressed surprisingly in loungewear and slippers; the parents scooped boiled noodles and meat slices for their children, as the younger kids ran about and knocked into things. There was a group of salarymen seated at the back, trading jokes over two large pots, as a phonograph stood by the main doorway, playing music from another era.

Takao asked for a table for three. A waiter led us to a table, situated beneath a framed poster. Printed on the poster was a black woman, from what seemed like the sixties: she had short and curly hair, and wore a lime green dress. There was a caption printed across her bosom, in red and yellow characters: *I search for my heart in Perdido.*

"It's lively, isn't it?" I said to Junpei. He didn't respond.

Takao took a quick look at the menu, and placed an order with the waiter. The waiter walked away.

"I thought it'd be quieter," said Junpei.

Takao smiled, and hung his baseball jacket over the back of his chair. "Nabe is nice when you have it all to yourself. But it's even better with friends. It's a dish that's meant to be shared."

Junpei nodded. The waiter reappeared, with a jug full of stock.

"Do you ever have nabe with other people?"

"You mean, like, people apart from the two of you?"

Junpei nodded again. The waiter poured the stock into the hot pot, and set the remainder aside. The waiter then adjusted the dials on the electric heater.

"Well, sometimes," said Takao. "Not too often. I prefer your company a lot more, if I have to be honest."

"You mean to say, me and my sister?"

"Well yeah," said Takao. "You and your sister both."

The waiter went away and came back with an array of ingredients: shiitake and enoki mushrooms, tofu and fresh eggs; there were also a couple of leafy vegetables, as well as some sukiyaki slices of beef and pork. But the broth, still simmering, had yet to be brought to a boil.

"Can I ask you something personal?" asked Junpei.

Takao nodded again. "Sure thing, kiddo. But you'll have

to speak up."

I watched Junpei as he tried to find the words.

"Do you have any family in Tokyo?" he asked, his voice a little louder.

Takao paused.

"Well, you know I'm originally from Kagoshima. You can tell from my accent," he said.

"Does that mean your family's still there?"

"Well, my parents are dead, if that's what you're poking around for. But I have two other siblings."

"And?"

"They've moved on to other places. Just like me."

"So they don't live in Kagoshima anymore?" Junpei asked. Takao shook his head. "And nobody followed you to Tokyo?"

"None," said Takao. "Nobody followed me anywhere." He then picked up the mushrooms and the vegetables, and dumped half of it into the stock. The liquid had just started to boil at that point. "Anyway, enough about me," said Takao. "Let's talk about you, Jun. What did you do today?"

Junpei paused. He told Takao about how he had been reading Chiba Mari's manuscript ever since he woke that morning.

"It's her latest novel," he said, "about a notebook that a young man purchases at a bookstore. He buys it, thinking that it's empty. But when he opens it, he realises it's filled with the diary entries of some other person. The more he reads this diary, the more he realises that it's about a person who'd run away from home at the age of sixteen, only to find himself unable to return when he wanted to at the age of twenty-five."

Takao began to serve us the enoki mushrooms.

"So does the young man end up trying to find this person?" he asked. "I assume he feels bad about coming across this guy's diary, or at least curious as to who this person might be."

Junpei shook his head. "The diary is only half the story," he said. "In the other half, the protagonist is too unmotivated and lazy to lead a fulfilling life. But you get this feeling that he wants to murder his neighbour's dog."

"The dog?" said Takao. "Really?"

Junpei nodded. "Chiba Mari is fascinated with household pets, I realise. She once said in an interview that pets are given this illusion that they're a part of something, although in reality their lives are mostly governed and led by the choices of others. She thinks their only purpose is to fill up the pockets of space in other people's lives. There's a lot of cruelty in that arrangement, according to her point of view."

"Well, that's certainly a unique perspective," said Takao.

"It is," said Junpei. "For example, her fourth novel was a family drama centred on the death of a pet goldfish. It was the kind of goldfish that won many prizes for being really beautiful."

"I see," said Takao. He looked towards me. "You know, this Chiba Mari person—she's pretty famous, isn't she?"

"She's quite famous, yes," I said.

"So how does a sixteen-year-old like Jun get his hands on the manuscript of her latest novel?" he asked. "I imagine you had something to do with that."

I smiled at him. "Chiba Mari told me at the café that she was hard at work on something she had never thought of doing before. She wanted a real fan of her work to read it and give her feedback before she showed it to anybody else, and proceeded to ask me about Junpei. She needed somebody both smart and trustworthy—someone who could compare this manuscript with her previous four novels, and who was also loyal enough to be understanding and yet impartial. She asked if my brother fit the bill."

"And you said yes?"

I nodded.

"And then she gave you her manuscript, just like that," said Takao. I nodded again.

"She gave me instructions to pass it on to him, as well her business card in the event either of us wished to contact her. This happened last Thursday, I think."

"The thing is, she expects me to finish reading her manuscript by the end of this weekend," said Junpei. "That's why I did nothing but that today."

"Right," said Takao. He took the plate of meat, and dropped a few of the slices into the broth. They turned grey in a matter of seconds. "So what do you think, Junpei? Does the protagonist kill the neighbour's dog in the end?"

Junpei fished out a slice of beef with his chopsticks. "I'm not entirely sure, to be honest," he said. He then placed the beef in his mouth.

Takao looked confused. "Why aren't you sure?" he asked, and Junpei answered after he swallowed.

"I'm getting the sense that he might kill himself instead," he said.

"But why?" asked Takao. "Why would he do that?"

"I'm not sure," said Junpei. "I'm not done with the manuscript. But I think it's because he identifies with the dog in some way."

"More than he would with the guy in the diary?"

"I believe so," said Junpei. "In some way, the fortunes of the diary-writer run contrary to the protagonist's. The protagonist, whose life revolves around his house and his neighbour's, remains transfixed in a prison of his own making, whereas the diary-writer travels across the country in a bid to retrace his steps. The writer's journey to and fro seems almost too exciting to be true, and so the protagonist sees more of himself in the dog next door than in the person he reads about in the diary."

Takao grew quiet. He began to gaze at the food before him. I scooped a ladleful of broth and poured it into my own bowl.

"A penny for your thoughts, old man?" I asked. Takao raised his head and looked towards me. He didn't say a thing for about a minute or so.

"Can humans really feel that way, sometimes?" he asked. "Like they're lost, even when they're not? Even when they're at the place where they're absolutely meant to be?"

I thought about the question. I then looked at him, still staring at the pot. "I guess so," I said, and left it at that.

It was nearly ten o' clock when the train stopped at Horikiri station. Junpei took down the restaurant's address, just before we left the place, and passed the details on to Takao. "Now you'll know your way back to Perdido," he said. As we walked out of the station, Takao asked if either of us would like to stay for a while, perhaps go on a walk with him. Junpei said he had to go home.

"Is it the manuscript?" Takao asked, and Junpei said it

was. "Are you close to the ending, Jun?"

"I'm nearly there," he said. "Just about a quarter left."

Takao smiled. "Let me know how it goes, okay?"

Junpei said he would. He then left. Takao turned towards me.

"Does the novel have a title, by the way?" he asked, and I shook my head.

"Chiba Mari's still deciding, I think. I don't recall seeing a title on the first page, when I had handed the stack to Junpei."

A wind blew towards us. Takao drew his jacket tighter around him, and pulled the zip up even higher.

"Maybe it's not meant to have a title at all," he said. "Maybe that's been Chiba Mari's plan from the start."

I laughed. "Perhaps," I said. "We'll never know."

We began to walk: we went back into the station and came out through another exit, climbing up the steps to the side of a long, long road. It seemed to have no end at this time of the night; it stretched, endlessly, towards a point where I couldn't make out anything anymore. I realised that Takao was taking me to his park—the one beside the river. We stood by the roadside, and waited for a taxi to pass before crossing.

The park was freshly mowed, with the sight of the Arakawa River before it. Takao and I were the only ones there that night, hugging our knees against the sharp, chilly breeze. Distant were the sounds of the railway and expressway, swirling around and behind us, as though the sounds were drifting on the wind.

"It's nice," Takao said softly, as though he were speaking to himself.

"It is," I said. I tried to make out the expression on his

face, but it was hard to do so without any light. "Have you ever had company before?" I asked. "Here in this park?"

"No," he said. "You're the first."

"I see," I said. I looked at the expressway on my right, and saw how it made one large curve around the horizon. "I can see why you're drawn to this place."

"You can?" said Takao. "You're nice. But it's such a typical thing for a kappa to do. People sometimes mock me for it."

"Do they, really?"

"They do," he said, with a hint of a smile. "Sometimes I notice people here as well, and then they notice me back: they see a lonely guy at first, seated all by himself, and then they notice the hole in my head. They keep clear of the place, as though they're trespassing or something. And to think my actual house is right over there," he added, pointing beyond the expressway. "I can't help but laugh sometimes, just thinking about it."

I thought about what he said. "You know, humans do it too. They like to be around rivers and oceans and seas as much as any other kappa. Think about it," I said. "I work in a café by the river, and there are quite a number of regulars there. And I'm sure they're not just there for the coffee. Some come because of the scenery."

"Really?"

"Really."

"That's interesting," said Takao. I could feel the weight of his gaze, boring into the side of my face. "I wonder why."

I shrugged. "It's just something we share, I guess. Is that why your family was originally based in Kagoshima? It being by the sea and everything?"

"Yes," he said. "We lived near the bay, actually, with Sakurajima rising from the centre."

"Sakurajima's a volcano, isn't it?"

"It is," he said. He then lay down on the grass, and folded his arms behind his head. "In order to support me and my siblings, both of my parents worked at a hotel located on the southern coast of the volcano. And in that hotel was a famous onsen, right at the edge of the sea. Some considered it spiritual, a holy sort of place; men and women both would wear robes and bathe together, and enjoy a direct view of the sea." He sniffed. "When we were kids, my siblings and I would go there and have fun whenever the hotel guests weren't expected anymore."

"That sounds wonderful," I said.

"It was, yeah. But my mother in particular used to tell us scary tales about human beings. According to her, all the humans secretly wanted to eat us; they'd cut us up and boil us in their hot pots whenever the weather got cold." He paused. "That's why we could only go to the hotel's onsen when the humans weren't around. If they saw us jumping around in the hot water they might feel tempted to snatch us away and eat us."

I thought carefully about what to say next; Takao had never spoken so openly about his past before.

"Is that why you keep eating nabe? So you can be more human?" I asked.

"No," he replied, shaking his head. "No matter what I do, I will always remain a kappa."

"Then why?" I asked.

He took in a deep breath, and let out a sigh. It was the

kind of sigh you hear at first, and then nothing at all, nothing until it goes away. He said, "I had a feeling that the more I eat nabe, the less afraid of death I will become. But I am never not afraid of death. And I will never stop thinking about dying. I know that now. That's why I eat nabe all the time, whenever I can afford to."

I let out a laugh. "Oh, Takao," I said. "Does nabe even taste good to you?"

He laughed as well. "That's the weirdest bit, kiddo. It's the best thing in the world, and I can't get enough of it. I will never be sick of it. I could have it any time of the year."

I laid myself down on the grass beside him. I turned on my side so I could continue to watch him. The grass, short and spiky, smelt of fresh dirt and water.

"Have you ever thought of returning to Kagoshima?" I asked.

"I have," he said. "But there's no reason for me to go back anymore. Both of my parents are dead. All my siblings have moved away. Even the hotel where my parents used to work at is gone."

"Gone?"

"Yeah," said Takao. "The hotel management filed for bankruptcy a few days ago, if I remember correctly. It wasn't making enough money, in spite of its famous onsen. The court just accepted their filings today."

"Today?" I repeated.

"Yes, today," he said. "Which means the hotel is probably closed forever."

We fell into a short silence. I watched him as he continued to watch the sky above us, the hair of his fringe whipping about in the breeze. I held my own hair down with a hand, to keep it from getting into my eyes.

"Takao?"

"Yes?"

"Could you close your eyes for me?"

"Sure."

"Thanks," I said. "Can you imagine something for me?"

He nodded.

"I want you to imagine us going to Kagoshima," I said.

"Right now?"

"Yes," I said. "Right now. Imagine the two of us taking the bullet train down south, across the entire length of the country. How crazy and irresponsible that would be."

"Oh yeah," said Takao. "Really irresponsible."

"Imagine the both of us, finding our way to Sakurajima. We'd take a taxi, try to find the hotel where your parents used to work."

He smiled.

"We'd have to board a ferry first," he said. "The port's right next to the station."

"Fine," I said. "We go to the port. The ferry comes, and we board it. The ferry stops at Sakurajima."

"It must be scary at night," said Takao.

"Just a little," I said, even though I was not afraid of the dark. "A taxi soon arrives. You tell the driver the address of the hotel."

Takao scratched the tip of his nose. His eyelids were still shut.

"He drives us there," he said. "But the taxi driver doesn't know the hotel is closed for good."

"That's right," I said. "The stupid driver doesn't know anything. He drops us off at the hotel, and we find that the doors are unlocked."

Takao laughed. "That's convenient."

"It is, isn't it? Anyway. We find the lobby, take a look at the signs. The signs point us in all sorts of directions. But we manage to find our way to this onsen of yours—which you and your siblings used to play in as children, when all the guests have gone to sleep."

Takao paused. "I take off my clothes," he said. "You take yours off as well. We put on our bathrobes." He paused again. "We push through the door and realise we're outdoors."

"We're outdoors?"

"Yeah," he said. "We're outdoors. We walk down a flight of stairs, down to the bottom of the slope. Down to the coast. None of the lanterns are on, so there's no light at all. But you can hear the sea all around us."

"And then we enter the water," I said.

"We enter the water," he said.

"The water is warm."

"The water is warm."

"You notice the sea is all black in the night."

"It's all black," said Takao. "And the wind from the sea is cold."

"It is?"

"It is," said Takao. "I walk to the edge of the bath. I spread open my arms." He then spread his arms open, his right hand hovering above my head on the grass. "Like this," he said.

"That's right," I said. "You spread your arms open, and I watch you from behind. I'm watching you from behind,

Takao." I then took his hand, used it as a pillow. His fingers were strong and warm against the side of my ear. "And how do you feel, old guy? How do you think you feel?"

He didn't say anything for a while. I felt his thumb, roving around the edge of my earlobe.

"It's a particular kind of loss," he said. "Something I can't quite put my finger on, but it's there. The more you look into it, the more it stares back at you, leaving you cold on the inside." He paused. "It feels like a void of some kind, the kind that hurts around the edges—and yet the longer I stand there, the less I can feel it hurting. The fuller I feel I'm becoming."

His thumb stopped moving. I smiled to myself, and pressed my hands against my eyes. I asked the old guy if it was true, if he could really feel it happening to him—and he said it was true, he said that he could. As though he were really there, standing at the edge of the world, letting the water fill up the void inside him. He could feel it all, while I felt nothing. I felt nothing whatsoever.

PART TWO

5

LOVER MAN

DECEMBER 2012

Sugimura

The intermission was nearly coming to an end, and the boy said he needed to pee. I looked at my friend, seated on his other side. He looked back at me. "C'mon," my friend said to Goro. "Let's go."

It was the New Year's Eve concert, held at the Fumon Hall in Tokyo. All my life, I had never stepped foot in a concert hall as big as this one, and now, as the crowd gradually dissipated, I found myself one of the few people remaining, seated in the middle of this great chamber. I noted an old couple seated together, down the row to my left, thumbing through the programme. In the row before mine, a couple of seats down to the right, sat Mr Five. I didn't know him then, but I would soon enough.

He was a kappa in what seemed like his fifties, the hole in his head positioned several inches above his left ear. Large boils of various sizes covered his face and his neck, each boil catching the light differently, causing his profile to be cast in an array of splintered shadows. It was such a curious effect I couldn't help but stare, until Mr Five looked over his shoulder and established eye contact with me. I was too transfixed to look away. Caught in the act, I ended up smiling at him, and he smiled back. The kappa then got up from his seat, walked down to the end of his row, and sat himself in the vacant one next to mine.

"I am Mr Five," he said with a short bow. I bowed back.

"Mr Five?" I asked.

"Yes," he said. "Mr Five, as opposed to Mr Four, or Mr Six. It is a nickname." He then said he was here to support a friend; a member of a jazz quintet he had most recently joined. "I am the fifth member of this quintet, and thus: Mr Five."

"Interesting…" I told him I was here to support a friend as well.

"Oh? What does he play?" he asked.

"The saxophone."

Mr Five blinked, and smiled even wider. He seemed taken aback by my answer.

"Same here," he said. "My friend plays the sax, while I play the trumpet."

I shifted in my seat. "Are you… a member of an orchestra as well?"

He pursed his lips and shook his head, as though it was a matter of great sensitivity to him. "I find it particularly hard to relate to classical music," he explained. "It lacks all of the things that make jazz so great: the spontaneity, the cool, the unpredictability. But I must admit I was very moved, halfway through the first set."

I began looking through the programme. "You mean, during the Gustav Holst…?"

"Yes," said Mr Five. "There it is: the Second Suite in F. Are you fond of classical music yourself?"

"You could say so," I said, closing the booklet. "But I prefer jazz as well… I owe this to my friend's influence."

"Was he the one you came with?"

"Yes… He's in the toilet now."

"I see," said Mr Five. He paused for a while, looking towards the empty stage. "I hope you do not mind me asking, but was that your son, seated between you and your friend? I could not help but notice earlier, just before the concert started."

"Ah, he is," I said. "My son."

Mr Five kept quiet once more. His eyes remained directed towards the stage. There were nothing but chairs and music stands, the conductor's podium. Mr Five scratched a large boil on his chin, in a thoughtful kind of way. "How strange then," he said to me, "for a kappa boy to have a human father."

I scratched my lip. It wasn't the first time I had been asked that question. "It's hard not to notice him… especially when the hole in his head is so big."

Mr Five crossed his arms. "I have never seen anything like it before, if you do not mind me saying. It is as though the boy had stepped out of the Edo period. Kappas like him are not meant to exist today, or rather, they just do not anymore."

I nodded my head. I didn't know what to say.

"Anyway," said Mr Five, getting up on his feet. "It was

nice chatting with you, Mr Sugimura. I will return to my seat." I then watched the back of his coat as he ambled away, down to the far end of the row, just as the other concertgoers streamed back in. Briefly, I wondered how the man had known my name.

•

Goro's homeroom teacher called me down once, to speak to me privately at the elementary school. It was during the last week of November, about four to five weeks ago. Classes were still ongoing that afternoon, but it was a free period of hers, and so we had a good hour of time entirely to ourselves.

"Shinichi's parents just had him transferred," Goro's teacher said. We were seated in the art studio, located on the third floor; she sat in a chair two metres away from me, the both of us at one end of a window. It was nearly two in the afternoon, and the room was filled with a clear, cleansing sort of light. "It was only a matter of time. They sent him to another school in a neighbouring city," she added.

"Is that so…?" I was dawdling again. "Was he treated badly? Because of what he did to Goro?"

The teacher tilted her head to the side. She was in her early fifties, possibly even later, but she had a girlish manner about her. She spoke slowly and gently, and had a fairly high voice register. She taught mainly mathematics at the school. Her students knew her as Ms Itsuko.

"It's only natural, considering what he did to your child. The kids made sure that Shinichi wouldn't go unpunished. Shinichi even seemed to welcome it at times," she said.

A few seconds of silence passed. Ms Itsuko brushed a piece of lint off her skirt. She then went on.

"Apparently one of the teachers had asked Shinichi if he was sure he wanted to leave, and he said that he did. Excuse me, Mr Sugimura—but he said he didn't feel safe."

"From his classmates…?"

She shook her head. "Shinichi said he could feel another person inside him; a person who could take control of his every movement. But of course we're not here to talk about him, Mr Sugimura. We're here to talk about your son."

"Right," I said. "Of course."

Ms Itsuko crossed, and then recrossed her legs.

"I'm sure you understand, however, that if we are to talk about your son, we will have to talk about the incident that happened in September."

"Of course," I said. "That goes without saying."

She smiled. "I apologise. I don't know if you remember all the details, Mr Sugimura, but it was right down this hallway, in the boys' restroom. Shinichi had just come out from one of the stalls, while your child was in the midst of washing his hands. And then something came over Shinichi: a violent impulse he couldn't contain. He took the back of Goro's head and smashed it against the mirror."

"I remember," I said to her. "There were…there were three other kids in there as well."

"That is right," said Ms Itsuko. "Three other witnesses to the incident. Two of them were Goro's classmates. All three of the boys said Goro had done nothing to provoke him. All Goro had done was wash his hands in the sink like he was supposed to."

Just then I heard a sudden *ping*—the sound of a bat hitting a ball outside. From the window, I could see a bunch of kids practicing baseball on the field. A round of applause rose from the stands, as the coach shouted something encouraging.

"Shinichi said it was the hole at the back of Goro's head that had agitated him." The batter began running towards the base. "He said he had never seen a cavity that big before in his life."

I nodded. Ms Itsuko turned towards the window as well, just as the batter scored a point.

"Sorry to ask, but—it's five inches wide, isn't it? More or less."

I nodded again.

"And how big was it, when you first adopted him?"

I tried to remember. It had been four years earlier. "Around three inches, I think…maybe three and a half."

"And do you think the hole in Goro's head will continue to grow, Mr Sugimura?" She tore her gaze away from the field. "I can only assume that would be the case. The boy's only eight, after all. There's still a long way to go before puberty."

The next pitcher assumed his position on the mound.

"It'll stop though," I said. "Won't it?"

Ms Itsuko didn't seem to know for sure. "My fear is if it gets any bigger it might invite more trouble in the future. I hope you understand," she said.

The pitcher swung his arm: the ball flew in a straight, white line. The pitcher couldn't have been older than twelve.

"I'm scared," I said.

Ms Itsuko smiled once more. I saw it in her reflection on

the windowpane. "That's natural, Mr Sugimura. Fear is the one thing all parents share."

It had been around eleven in the morning when I first found Goro, after a three-hour hike in Aokigahara. There was a car, parked at a clearing intended for vehicles coming down Lake Saiko: a banged-up, yellow Toyota Prius with the bumper half-missing. The real reason it caught my eye though was the envelope I saw, pinned beneath the windscreen wiper, and the boy looking out the window from the backseat. He opened his mouth. He was trying to say something, but I couldn't hear him; Wagner was blasting from the car's speakers—the third act of *Tristan und Isolde*.

All this happened four years ago. According to the officials, the boy was an enigma: without any proper identification, they didn't have a way to access his birth records. The only clue they had was his name—Goro—and the company that had rented the car out to his mother, but that proved to be another dead end: the mother had settled the deposit with cash, and the second-hand dealer, a shady sort of start-up, had neglected to ask for her ID card. A search for the mother's body through the forest had turned up nothing as well. The only good that came out of the situation was the boy himself, whom the doctors had pronounced a healthy, ordinary kappa. They noted that he had an unusually large hole in the back of his head—it was the size of a baby's fist, already larger than most adults'—but it was just a physical trait, the doctors had stressed. It had nothing to do with anything else.

Assured of his well-being, the social workers began to

make arrangements for foster care, and suffice it to say, I followed the proceedings with a fairly keen eye. I adopted him. I had failed at being a father once, and that failure had left a void in my life: I saw it every day whenever I came back home (the absence of it, the simple lack) and in many ways Goro felt like a second chance. That, and something told me the boy needed a home.

Ms Itsuko coughed lightly into her hand. She reached into a pocket and took out a packet of tissues. "I'm sorry," she said. "Excuse me."

I watched as she held onto the tissues in her hand.

"Goro changed after the incident, didn't he?" said Ms Itsuko.

"Hmm."

"Everybody noticed," she said. "Goro used to be such a cheerful kid. He was so eager for everything. So enthusiastic, energetic. And then suddenly, all of that disappeared."

I had been notified immediately, after the incident occurred. The school nurse examined Goro and had him sent to the hospital, just to be on the safe side.

"The doctors said he was fine," I said.

"Did they?"

I nodded. "It was just a bad case of bruising, a slight wave of dizziness… Goro was told to stay at home and rest."

Ms Itsuko sighed. "What was he like before? At home, I mean."

"He was cheerful… Just like what you said."

"And what did he like to do?" she asked.

"All kinds of things," I replied. "He liked getting out of

the house. During the summer he'd walk around the park and collect insects, put them into boxes… Every night at half past eight, we'd head down to the local bathhouse."

"To meet other kappas?"

I looked at Ms Itsuko. I was surprised. I asked her how she knew, and she smiled again.

"The bathhouse is my husband's favourite place in the whole town. That, and the hot spring motel he frequents," added Ms Itsuko. "My husband is a kappa."

I told her it was unheard of, at least in my experience. "How did the two of you meet?"

She shrugged. "I'm sorry, Mr Sugimura. I don't remember. It was such a long time ago that I've completely forgot."

"I'm sure it hasn't been an easy marriage," I said. Ms Itsuko held her hands together, and set them on her lap.

"It's impossible to conceive a child," she said. "That's the part, I think, that I found the hardest to accept. Everything else has worked out just fine."

A disquieting change took over my child, the week after the incident. It was like what Ms Itsuko just described: as though he had left a part of himself behind, like dead weight he didn't need any longer.

"I saw a lot of my old self in him, in fact."

"What do you mean?" asked Ms Itsuko. I tried to think of the words.

"It wasn't that the divorce made me angry or depressed… It just changed me," I said. But there was more to it, of course: after the divorce, I felt as though somebody had drawn a complete blank over my life, had left me with no real purpose to carry on from one day to the next. Each day I felt as though I was sitting next to the cliff of a deep chasm: just the constant feeling of falling down, when in reality I was going nowhere at all. I can't think of any other way to describe it.

"Goro spaces out for long periods of time," she said. "In class he'll either look out of the window, or stare vacantly at the blackboard. That is the worst, I think. You think he's paying attention to you, but he isn't."

"I heard he made a girl cry," I said.

"How did you know?"

"Goro told me," I said. "He came back home after school, said he made a girl cry… why she cried, though, Goro didn't know. He said he felt sorry for her."

Ms Itsuko's smile had left her face.

"You said over the phone, Mr Sugimura, that before his episodes at school began, he had his first one at your friend's apartment?"

"That's right," I said.

"Could you please tell me what happened?"

"It was the second week of October… A friend of mine had bought a new set of speakers and wanted me to check them out. He lives alone in a spacious apartment, located in the middle of Kofu city. Bachelor. Typical artsy guy: long, greying hair, clothes entirely in black… I brought the boy along and we went over for dinner," I said.

"How did you meet this friend?"

I tried to remember. "A few years ago I met up with a researcher at the local college, a cartographer who was interested in the local region… She introduced us to one another. She said, 'I think you and Hajime would make good friends.' And we did. We've been friends ever since."

"What kind of guy is he?"

"He's caring, easy-going… Our friendship mostly takes place at dinnertime, over at his apartment." We followed a fairly simple pattern, my friend and I: we would sit back, trade stories with one another, and listen to music. Recently he had taken to vintages as well, so we'd share a bottle amongst ourselves. That evening, he served us aglio olio with grilled prawns, followed by tiramisu from the supermarket. The wine was a smooth white, specially imported from a Spanish vineyard. That night he played 'Lover Man' on his new speakers."

"Billie Holiday?"

Again, the feeling of surprise. "No," I said. "Sarah Vaughan. You know the song, Ms Itsuko?"

She smiled. "You and I were born in the sixties, Mr Sugimura. It was a great time. Barbra Streisand recorded a version, I think, in *Simply Streisand*. How was the sound quality?"

"Flawless," I said. "You could hear every breath Vaughan takes, every single trill she makes with her voice… It's as though she has her mouth right beside your ear."

Goro had seated himself before the speakers that night, eating the pasta on his own. He'd asked my friend who the singer was, and my friend had told him. The boy turned.

Who?

She's American, said my friend.

Is she popular?

I think so, my friend had replied. *She used to be, at least.*

The child blinked. He asked what had happened to her, and my friend said she had passed away, more than twenty years ago. *Cancer in the lungs*, he added. *Though I'm not sure if you know what that is.*

"Goro didn't speak for a while," I said to Ms Itsuko. "My friend and I watched him, as he turned back to face the stereo. And the song was just growing, bigger and bigger... 'Lover man, lover man,' she sings. 'Where can you be?'"

"The virgin," said Ms Itsuko, "dying to be loved."

I nodded. "My friend said something then. 'It's huge,' he said out of nowhere. And then I realised he was referring to the hole in Goro's head. My friend was practically staring at it."

Ms Itsuko tilted her head again.

"Do pardon me for asking this, Mr Sugimura—but would you say he was drawn to it? Much like Shinichi?"

I wanted to wince. "I don't know," I said. "I wouldn't know what to tell you."

Half an hour later, my friend and I had relocated to the living room. We listened, attentively, to the last of the LP. We were seated on the floor, a cushion behind each of our backs, nursing a glass of wine each. Goro wasn't there with us at the time; he had gone to the toilet.

"After the record came to an end, my friend and I realised that Goro still had not returned... He was taking a lot longer than he should have."

"Did you both go to the toilet?"

I nodded. "We opened the door and found the boy, curled up beneath the sink. The tap was still running... I turned off the water and knelt beside him. 'Look in the mirror,' the boy said to me. But I looked and I saw nothing."

Ms Itsuko raised a hand to her lips. Her eyes were wide with attention.

"So that was the first episode," she said to me. She lowered her hand back down. "I see," she said.

It had been forty minutes since we had started our conversation. Ms Itsuko laid down the facts of the situation.

"Over the past two months your son has had three separate episodes at the school. These episodes do not include the one that had happened this morning."

"I understand," I said.

"The first time it happened, nobody knew where he went. It was his art class that morning, and he had asked the instructor if he could excuse himself and use the restroom. The instructor said that he could. Ten minutes later, however, Goro had not returned. This worried the instructor."

"Yes…"

"She sent a student to bring him back, and he did. Nothing much was made of it. After class, however, the student went up to the instructor and told her what he saw."

"Goro was just staring at the mirror, wasn't he?"

"Like I said: nothing much was made of it. The instructor didn't think it was necessary to pass the information on to me," said Ms Itsuko.

There was a pause. I waited for her to continue.

"The second episode was exactly the same," Ms Itsuko went on. "Except this time it occurred during my own class. This upset me, of course, but I didn't know what to do about it. I let it pass."

She coughed once more. She took out a tissue from the packet.

"Excuse me," she said. "I am not very used to this room."

Various paintings had been left to dry, on the easels in the art studio, while others were framed and hung on the walls. From the window, I could see that the students had vacated the field; baseball practice was apparently over.

"His third episode was particularly bad," she said.

"He threw a rock, didn't he?"

"Yes. Normally something like that would have led to a suspension," Ms Itsuko said. "But we reconsidered that, in light of what Shinichi had done to your son. Trauma, the school counsellor told us. It never fully goes away."

"He promised he wouldn't do it again," I said to Ms Itsuko. She smiled.

"He was just frightened, wasn't he? Of the stranger in the mirror." She looked towards the window: she was looking at her own reflection. "This morning, he hid in the toilet stall and would not come out. I had to climb over the cubicle wall and unlock it with a broomstick."

I bowed. "I'm so sorry," I said to her. I bowed again. "I apologise for all the trouble I've caused you…"

She merely shook her head.

"It's all right, Mr Sugimura. It makes my life more exciting." She turned away from the window. "Are you familiar with the Blue Room, Mr Sugimura?"

"The Blue Room?" I asked.

"That's right," she said. "Has he ever talked about it before?"

I tried to think back. "This is the first time I've ever heard about it," I said.

"He says he sees it in the mirror, Mr Sugimura. A room entirely in blue, without any furniture whatsoever. Just walls. And in that room is a person, walking towards him."

"What?" I said. "No... No, I've never heard of something like that at all."

Ms Itsuko pursed her lips. "It cannot be helped, then. We will just have to adapt. Shinichi's transfer has just been finalised, and so the child is gone for good. I had hoped that Goro would somehow do better in his absence. But that was a silly thing to assume."

Ms Itsuko then rose from her seat. She walked over to the drawer, and pulled out a large folder. Inside it were a number of students' drawings, done in paint and crayon. She took them out, one painting at a time, and showed them to me.

"As you can see, these are all goldfish," Ms Itsuko said to me. "That was what they had to paint the day before." She then took out the final drawing. "This is what your son painted."

I looked. It was just blue: an empty tank of water. In the middle of it was a rough sketch of something in beige.

"Is that a man?" I asked.

"It is somebody," Ms Itsuko said. She sat back down in her chair. "I know this may sound unorthodox, Mr Sugimura, and I do apologise for suggesting this. But I could get my husband to see your son, I believe. Have one kappa speak to another. I think he would be very interested in meeting your boy."

I handed the painting back to her. I felt bad, to say the least. And guilty. "It's okay," I said. "Thank you for the offer though…"

Ms Itsuko smiled. She seemed almost disappointed. "You are welcome," she said.

●

My friend called, later that evening. I was wrapped in a jumper, with socks over my feet. It was during the evenings when I was reminded most that winter was approaching. I told my friend about everything that had happened.

"The teacher had to get him out of the toilet?"

"Yes."

"Man," he said. "That is rough. I wonder why the boy felt he had to lock himself in, though."

"She said something about a Blue Room…"

"A what?"

"A Blue Room," I said. "A room entirely in blue, with nothing but a person seated on a chair… He sees it in the mirror, she says. Have you ever heard of it?"

"I ain't got a clue."

There was a pause. I was in my living room, seated on the couch. I switched the television on. Advertisements played across the channel.

"You know, it's not that strange of a situation," my friend said.

"What are you talking about?" I said. "It's strange enough as it is."

He laughed. "You see, everyone has got their own set of issues. It just how we deal with 'em, that's all."

I stared at the TV. "So what does that say about Goro, then?"

"The kid's just handicapped," he replied. "We all are."

"Yourself included?"

"Of course," my friend said. "You know about the washroom I never use?"

"The what?"

He laughed again. "It's located at the end of the floor where I teach. It's pretty small, so it's only got two stalls, and one of them always seems to be occupied. And yet somehow it's always completely quiet."

"What do you mean?"

"It's completely quiet," he said. "There's no sound. Nothing from that stall at all. There's no squeak on the seat, no zip of the pants, no tearing of toilet paper. Nada. Zilch."

I picked up the remote. I switched the channel.

"Maybe you're just imagining things," I said. "The door could just be closed, after all… It doesn't have to mean someone's there."

"That's the thing, though: there *is* somebody in there."

I switched the channel again.

"But how do you know for sure?"

"I don't," he said. "That's the whole point, Sugimura. I know and yet I don't know. So where does that leave me? It's a purely irrational thought, and yet something in my gut tells me that no matter what I do, I should never use that washroom again. Because there will always be somebody inside it, somebody whom I can never see or hear or touch. And so now I avoid it completely."

I sighed. There was nothing on the TV. I switched it off.

"Maybe we're all crazy… It's the sane ones we have to worry about."

"Perhaps," he said. He paused. "Whatcha doing right now?"

I stared at the empty television screen. "Nothing," I said.

"Come over to my place then. Goro's asleep; you're not. And I've just got my hands on something that you absolutely have to try."

I started the car and drove over to his apartment. It was a bottle of red, it turned out: a 1998 Vega Sicilia Unico, as written on the label. From the oven he took out a warm slice of chicken pie, reheated and ready to eat. I'd never had anything like it before. "It's from a nearby bakery," he said to me. "A Kofu city secret."

"It's amazing," I said.

My friend dug into his slice. "Crust is light and flaky, without ever turning soggy. And the filling goes wonderfully with the wine," he added.

I nodded. I then held up my glass, high enough so I could see it against the light. "How did you manage to get that bottle, by the way? I've never seen the label before…"

"I got connections," he said. "I'm not boasting or anything. I just so happen to know all kinds of people."

I felt sceptical. "And these people… they recommend you things like this all the time? Like wine and pie?"

"Sometimes," he said. "Once in a while they render me special services as well. Special favours, things like that."

"What kind of favours?"

"Er, things I need doing that I can't do myself. I know a guy who's very good at locating people, for instance. It's a gift that he has. Helped me track down a writer who became something of a shut-in, recently. That was the first time. Second time, he found the daughter of someone who had gone senile; I needed the guy's records, and his daughter happened to be the only person I could ask."

"That's wonderful," I said. An idea then occurred to me. "Could you ask this guy of yours to do me a favour?"

My friend gave me a curious look. "Sure, man," he said. He was refilling his glass of wine. "Is there somebody in particular you wanna find?"

"It's to do with Goro…"

"Go on."

I scratched the edge of my nose. "I'm wondering if this contact of yours could find somebody related to him."

He took a sip of his wine. "You talking about family, right? Biological relations?"

I nodded. *Have one kappa speak to another*, I recalled Ms Itsuko saying. "I think talking to one of them might help," I said. "Shed some light on his issues… Maybe they'll know something about the Blue Room that I don't. Or at least something about his background, his family history…"

My friend took a look at my glass, and proceeded to refill it as well. He poured a little more than he should have. "You will want a number, I'm assuming?"

I told him that would be great. My friend smiled.

"Gimme a week or so, will you? I'll see what I can do."

Goro called me at work, two days before Christmas Eve. He told me I couldn't come back home. "Why not?" I asked, and he said that I just couldn't. "It's dangerous," he said.

I racked my brain for a few seconds. "Is it the person in the Blue Room?" I asked.

"Yes," he said.

"And you saw it where…?"

"The toilet."

"How long ago?" I asked. He didn't reply. "Are you scared?" I asked.

"I'm scared," he said. "I'm heading to the bathhouse."

"You are?"

There was a pause.

"I'll take the keys," he said. "I'll stay there and wait for you."

"All right," I said. "Don't go anywhere else."

I hung up and called my friend. I asked him if Goro could spend the night at his place, and quickly relayed the situation. He told me it was no problem.

"Your timing's perfect, by the way."

"How so?"

"My contact just got in touch with me."

My heart pounded. "And…?"

"He just sent a number to my inbox. Says it's the number to the little guy's uncle."

I felt my chest go tight. "His uncle?" I asked. "On the mother's side?"

"That's right," he said. "She's got a younger brother and an older sister, as a matter of fact. But the sister is nowhere to be found—my guy thinks she might be living in a commune, somewhere in Eastern Europe. My contact doesn't know for sure. The brother, on the other hand, is right here in this country."

"That's incredible," I said. "Is there a name?"

"No name," my friend said. "I think that's just how far he's willing to do a favour, I'm afraid. I think he expects you to do everything else on your own."

"No, no," I said, "that's fine." I'd figured things like names and such could be sorted out later. "Could you forward the number please?"

"No problem," he said. "Anyway, I've got a department meeting in a few minutes. I'll probably be done in an hour or so. Lemme know when Goro will be arriving."

The boy was waiting at the front of the bathhouse, drinking a box of juice the owner had given him. I thanked the owner, got Goro into the car, and drove him to the block of my friend's apartment. It was half-past four in the afternoon, and the sky had started to turn; the radio, tuned to a classical FM broadcast, played the prelude to Wagner's *Tristan und Isolde*. An uncanny coincidence, I thought. For a while, we sat in the car and listened to the swell of the orchestra, wondering when my friend would arrive.

"Do you remember this music?" I said.

The boy nodded his head. He then looked at me. "I'm sorry," he said.

"What for?" He didn't answer. "There's nothing to be sorry about," I said.

He shook his head.

"But I brought it home," said Goro. "That wasn't supposed to happen."

I turned the radio down.

"Is it okay if I ask about the Blue Room?"

The boy looked at me. He then looked at his lap. "What do you want to know?" he asked.

"I want to know what the room is like... the kinds of things you see in there. Stuff like that," I said.

"But there's nothing in the Blue Room. Just walls."

"Just walls," I said, echoing his words. I looked at the sky outside. It was dusk, I saw: a single yellow cloud, drifting lonesome across the sky.

"Hey," I said to the boy. "Can I ask you one more thing?"

He nodded.

"This person in the Blue Room… is it a woman?"

"A woman?"

I nodded. "Your mother."

He shook his head. "Not a woman," he said. "Not my mother. It is a man."

"A man?"

He turned his head towards the window; he saw his own reflection gazing back at him. "He's coming to get me," the boy said.

A pair of lights grew brighter in the rear-view mirror. It was a bus, and it stopped about ten metres behind the car. My friend alighted from the exit, wearing a long grey scarf and a large trench coat. Goro and I got out of my car.

"Have you called the number yet?" my friend asked. I told him I planned to afterwards. My friend nodded and placed a hand on the boy's back. "Hey buddy," he said to Goro. "Let's go."

I took my phone out as soon as I got back into the car. I had the number before me, written down on the back of a receipt. My hands were slick with sweat as I keyed in the digits. The call connected: it started to ring. I silenced the radio.

"Hello?" a voice said. "Who's this?"

"Good afternoon," I said. I introduced myself: I told him my name, and where I was calling from. I told him I was a researcher. "I conduct field studies," I said, "on the local terrain and such…" When the voice replied, he sounded somewhat amused. He asked why a guy like me would call someone like him. "We've got nothing in common," the voice said.

"Ah, well… that's true," I said. I asked if he had an older sister, by any chance. The voice didn't immediately answer. He then said he had two older sisters, neither of whom he had seen since he had gone to university. He wanted to know which one I was talking about.

"Your second sister," I said. "The younger of the two."

"Right," the voice said. "So what about her?"

My hands continued to sweat. It was a mobile number based in Tokyo, but there was a peculiar accent in the voice that was a little hard to place. I wiped my hands on my shirt.

"Your sister had a child in 2004," I said. "A boy. He's in second grade right now, and I am currently the boy's guardian."

"You're saying I'm an uncle?"

"Yes," I said. "You're an uncle." I then explained how his nephew seemed to be in some kind of trouble. "I'm not a kappa, you see, so there are some things that I find hard to deal with at the present… I was wondering if you could help me, somehow."

He said nothing for about a minute.

"You're a human?"

"Yes."

A pause.

"Where did you say you live again? Yamanashi, am I right?"

"That's right, Yamanashi prefecture."

"Okay, I understand," the voice said. "Could I crash at

your place tonight? I can go home, grab my things, and take the first train to Yamanashi. That okay with you?"

I was taken aback. "Yes," I said. "I don't see why not." He then asked for the boy's name, and I told him.

"That's my father's name," the voice said. "I can't believe she named the kid after him." He then asked after his sister. "Where is she? Why isn't she calling me instead?"

I told him about the car by the forest, four years ago.

"And the father?"

"Nobody knows."

"Damn it," the voice said. "Shit. God damn it." There was another, longer pause. I bent my head over my knees and waited, with the phone in my hand. I thought I was going to throw up. Finally he spoke: he said it was all right. "She's been dead to me a long time, anyway."

Before we hung up he asked about my job. "You said you're a researcher, right? Local terrain and stuff like that?"

"That's correct."

"Interesting," the voice said. "I'm a musician."

"A musician?"

"Yeah," said the voice. "I play the sax. Name's Takao."

It was nearly ten o' clock when I picked him up from the station. Takao turned out to be big and tall, and seemed to be in his late thirties. It was only two degrees Celsius that night, but he somehow seemed warm enough, wearing nothing but a baseball jacket over a white T-shirt. He had a duffel bag slung over his shoulder.

"I've only packed for a day or two," Takao said, as he got into the passenger seat. He had to adjust it back to make room for his knees. "I hope you don't mind."

He took off his cap. There, at the back of his head, was a hole no larger than a five-hundred yen coin. Goro's was probably three or four times bigger. I stepped on the pedal and began driving to my friend's place.

"Why's he there again?" Takao asked. "He thinks your place is haunted?"

"Something like that," I said. "It's hard to explain… I was hoping you might have a better idea, actually. You could try asking him about it, when the boy wakes up tomorrow morning."

"Now's his bedtime?"

"That's right," I said.

He shook his head, and began biting on a nail. He then burst out in a spate of cursing. "Fuck!" he said. "Shit!" He placed a hand over his mouth. He started pounding his fist against the window. "Shit, shit, shit, shit!" Takao then leant back against the seat to collect himself. "I'm sorry," he said. "I'm going nuts."

"I understand," I told him.

Later, I stood in front of my friend's guest room, as Takao pushed the door open by a crack. My friend kept himself busy in the kitchen, washing up the dishes, as Takao looked inside,

"He's eight, yeah?" Takao asked.

"That's right."

He kept quiet as he continued to look. The boy didn't stir.

"You said somebody hit him at school?" He mimed the act out, with that big hand of his. "'Cos of the hole in his head?"

"Yes."

Takao looked for a few more seconds, before closing

the door shut. We moved towards the living area. Takao noticed my friend's LP collection, mounted beside the stereo equipment, and began looking through the titles.

"You've got some great stuff here," Takao said. My friend thanked him from the kitchen. "You like music as well, Sugimura?"

I shrugged. "Sure… Music isn't hard to like."

Takao smiled. "I'm glad," he said. It was sometimes hard to remember that a guy in a baseball jacket was a sax player in an orchestra. "Does the kiddo listen to any of this stuff when he's here?"

"Most of the time he doesn't have a choice," my friend said. He'd returned from washing the dishes, wiping his hands on his apron. "But he's taken a liking to Sarah Vaughan, methinks."

He smiled. "That's awesome," Takao said. "That's nice to know."

When we were back in the car, on the way to my place, Takao told me about how music had run in his family. "My father used to frequent a jazz bar, ever since he turned legal. He'd go there whenever he had nights free. It was located in the basement of a sukiyaki restaurant, I believe, right in the heart of the bay area. My father loved that bar because that's where he met all his friends, he said. It was also where he met my mother."

Takao fell quiet for a bit. The radio was still tuned to the classical FM broadcast.

"We barely had any mirrors in the house," he said. "My mother was quite sensitive about those things. She said she didn't like them very much."

I asked him why. Takao said he had a hunch.

"She wanted to be a singer. That's why my father found her at the jazz bar. She wanted to sing but she didn't have the voice."

"What does that have to do with mirrors...?"

"A reflection in a mirror can't sing," he said. "I think that's why."

I said that was sad. Takao nodded.

"It's a kappa thing," he said. "Kappas generally hate what they see in themselves. They also hate what they see in one another."

"Ah," I said. "Is that why they tend to be alone, all the time?"

He nodded again.

"There are instances, of course. When kappas manage to form groups with one another. I find that admirable. And I think that's what my father tried to do, with a family as big as ours. That was his aim. And my mother did her best to support him."

I slowed the car down; the traffic light had turned red. There were barely any vehicles before us, in the long stretch of road ahead. There were hardly any behind us either. Soon we left the city behind as we travelled down the highway.

"Is that why you and your sisters parted ways?" I asked. "Because the three of you preferred to be alone?"

"Yeah."

"Even now?"

He shook his head. "Now I'm not so lonely," he said. "I've got friends. And I'm in an orchestra as well, which is about seventy members strong. Eighty, possibly. I've got friends there too."

"Are there are… other kappas in the orchestra?"

"Just three others," he said. "We talk from time to time." Takao then looked out of the window. There was nothing to see.

"Which forest did my sister go to?" He turned towards me. "Was it Aokigahara?"

I nodded. "It's where I found Goro, in the car that she'd left behind."

"Okay," said Takao. He took his cap off, and then put it back on again. He adjusted it to the side. "She left a letter behind as well?"

I nodded again. "I'll show it to you later, when we're back at my place. I have it in one of my drawers." I switched gear again, signalled to the right. "Shouldn't be long now."

It was a little past midnight when Takao was done reading the thing. He handed it back to me, and watched as I put it back where I normally kept it. He said, "It was the mirror in the toilet, wasn't it? Where Goro saw the Blue Room."

The both of us went inside. It was a simple toilet, with a sink and a bathtub, and a floor that dried easily. At the corner were a stool and a washing basin, as well as the basket where the bottles were stored. Towels hung on the rack. Takao and I stood before the mirror nailed above the sink; I asked him if he saw anything special in it, and he said he didn't see anything.

Another minute or two we stood there, watching ourselves in the mirror. We waited. Time passed and Takao asked, a little sheepishly, if he could possibly run a bath.

"I know it's a bit sudden," he said. "Sorry."

I told him it was okay. He could take as long as he liked. The towels were his to use.

"Thanks," said Takao. He turned the taps, and the tub started to fill. "You can stay, you know—if you're not feeling sleepy. We could still chat."

"Sure," I said. "I can stay up a while longer."

I sat on the stool and watched as he took off his clothes. He stepped gingerly into the bathtub. Steam filled the room as hot water poured steadily from the tap, while I folded his clothes and set them aside. "This is great," he said. He closed his eyes. "I haven't had a proper bath in ages."

"Why not?" I asked. "You're a kappa, aren't you?"

He made a face. "Something's wrong with my tub, back home. Makes a weird noise whenever I turn the tap."

"Have you called somebody to fix it?"

"I told the landlord," he said. "He says he'll send someone to check it out in a few days' time. I'll have to be home for that."

"You live alone?" I asked.

He said that was right.

"You have a girlfriend, though?"

The guy smirked. "I don't know," he said. "It's complicated."

"How so?" I asked. Takao opened his eyes and turned his head towards me.

"I care a lot about this girl," he said. "But sometimes I confuse that with love."

"Do you want to have sex with her?" I asked.

"Sometimes," he said.

"Is she kappa or human?"

"Human. Early twenties. The kind of girl who should have nothing to do with me." He placed a hand over his eyes. "She said something to me once, out of the blue. First time we ever met. Spoke to me as though she'd known me her whole life. Her friends were all waiting outside then, standing around the restaurant. She asked me why I was eating nabe all by myself."

I smiled. "You had nabe all by yourself?" I asked. Takao waved his hand in the air, like it was no big deal to him.

"I've always been a loner," he said.

A while later he asked what my life was like before Goro came along, and I told him I had lived on my own as well. "For about three years, I think… I got divorced in 2006."

"You had a wife?" Takao asked.

"Two sons as well," I said. "Twins. They should be in high school by now."

"Why did she leave?"

"My job," I said. "Too much bad luck all over it…"

Takao said nothing for a bit. "You know, all my life, I never really knew what it meant to be close to somebody. I had no real idea of what a family was supposed to be like."

I nodded. I knew his pain. I said to him, "There are all kinds of families, Takao."

Takao looked at me. He had the saddest eyes I had ever seen.

"There's a custom we have," Takao said. "Whenever a kappa shares a bath with another. Do you know it?"

"I think I do…"

Takao smiled.

"Could you do it for me?"

I got up from my stool. Takao moved in the tub.

"I scoop the water with my hands, yes?"

"Yeah."

"And then I pour it over the hole in your head?"

He nodded. "Yeah."

"Like this?" I asked, and he said yes. Yes. "Thank you."

•

The concert was over, and the three of us stepped out of the hall. The foyer was crowded with concertgoers, and we stood amongst them in a rosy haze of feeling. The New Year was upon us, and I could almost feel it, like a warm draft passing through.

We spotted Takao at a distance, talking to a young woman. Her hair was tied up into a bun, and her smile was open and friendly. Behind her stood an even younger man, a teenager, perhaps. Goro turned towards me, and I placed a hand behind his back. "Go ahead," I said to him and my friend.

"Where you off to?" my friend asked.

"The washroom… I'll find you when I'm done."

The washroom I went into was located at a fairly quiet corner of the building. When I went inside I noticed, immediately, how there was no one else aside from myself. There were no urinals either; just a sink and two unoccupied stalls. I went into one of them. Seconds passed as I went about my business, which was probably when I felt it. I can't explain how, but it was a feeling that began slowly, and then quickly, all at once: it was the undeniable presence of another person, here in this small, walled-off space. I shuddered. I grew cold, and nervous. Was this what my friend had felt, back then? This paranoia? This anxiety? This great silence, this caving in of the ears? I felt the hair on my arms stand as a nagging, persistent realisation dogged me to no end: that there was a second person in this washroom, a person I hadn't noticed before, standing right outside my stall—and I had no idea when he or she had come in. Or maybe, just maybe, that person had always been there, waiting for me to be done.

I zipped up my pants. I flushed. And then I heard it—the sound of the automatic tap, releasing water into the sink outside. I opened the door.

"Ah, Mr Sugimura. We meet again."

Mr Five had a comb in his hand, its teeth wet from the tap's water. He proceeded to brush it through his hair.

"I hope you found the concert enjoyable," he added.

"I did," I said. "And you?"

"To a degree, yes. What a terrific finale. To be utterly frank, I have never heard anything by Johann Strauss the Second before."

I nodded. I didn't exactly know how to respond. I was uneasy, to say the least, and my breath had turned shallow. Mr Five continued to comb his hair, with a movement both slow and careful. I stood behind him and watched.

"Are you going back to Yamanashi prefecture by any chance, Mr Sugimura?"

I stammered out a reply. "N-not tonight, I'm afraid… The three of us have a room booked in a hotel… We'll be spending a couple of days in Tokyo."

"I see," said Mr Five. "Would you be needing a ride?"

I told him it was fine. "I have my car parked somewhere."

The kappa smiled. He ran his comb beneath the tap once more.

"You remind me of someone I once met," he said. "A

woman I came across six months ago, in the lobby of a hotel I frequent. It is an uncanny resemblance: the way you walk, the way you stand, your overall mood. Even the way you look at things. I have been thinking about this ever since the intermission."

"And where is this woman now?" I asked

"Gone," he said. "She was just a tourist, after all. She was only there for a couple of days."

There was a pause. I ventured another question.

"Is there anything else to this woman?"

"She is a mother," said Mr Five. "And a wife. But all of these things have been taken away from her. Loss after loss. Now she is searching for a way to overcome this."

I nodded. I could feel an old ache, stirring in my chest. I could call it back like an old friend. "I would like to meet this woman one day," I said.

"You would, Mr Sugimura?"

I nodded again. "There aren't a lot of people like me, I think."

"And what makes you say that?" he asked. I balled my hands into tight fists.

"Everything I do now, I do in light of what I've done before… And there aren't a lot of people who've gone down the path that I have. That this woman and I both have."

Mr Five smiled once more. Done with his hair, he stashed his comb in an inner pocket of his jacket. But he remained in the same position, standing firmly before the sink and the mirror. His eyes were now entirely focused on me.

"Is this a path you have come back from? Or have you gone past the point of no return?"

I didn't exactly know how to answer his question. "We can't go back to the past, Mr Five… it's not a hallway in which you or I can walk however we want. There's only one way forward for all of us." I looked back into his gaze. "It's cruel, but… it gives me hope, for some reason."

His smile softened. An ambivalent look remained in his eyes.

"Death is a clock with no hands, Mr Sugimura. You would do well to remember this." He turned towards the door. "It was a pleasure talking to you tonight. Goodbye."

I watched him go. I placed a hand on my chest. I could feel my heart, beating through my ribs.

Takao was saying something about music to Goro, in the back seat of the car, and my friend and I laughed. Takao was still learning how to talk to an eight-year-old, and he'd been treating Goro as though he were a depository, rattling off the names of various musicians: Jimmy Garrison, Elvin Jones, McCoy Tyner. "I don't understand what you're saying," Goro said to Takao. "But it sounds cool."

We were about halfway to the hotel, where the four of us had booked a room: the plan was to stay up all night and watch the New Year's Eve programmes together. I took a quick glance at Takao in the rear-view mirror and managed to catch his eye.

"I have a question… You know of any sax players in your orchestra trying to form a quintet?"

"Like a small band?" he asked.

"Yes," I said. "Jazz music. Group of five players and everything."

"I haven't, sorry. Not as far as I've heard of." The guy was sprawled all over the backseat of my car, and Goro fit just right beneath his arm. "It'd be nice though, if something like that were to happen. I'd love to play jazz with a few other guys."

"You would?"

"Sure I would," said Takao. "But not in a quintet, I think." He shook his head. "A quartet would do better."

"With four people?" my friend asked.

"Yeah," said Takao. Looking at him once more in the rear-view mirror, I could see the amber of the streetlights in thick lines, passing over his face; he was looking at the boy, who was looking out of the window. "Four people would be perfect," he said. I looked away, and kept on driving.

6

KITCHEN TOWN

APRIL 2013

Mr Shimao

Ahab had a hole in his heart as a kid; it had long healed since then, but he believes he's the way he is because of it.

"You've ever read this manga by Ito Junji?" he said. He had gone behind a tree to take a piss, about a few metres away. "It's about this fault in the ground, yeah?" A pause. "It rises from the ground after an earthquake, this huge slab of rock, and all across it are tons of man-shaped holes. You've ever read anything like that?"

"Who is it again?" I asked. Ahab's Singaporean, so his Japanese always sounded strange. "Plot sounds familiar," I said.

"Ito Junji," he said again. "You know him?"

I shook my head. "Never heard of him." Ahab came walking back.

"Isn't it your job to read all kinds of stuff?"

"My business is with novels, not manga," I said. I looked at Sugimura, seated on the other side of the fire. He was boiling instant noodles with a metal saucepan. "You know it?" I asked him, and he shook his head.

"Oh, well," said Ahab. "You guys should read him. He's amazing."

"Noted," I said. I looked at Sugimura once more, his face as impassive as ever. He cracked an egg over his noodles. Sugimura was here to guide us, not befriend us, and he made sure he stuck to his role the entire time. He never really approved of killing, after all.

●

Sugimura has a kappa for a son. He's forty-eight, divorced; the ex-wife got the twins. He adopted the kappa three years later. The first thing I noticed about him was how tanned his skin was, as though he had spent every waking hour under the sun. The skin on his face and arms looked almost leathery in his camping gear, all buckles and straps and khaki. There was a pale band of skin around his ring finger.

"My boy is a kappa," he repeated himself to me. "I don't like this at all…"

This was about a week ago, when I was in search of a person who could guide us through the forest. Sugimura and I were seated in a café in Kofu city. The only food it served was chicken pie.

"I wouldn't need you if this wasn't a matter of urgency," I said to him. "But it is. You said so yourself. A kappa has been spotted in the forest, and unfortunately it's looking for prey.

We need to be able to avoid it before it catches up to us or Kawako, and nobody knows the forest better than you do."

He didn't look pleased. "And if it does catch up to us? What will your guy do?"

I didn't answer. Sugimura shook his head.

"There's something I don't get," he said.

"What's that?"

"Why would the kappa go to Aokigahara, of all places? Wouldn't Lake Saiko be more, how do I put it..."

"Fitting?"

Sugimura rubbed the side of his head. "This isn't the first time either," he added.

I knew what he was referring to. My contact had told me all about the boy's mother, and the yellow Toyota Prius she'd left him behind in.

"I don't know," I said to him. "Kappas haven't made ponds or lakes their homes for a very long time. They've adapted to the human way. Maybe that's why. And maybe that's why people assume they're not dangerous anymore."

Sugimura said nothing for a while. He moved in his seat.

"Some people say it's easier to steal a shirikodama... if its owner is willing to dispose of it." He paused. "Do you think there might be any truth to that claim?"

I shrugged. I asked him, "How many bodies have you found? Across all the times you've hiked in the forest."

He said sixteen.

●

Nobuo and Akiko came back with the water, three jerrycans

loaded. "These should last us for another while," Nobuo said. They were drenched in sweat.

"Was it tough?" Ahab asked.

Nobuo made a face. "Well, I'm definitely not a guy with a lot of endurance," he said. "Akiko?"

Akiko made her way back to the tent. "I'm going to lie down for a while," she said. "Tell me when we have to get going again."

"Okay," Nobuo said. "I'll let you know."

We had set up camp about eight kilometres away from the nearest path: Nobuo and Akiko in one tent, Ahab and me in another. Sugimura had a tent all to himself. We were as close to the centre of the forest as we could get.

"So we're covering the west this time?"

I nodded. "Most of the eastern side's been accounted for. Right, Sugimura?"

He was slurping up his noodles. He nodded back.

"We'll take turns as usual," I said. "We'll go out in two pairs and rotate our partners. One person stays at the campsite."

"The west is a lot bigger, yeah?" Ahab asked.

"We could find ourselves searching for up to a week," I said. "Hopefully we'll take half that time."

"Because of supplies?"

"That's one of the reasons," I said.

Nobuo opened up one of the trunks, and took out a custard bun. He sat beside Sugimura and ripped open the plastic with his teeth.

"How much longer till we set out?" he asked.

"Thirty minutes?" Ahab said. He looked towards me. The guy had one foot constantly tapping the ground, wearing away the moss beneath his boot. "That's good, yeah?"

"That's good," I said.

Thirty minutes later, Nobuo woke Akiko up. "It's time," he said to her, through the opening in their tent. Akiko got out and put on her boots.

"I never slept," she said. "I just lay there."

Nobuo and I set off at a hundred and eighty degrees on the compass, Ahab and Akiko at a hundred and ninety: the seventeenth and eighteenth cardinal points, respectively. The aim was to keep going in a straight line for four hours and then head back in the exact same direction. We'd do this for every cardinal point on the compass.

It was Sugimura's turn to keep watch over the campsite. "Remember," he said, wiping his saucepan clean. "Avoid stepping on the roots, if you can... They're pretty weak, the trees in this forest."

Nobuo and I began our route. Neither of us spoke for about thirty minutes.

"I'm going a little mad, truth be told." Nobuo was sweating badly. "All the trees look the same to me."

We were moving at a steady pace, stepping over mounds and roots that snaked across the forest floor. The soil was rock solid beneath our feet, cushioned somewhat by the green moss. All around, the trees stood tall and narrow, a sight that repeated itself as though we were in a hall of mirrors. It was enough to make anybody's head light.

"You've ever been camping?" I asked him. He shook his head.

"I was born and raised in Tokyo."

"Didn't you ever climb Mount Takao?"

"Well, a few times, when I was a kid," Nobuo said. "But that was it. You went up to see the summit and visit the temple. I hardly know anyone who went beyond Takao and camped in the mountains."

We kept on walking.

"It's dizzying, isn't it," I said.

"Yeah," said Nobuo. He wiped his brow with the sleeve of his shirt. "To be honest, I really enjoyed going back to the visitor centre and getting our water filled. It was so great to see another face."

I nodded. "We really shouldn't take more than a few days," I said to him. "If Kawako brought any supplies with her, they would have run out by then. There would be no point in staying in this forest."

Nobuo stiffened. He said he understood.

"I'm not having second thoughts, if that's what you're thinking. I'm just tired, that's all."

I nodded again. There were a number of tree roots, sprawled across the soil. We avoided stepping on them like we were told.

"How did you know my uncle again?"

"Business," I said.

"What kind of business?"

"He didn't want a book published, if that's what you're asking. I am more than just a literary agent." A pause. "He wanted to track somebody down. He needed to, from time to time."

"So that's really your specialty?" asked Nobuo. "Tracking people down? Finding people?"

"I do my best," I said.

We kept at it, the walking. Once, we stopped to inspect a boot, a wallet, a baseball bat. A length of rope, looped over a tree branch. Nobuo sighed.

"We did a story about this place," he said to me. "Back at the newspaper. One of my colleagues even had photos of a body."

"That must have been bad," I said.

Nobuo tugged on the rope. The branch made a cracking noise. Nobuo stopped.

"There's a shared photo archive that all the reporters can access," he said. "It caused quite a stir in the office, but it didn't really affect me so much."

"You used to work the local crime beat, didn't you?"

He nodded.

"All the bodies I saw were the bodies of strangers. Six months into the job, and I found I could actually tolerate the smell of a crime scene without even trying."

There was another pause; I didn't know what to say.

"Have you ever failed to find a person, Mr Shimao?" He turned towards me. "You don't have to answer if you don't want to."

I looked at him. We resumed walking. We left the branch with the rope behind.

"Of course," I told him. "But: whenever I fail to find someone, I end up finding somebody else. So I can't really call it a failure, per se."

Nobuo didn't say anything, for about a minute or two.

"Everywhere I turn, I see Kawako, standing behind a tree," he said to me. *Do you see her dead or alive*, I wanted to

ask, but I kept the question to myself. We still had plenty of
forest to cover.

We made it back to the campsite, as the sun began to set.
Ahab and Akiko had returned long before we did, and their
search too had yielded nothing. Sugimura was busy preparing
a bigger fire. We handed our radios back to him.

"Tell me if you guys need the generator tonight," he
said. "Dinner's in the pot over there." He then turned back
to the flame.

We had dinner. Nobody felt like making conversation
that night, so we returned to our tents. Sugimura remained
outside. Ahab and I got changed and kept our eyes on his
shadow, his figure hunched and exaggerated over the fabric.

"I know how he feels about me," Ahab said, pulling
on his jumper.

I unzipped my sleeping bag and slid myself in. I switched
on my flashlight and took out Chiba Mari's final draft. We
were a month away from printing; I had a red pen in one hand
and a highlighter in another. I told Ahab it wasn't personal.

●

Ahab was the first to wake the next morning. "Come on," he
said. "It's you and me today, yeah?"

It was Akiko's turn today to stay behind.

"Remember to radio us immediately if you see something
suspicious," Sugimura said to her.

"I will," she said. She was setting up a laundry line, to air
some of our clothes. It was a fairly big pile. For some reason

she had on a raincoat and a pair of wellingtons. "Take care when you're out there, Nobuo."

Nobuo turned. He and Sugimura were already more than ten paces away.

"See you," he said to her.

Nobuo and Sugimura took the nineteenth cardinal point that day, while Ahab and I did the twentieth. Before we set off, I caught Ahab looking at Akiko.

"What?" he said, smiling. "Let's go."

We went. I looked over my shoulder, just before we lost sight of the campsite. Akiko was standing absolutely still; she had a pair of jeans in her hands. She was watching our backs.

"Did something happen between you and Akiko?"

"What," said Ahab. "You mean, yesterday?"

I nodded. It was chilly, that morning. We stepped over a fallen tree.

"We just talked," he said.

"About?"

We walked—nothing but green, for miles and miles. With Ahab you had to double your pace, lengthen your stride; the man was long-legged and toned, and built like a panther. Sometimes I forget he used to have a heart condition.

"Akiko told me about stuff. About her relationship with Kawako."

I kept quiet. He went on.

"Akiko told me she has a fantastic memory. Remembers all kinds of details. Lately though, she's been starting to forget."

I frowned. "Forget?"

Ahab stepped over a root. "They met way back in university, yeah? Akiko and Kawako."

"That's right."

"According to Akiko, Kawako was different back then." He stepped over another root. "Completely different. I mean, she's always been the same person, technically speaking—but right now there's a large gap between the Kawako of the present and the Kawako of the past. It was as though she'd lost something along the way, except it wasn't just one thing. It was many things. That's how Akiko put it."

We kept on moving. We sidestepped a tree, followed by another. The forest was getting dense.

"And?" I said to him. "So what about Akiko's memory?"

He hopped over a mound of dirt.

"Akiko can't remember," he said. "Why she'd loved that Kawako in the first place. And she kept saying this one thing about herself."

The thicket of trees grew denser. "What was that?" I asked. He shrugged.

"That she was a monster," he said.

●

Ahab kept a large knife with him, wherever he went. He owned a parang in Singapore, a Malay machete, but obviously he couldn't bring it to Japan. I had to get him one of those absurdly long knives chefs use all the time, in a store I found in Kitchen Town. Ahab said that was good enough.

I got the call on the third of April. It was from Nobuo. It had been more than a month since Haruhito Kawako's twenty-ninth birthday, when she had refused to celebrate the occasion with any of her relatives. In fact, she hadn't seen a single one of them since her father's funeral. Only her flatmate, Akiko, had any access to her. Nobuo met up with Akiko one day and asked if he could check in on his cousin, let him into their apartment. Akiko said it wouldn't be a problem.

"It's not like Kawako's a shut-in," Akiko had said to Nobuo. "She goes to work and comes back home. Sometimes we go out, have a drink, watch a movie together. I actually don't know why she refuses to see any of you guys."

Out of instinct, Nobuo asked Akiko if she had ever returned to Akishima city, after she'd made the move to Nakameguro. Had she ever gone back to see her family? Akiko blinked. She then gave him a smile.

"You caught me," she said to Nobuo. "We're awfully alike, aren't we."

On the day Akiko had agreed to bring Nobuo to their apartment, Kawako was nowhere to be seen. It was the thirty-first of March. A Sunday. Both of them had assumed that she'd simply gone out for the day, and waited for her to return. She did not come back.

"Kawako didn't report to work the next day either," Nobuo said over the phone. "Naturally we got a bit worried. We checked for any clues we could find, from her room to her toilet and the kitchen. We concluded that she probably packed a bag and left. As to where she went, nobody knows."

"I'm assuming she didn't leave a note," I said.

"She didn't, no. It's like she just vanished."

I paused at what he had just said.

"People do that sometimes," I replied. "One moment they're there, and in the next they're not."

"But Kawako's been doing nothing but running away," he said to me. "She ran away from me. She ran away from my family. She's been taking herself out of our lives and now she finally did it to Akiko as well. I can't let this go on any longer."

He then made it clear that I owed him a favour, after what I had asked him to do for Chiba Mari. And so I was left with no choice.

The next day, I sent out a couple of my usual feelers, and found that she'd taken herself to Yamanashi prefecture—to the forest northwest of Mount Fuji: Aokigahara. But another feeler in Kofu city had informed me that there was a kappa in there, hunting for humans to prey on. Tourists had been told to stay in groups, and to never venture away from the paths. Once you did, there was no guarantee of ever returning.

I called Ahab, the day after I'd gathered all my information on the situation. "If we want this woman to survive, I'll have to assemble a search party as fast as possible," I said to him. "You know how it goes."

"No cops?"

"No cops," I said. "So you can do whatever you have to."

"Heh heh. But we're not killing this woman, yeah? So what do you need me for?" he asked.

"The kappa," I said. "It could either attack Kawako, or it could very well attack us."

"While we're out searching for her in the forest."

"Yes."

"Right," said Ahab. "I get it." He then paused for a few seconds. "I can fly out first thing tonight."

"That's great," I said. "Thank you."

"Truth is—something similar is happening in Singapore. Something just as bad, possibly worse. A colleague and I are doing our best against this guy, so I could use the experience, I think."

"But 'this guy'," I said. "Is he a kappa?"

"No," said Ahab. "But he's after the same thing: a shirikodama. As far as I know he's already attacked one guy, who died on a plane soon after—who knows if he's gotten to other people?"

"Right," I said. I felt a memory stirring. "I know of a man. He died on a plane as well. Nobody really knows why."

I heard Ahab sigh.

"Our trail has gone cold for a while now. He's gone into hiding, and he's doing it well. We could certainly do with a man of your abilities, but we'd like to avoid getting other people involved." A pause. "If I'm flying to Japan, Mr Shimao—I'll need a knife."

"A knife?"

"Yeah," said Ahab. "A good, long knife. Get me one and we'll do just fine."

I took the metro to Kitchen Town, after we'd confirmed his flight. I went from Jinbocho to Ueno and made my way down to the main street. It was lined with appliance stores, supplying Tokyo's widest range of kitchenware; it was also a shopping district run entirely by kappas, but I had to set aside that fact for the time being. I entered a store and began browsing through a rack of knives, hung against a wood-panelled wall. The lighting, dimmed inside the store, lent a certain lustre to the hardware.

"Do you need any help?" a store clerk had asked. I looked at her. She had medium-length hair, tied up in a small bun, which made it impossible to see where the hole in her head was. She could pass off as human any day of the week. I told her I was looking to buy a knife, something light but sturdy.

"What ingredient will you be using it for?" she asked. "Fish, or meat?"

I didn't know what to say. I turned back towards the knives. It was hard to choose, in that particular moment. I went ahead with meat.

•

The knife swung by Ahab's side as we walked. He wanted to talk about the Ito Junji manga again.

"So the story's about this one guy, yeah, who travels to the site of the fault."

"Sure."

"And when the guy's there, he's all like, whoa, look at all these man-shaped holes! It's crazy."

"Yeah," I said. "Crazy."

"So he meets this other girl, who had come down to the fault site to check them out as well. The two of them hit it off."

"All right."

"They're talking about the holes and stuff, until they see this other guy, this total stranger, saying that he's here to find his own hole."

"What do you mean?"

"Meaning, this stranger here believes that there is a

hole made perfectly for him. And then he shows it to the couple. 'See?' the stranger says. 'It's in the exact shape of my silhouette. It's perfectly made for me.' He then does the craziest thing: he takes off his clothes and steps into the hole. And he gets totally sucked in."

"Sucked in?"

"Like a vacuum cleaner," Ahab said. He makes a slurping noise. "He just goes right in and disappears. Everybody freaks out."

"Understandably."

"They're all like, somebody save him! Somebody get him out! But he's disappeared, yeah, to god knows where. Nobody can get him out. And then it starts a whole chain of other people stepping into their holes. They find their own specially-shaped hole and disappear for good."

"I bet the girl finds her own hole as well."

"Oh yeah. She finds it. But the main character is like, don't go, please. Once you go in you can't come out. And so she stays with him in his tent, for a couple of days. They make love. But eventually she goes to her hole and steps inside. She does this in the middle of the night, leaves her clothes behind and everything. The main character is devastated."

I nodded.

"He's crying and everything, going why, why, why? Why did you leave me? And then, all of a sudden, he sees it."

"His own man-shaped hole?"

"Oh yeah," said Ahab. "He finds it. And there are all these voices telling him to go in, but he resists. Ultimately he's overcome by madness and despair."

"Whatever is empty needs to be filled."

"That's right," said Ahab. "Whatever is empty needs to be filled."

Our pace slowed incredibly, this time. There was barely any room to walk between the trees, let alone for two people. I led at the front while Ahab kept the rear, his knife catching the light and glinting at the blade. It began to feel like rock-climbing, only horizontal: there was hardly any flat ground to find stable footing. Once in a while, the sole of my boot would chip away at a root.

"What happens when you step inside the hole?" I asked Ahab. "Is that revealed in the manga?"

"It's a nightmare," he said. "A never-ending route, carved out of the exact shape of your own silhouette; you can't ever turn back and look behind you. All you can do is keep going. Do you know how that feels?"

I shook my head. "Do you?"

"No, man," said Ahab. "Thankfully, no."

It was dark when we returned. We were late. Ahab and I were about a hundred metres away from the campsite when I radioed the other pair.

"We're going to be late as well," Nobuo replied. "We thought we saw something that might have belonged to Kawako, so we spent a good amount of time searching the surrounding area. But Mr Sugimura reckons we're only seven hundred metres away. We shouldn't be long."

"Sure," I said, radioing back. "We'll see you there."

Just then I felt a hand on my chest: Ahab stopped me.

"Something's wrong," he said. His other hand reached for his knife. He unhooked it from his belt. The light of our campfire flickered and danced, just past the trees ahead.

"The fire's too weak," I said. Ahab nodded.

"The clothes line is still out as well. But I can't tell where Akiko is."

I strained my eyes to see. She was nowhere in sight.

"Radio her," Ahab said.

I held the comm set to my mouth and whispered. "Akiko," I said. "You there?"

There was no response. But there was a weird sound, coming from the camp. A strange sort of rustling. According to Sugimura however, strong winds don't exist in this forest. It's why the forest is so unnaturally quiet. Nobuo's voice came from the radio.

"Why isn't Akiko responding?" he asked. There was that strange rustling noise again.

I radioed back. "Ahab and I don't see her. Hurry, but be careful."

"We will," he said.

Ahab walked ahead this time. I followed closely behind. The fire was nearly out; whatever was in the pot, however, had burned to a crisp. Ahab took a couple of logs and threw them in to make the fire grow.

"This is her radio," I said, pointing it out. It was left behind on one of the chairs. "It explains the noise we've been hearing."

Ahab nodded. He then turned on the spot, looked over my shoulder.

"There you are," he said.

It was Akiko. She had stepped out from her own tent.

"I'm sorry," she said. "I thought I saw the kappa earlier,

before the sun had set. I went into my tent to hide and realised I had left my comm set outside. I'm a fucking idiot."

"The kappa came by?" I asked.

"A female," she said. "Long hair, brown linen dress. She had on a backpack and wore a pair of sandals, like she was going to school or something."

"What did she do?" Ahab asked. Just then we heard Nobuo and Sugimura running towards us.

"She was desperate for water, I think." Akiko nodded towards the jerrycans. There was only one left. "She drained that one and dragged away the other two. I saw through the opening of my tent."

Akiko said she was all right the next morning. She'd slept perfectly fine. "Sleep's for the brave," said Ahab. Nobuo and Sugimura had volunteered to refill the jerrycan before dawn, and came back with a second one in tow. "I always keep an extra one in the boot of my car, just in case," Sugimura explained. "This should do."

We stuck to the usual plan; Akiko didn't know where the kappa had retreated to, and Ahab didn't think circling the campsite was worth the effort. If the kappa had remained nearby, it would have attacked us during the night. Nobuo agreed.

"We're here to find Kawako, anyway. That's still our main priority."

Breakfast was canned tuna and diced onions, mixed with mayonnaise and ground black pepper. We spread the lot on salted crackers. The five of us huddled around the big bowl with our spoons.

"How old did the kappa look, by the way? How

tall?" Ahab asked.

"Not young," Akiko said. "In her thirties or forties, I think. About 1.7 metres high. Slightly taller than I am."

"Build?"

"Skinny. Like she'd been in the forest for a long time," said Akiko.

"How about the cavity in her head?"

"Located near the crown. It wasn't too big or too small; I only caught a glimpse of it."

Sugimura got up and walked towards his tent. He wiped his hands on his trousers as he did so. Nobody said anything as he zipped his tent open and stepped inside.

"It's me and him today," Ahab said. "Isn't that great." Ahab had been practicing with his knife all morning: he'd throw it towards a nearby tree and watch it pierce the bark. That or he'd move it through the air like a conductor's baton, with clean vertical and horizontal strokes. Akiko and I made the other pair.

"It's day six, isn't it?" Akiko said. The forest wasn't as dense today, compared to yesterday's route. "It's amazing how you haven't given up, Mr Shimao."

The air smelt like soil: both light and heavy. "It's my job after all," I said. She didn't press the matter any further.

I had met her for the first time last summer. We were outside a temple in Meguro ward, where Haruhito Daisuke's funeral was held. Akiko had a cute face, with short bronze hair cropped at the shoulder. I saw her approach the temple gates and called her over. In that instant, I deduced that she was the kind of girl who'd pay heed to a stranger's words. She'd come over to your side if you told her to. But there was something about her: a hard, tightly coiled fist of a thing she held inside. No matter what you did, you could never take advantage of a girl like that. Her coming over was just deference on her part.

"Kawako's father once told me something," Akiko said. We were a good hour in, and the weather was fine over the forest. We kept at a steady pace.

"What did he say?" I asked.

"He said that I had a bright soul. A really bright soul." Akiko seemed to smile at the thought. "Only Kawako and Chiba Mari know about this."

"You haven't told this to anyone else?"

She nodded.

"It was during Kawako's birthday party. About ten years ago, I think. Mr Haruhito and I only ever met that one time," she said.

"A bright soul, you say?"

She nodded again. "Last night I wondered if that was the reason why the kappa came. To take what I had for herself. Afterwards I wondered why she'd left without it."

I considered the situation. "Water was more important to her, I suppose."

"Perhaps," said Akiko. "Have you ever seen a dehydrated kappa before?"

I shook my head.

"They look like walking skeletons," she said. "Bony and dry as twigs, all shrivelled up. I was shocked, when I first saw it. I thought it was just another tree, except it seemed to be moving."

I looked at her. "You didn't mention it this morning. You

just said it was skinny."

Akiko shrugged.

"It's got all the water it needs now," she said.

For the next minute or so we kept up our pace, making long strides over the hard ground. There was no wind, no stirring, no sound apart from our footsteps. A bird chirped overhead, as though to break the silence.

"Sounds like glass," Akiko remarked.

Two hours later, we stumbled across a cave. There were a number of these, apparently, scattered across the forest. We chanced upon this one, thinking it was a large clearing we had spotted towards the right.

"Should we check it out?" I asked.

Akiko looked at the GPS, followed by her compass. Two hundred and forty-one degrees, it said: southwest by west. Anything beyond our right would be tomorrow's work. "It's a bit off our course," she said. "But let's take a look anyway."

The cave was more than twenty metres wide. The ground sloped steeply on the opposite edge of the cave. Where it ran downwards, the light could not reach.

"Do you feel that?" said Akiko.

"It's chilly," I said.

She looked around. "There are some trees over there, standing right at the edge." She pointed. "That one looks like it could fall in at any moment."

I looked. The sapling bent and curved, like a thick, wooden vine; its branches reached towards the inner hollow of the cave, as though it were a willow bent over a stream. But this was no stream. Akiko zipped open her backpack.

"I'm going to have lunch now, if you don't mind. It's more or less time."

"I'll have mine as well," I said.

Twenty minutes we spent, seated over the top lip of the cave, between the roots of a tall cypress tree. The air moved powerfully here. Lunch was onigiri packed into a Tupperware container. For a long while Akiko did nothing but look towards the cave, that big black hole in the ground. The perimeter of it was so wide and so vast it only seemed to grow: it grew to a point where the forest might as well be pushed back, continually, away from the reach of the cave.

Akiko ate a lot faster than I did. For a while, she barely even stirred. At that moment I noticed that she had on the same raincoat and wellingtons she wore the day before: they were both red in colour, a fashionable shade of ruby.

"Akiko."

"Yes?"

"Why are you here?" I asked. "The forest is no place for a young woman."

She turned and fixed me with her eyes. "I'm tough, Mr Shimao. I have my own reasons for being here."

It was half past one when I was done with my food. Akiko got to her feet.

"Let's go back," she said.

Nobuo kept guard by the fire. The rest of us had called it a night. Akiko sat next to him, keeping her words to herself. Neither of them spoke. Their shadows were cast high and far over our tent.

"Sugimura barely spoke to me the whole afternoon,"

Ahab said. I threw him a look.

"He's not here to make friends," I said to him. "He just owes me a favour. That's the only reason why he's here."

"Oh yeah?" Ahab said. He smirked. "What did you do for him that was so special?" he said. I told him it was none of his business.

At a quarter to ten, Nobuo came over and unzipped the front of our tent.

"I think I saw the kappa. Somewhere over there." He pointed southeast.

"You sure?" I said.

"Not really, to be honest." Nobuo was drenched in sweat again. "The figure wore something brown, though. Matched what Akiko said yesterday."

Ahab was out of the tent in seconds. "Akiko?"

Akiko looked at him. She was rooted to her chair beside the fire, seemingly out of breath.

"I'm not lying, Ahab."

Ahab and I quickly got flashlights. Nobuo held up an electric lantern. Sugimura and Akiko were to stay behind, and Ahab was to be our leader. "Follow me," he said. Somewhere behind, Sugimura called out, "Don't go beyond sight of the flame." Ahab crooked his jaw.

"First thing he's said to me all day," said Ahab. He waved the knife in his hand. "Come on."

The forest was completely dark: the canopy had broken the moonlight, rendering it useless. It just fell, diffuse, like dust over the ground. The only thing our flashlights revealed was just darkness, darkness, more of it—an endless supply of it lying ahead. The trees revealed themselves as white as bones.

Nobuo nearly tripped over a root. The light from his lantern swung back and forth, back and forth, back and forth.

"I'm going crazy," he said. I swore.

"I can't see anything."

"Shut it," said Ahab. He looked over his shoulder. "I can still see the campfire. Let's keep walking."

Barely a few seconds passed before I began to sweat. All I saw was tree, bark, root. Tree, tree, tree. All I could hear were my breath, my thoughts. Steps I took with my feet that I kept counting. "Nobuo," I said to him. "Nobuo." But he didn't reply.

I turned around. The two of them were gone. I didn't know where I was any longer.

"Nobuo?" I said again. "Ahab?"

I swung my torchlight. Nothing. No one. The light was so strong it bounced back into my eyes, blinding me for a second. I was completely alone.

"Nobuo! Ahab!"

I swung my torchlight again, and again. And then the beam of light landed on a wood-panelled wall. Mounted on it was a rack of knives, each one the same length but shaped a little different.

"What is this?" I said. I turned.

"Do you need any help?" a store clerk asked. It was the same clerk I had spoken to at Kitchen Town: medium-length hair, tied up in a small bun. I swung my flashlight towards her and directed it to her feet. We were in the forest all right. But as I swung my flashlight towards the rack of knives they were still there, each of the blades gleaming lustrous in the night.

"Sir?" the store clerk asked. I looked at her. The clerk was smiling at me. "Which knife are you interested in, sir?" Her smile then grew wider—it grew until her lips had stretched to her ears. Her eyes had turned to slits. "Are you fish or meat, sir?" she said. "Are you fish or meat?"

There was a shout. Ahab. I turned.

"Ahab!" I said.

He shouted again. And then I saw it: another strobe of light, waving behind a tree. I ran.

"I'm coming," I said. I cleared my throat. "I'm coming," I said again.

I ran faster. I didn't look back. My shoe caught on a root, but I quickly stepped over it and kept on running. I never wanted to look back. As I came up right behind them I realised I didn't have my flashlight.

"Where is it?" Ahab asked. I told him I had no idea.

Ahab and Nobuo were standing over something on the ground. I looked. It was the body of a man, its throat freshly slit open. Blood was still trickling from the wound. Nobuo raised the lantern over the corpse: its light was a moving circle, moving, moving, moving. It never stopped moving.

"Wearing a beige jumper," Ahab said. He knelt down and turned the body over. He felt through the man's hair. "Human." He looked up at Nobuo. "Did you mistake this guy for the kappa?"

Nobuo looked tired. But his gaze never broke: he kept it fixed on the body.

"We should leave tomorrow," Sugimura said. "We shouldn't stay here any longer." The five of us had carried the body back to the campsite. We placed it beneath a sheet beside Sugimura's tent. "Besides, we're running out of food and water. We keep going for another day, the search will turn futile."

Everybody looked at Nobuo. He was taking deep breaths, his chest rising and falling as he did so. He shook his head. "The situation's not that bad," he said. "We can still afford to keep going."

He waited for a response. Nobody said anything against him. I turned to Sugimura.

"When will the officials collect the body?"

"Tomorrow morning," he said. He looked pale. "I gave them our coordinates… They're setting off at eight, so they should be here by ten."

"I see," I said. I was still shaking, somewhat. I tried to hold it together. Sugimura and I were supposed to be a pair tomorrow. "They're going to ask us a lot of questions. Do you want to swap with Ahab and stay here at the camp? Liaise with the officials and everything?"

Sugimura shook his head. "No, no," he said. "We'll proceed as planned. Ahab will do fine with them."

Back in our tent I changed out of my clothes. Ahab came inside. He lay his knife down, and started to change as well.

"The guy slit his own throat open with a razor blade," he said. "He did it before we could catch up to him. He saw us coming and panicked, I think."

I didn't say anything to that. He then asked me what had happened earlier. One moment I was there, and then in the next I wasn't. It was as though I had just disappeared in the middle of the forest.

"I don't know," I said. I was trembling. Burned into my

eyes was that image of the light, moving, moving, moving. "I came back out," I said.

"You what?"

"I came back out," I said again. "I went in and then I came back out."

Nobuo and Akiko were assigned the twenty-third cardinal point, while Sugimura and I were assigned the twenty-fourth. Sugimura didn't look too happy. What he had said was true: we had no food, no water. Instead we had a body.

Ahab sat by the fire and began sharpening his knife. "I'll let you guys know, yeah? When the officials are here," he said.

I thanked him. We set off.

"See you later," Nobuo said to us. Akiko waved. She was in red again, with her boots and her raincoat on. I waved back.

"I don't know why she insists on wearing them," I said to Sugimura. "It must be uncomfortable."

He scratched an ear. "It's very noticeable, isn't it…"

"What?"

"I mean, you can't help but take note of her. Especially in a forest like this."

"Because of all the green."

Sugimura nodded. "Exactly," he said.

We kept on walking. There was a bird somewhere, here in this sea of trees; it made a call like a whistle. For some reason the forest felt sparser here.

"Akiko and I chanced upon a cave yesterday," I said.

"You did?"

"Yeah." I then described it to him: how big it was, how

wide. I gave him the coordinates Akiko had on her GPS that day.

"That's interesting… I'll take note of it," Sugimura said. "I've never heard of a cave in that location before."

According to him, there were a great number of caves throughout the forest, formed by lava and steam, some as large as the one I had described. Others were smaller. All this had happened during the Jogan period, after an eruption of Mount Fuji laid waste to the surrounding area. Ash had risen into the sky and fell back down in faraway places.

"The lava flowed across the middle of a large lake and split it in two," Sugimura said. "Over time it cooled down, and the forest grew atop it."

The forest, spanning more than 3,000 hectares, was built on a thin layer of soil only dozens of centimetres thick. "That's why all the roots are exposed," he said. "The ground's too hard and shallow… And yet the trees manage to grow, somehow."

"They hold on to what they can," I said. Sugimura smiled.

"This whole forest has been here for more than 1,200 years… That's hardly a life, if you think about it."

A minute passed. Sugimura went on.

"I remember going into this cave once, about a month after my divorce was finalised. I was asked to lead a group of undergraduates there as a tour guide of sorts. The cave was a tourist destination, famous for all the ice it had, even during the summer… In order to go in you had to climb down these narrow stairs and then climb back up."

"Was it fun?"

He shook his head.

"I was still bitter from the divorce," he said. "I had all these

feelings weighing me down, things I didn't want anymore…
They were a great burden to me. As we walked down to the
very bottom of the cave, there was a large fence across a dark
enclosure, and a sign on it that said, 'Hell Hole'."

"Hell Hole?" I said. Jigoku Ana. He nodded.

"I remember staring at the sign, transfixed… I'd seen
it before, of course, but this time I kept staring at it, even
though there were a bunch of students behind me, waiting for
me to say something. But I said nothing. I stood absolutely
still… There was a message on the sign saying that if you ever
slipped into this hole you'd never go back home again. And
then I thought about it: I thought about going over the fence
and jumping straight in."

He paused.

"It's true, what the sign said." He looked at me. "There's
no coming back from something like that."

They found her that afternoon. Nobuo and Akiko. They
found Haruhito Kawako in the end. They had walked by
the other side of the cave, the large one that Akiko and I had
chanced upon the day before, and found her clothes, neatly
folded in a pile at the edge of its lower lip. Her bag and other
belongings lay in a separate heap.

"We found her," Akiko said. Her voice was static, white
sound over the radio. In the background was an ugly, retching
noise. "It got her first."

7

SORA NO NIKKI

MAY–JULY 2013

I

ZHIWEI

A row of palm trees stood between the outer wall and the main road. The trees were brown around the base, and then green from the midsection up. There were eight of these trees, each one a perfect distance from the other, so that their leaves formed a canopy of sorts, a shield from the outer eye. The outer wall was of a white stone, smooth all around. It stretched from one corner of the eye to the next, forming a low perimeter around the estate. The sky above was a rare, cloudless blue.

I'd started going in the pool again. It'd been a week since the incident, after the authorities had cleared the body away and assured the residents that the water had been fully replaced. It didn't take long at all for me to settle back into my old habit. It was a thing I did, whenever I had nothing better to do: I'd step into the pool and float on its surface, my body half in and out of the water for hours at a time. Sometimes I would do a couple of laps, just enough to get the blood pumping. I'd been doing this ever since I was a teenager.

The pool had never been very popular to begin with. It was a centrally located facility, about twenty metres long and eight metres wide, and only two metres deep. Sectioned at one end was the Jacuzzi, just big enough for five or six people to sit inside. There were deck chairs on one side of the pool, with a view of the palm trees; each chair had its own parasol, striped in white and blue. But flanked on three sides were five blocks of flats, each block more than twenty storeys high, with a balcony attached to every apartment. This meant that any resident could look down at the pool whenever they felt like it, and nobody ever seemed to appreciate that kind of scrutiny. Sometimes I'd find myself accompanied by a mom or a dad, splashing about with their kids, teaching them how to swim. Sometimes I'd find the elderly man from Block B, who would have forgotten to do his usual laps that morning. He was a quiet man, with a flat chest and even flatter stomach, and he moved with a silent, slow-moving grace. Other than those people, though, it'd just be me, swimming about in the pool, my few belongings placed along the edge of the water—my keys, my phone, and my towel. Those were all the things I needed.

Over time, I found that a pool wasn't a place for worries. A pool was a place where things came to rest. All of one's anxieties and fears didn't matter once you were in the water, with a stomach full of air and your body swaying and bobbing on the surface. The water would lap continually into my ears:

there'd be a sucking, gurgling noise, followed by the swirling sound of underwater currents, powerful routes of movement unseen to the naked eye. All other sound would be cut away from my ears.

The only thing the water ever demanded was your ability to stay afloat. All it ever needed was for you to remain completely at peace. And all it wanted was for you to relax and remain calm on its ever-rocking, ever-changing surface. It would be all you'd ever amount to, just a thing to be one with, to be in equilibrium with. I learnt this over time as the surrounding blocks towered over my being, over and over again, like a memory I needed reminding of. With my ears in the water, it was all I could do, really, to hear me take my own breaths: to hear nothing but what was going on, to hear the reason why my heart could still beat.

Ever since the North East Line began operations ten years ago, the area surrounding the condominium had become prime real estate: from the guardhouse, you could walk to the nearest station in under five minutes, and to the nearby St Andrew's schools in ten. There was a kopitiam in the vicinity as well, where I could get nasi lemak for under three dollars. At various stages across the past decade, all the surrounding houses and condominiums had been torn down and built again, which meant that my idea of a neighbourhood had always incorporated the sound of the chainsaw, its high shrill cutting away at something, as well as the repeated sound of metal striking rhythmically against metal, keeping tempo to the daily music. Only the condominium where I stayed remained untouched as newer, fancier buildings rose around it, as though the estate—with its swimming pool, its white outer wall, and its tall row of palm trees—had remained oddly trapped in time.

Before the incident, I'd find myself in the pool about three times a week, sometimes four. My core modules had started to kick my ass that April, and the pool was my only way of unwinding from all that stress. After the incident had passed, my parents had advised against ever returning to the pool: they said something about bad luck, about how that kind of thing wouldn't go away, no matter how many times the water got drained and replaced. But I told them I didn't mind. That sort of thing didn't bother me, I said, and I didn't care if I would be the only one in that pool. But I was wrong.

He was slim and pale, with hardly any muscle on him. He looked to be about the same age as I was. The first time I caught sight of him, he was wearing a pair of yellow boxers, and reclining on the centremost deck chair. He had his long hair tied back with a hair band. It was the start of May, and the temperature that afternoon had been around thirty-four degrees, with only a couple of drifting clouds in the sky: it was perfect weather for swimming, and for sunbathing as well, except the guy seemed perfectly content reading the newspaper, beneath the wide shade of his parasol. He read it front to back, before calmly putting it aside. He then reached into the tote bag he'd brought with him, and took out a worn-looking paperback. Shortsighted as I was, I couldn't make out the author's name from my spot in the water.

Two hours we spent there, side by side but never speaking. Not once did either of us make eye contact: he was reading his book, whenever I stole a glance at him, and whenever he looked at me, my mind was probably somewhere else, my gaze kept focused on the sky above. I'd always been aware of the word azure—how it was supposed to describe crystal blue skies—and I believe I had only grown to understand what that word had meant that day. Those were the kind of thoughts that had run through my mind. The guy and I were so wrapped up in our own separate things, it hardly seemed to matter that only a few metres or so had stood between the two of us. We were like two boats docked at the same harbour, within reach of each other and yet never more than that. You could even say that I had come to appreciate his company: he was as much a part of the pool as the deck chairs, or the Jacuzzi, or even myself were. We valued the time we'd spent there, just as much as the other would. It was as good as being alone.

After that day, I grew to think that more people would come flocking back to the pool—that it was okay, really, and perfectly enjoyable. But I was mistaken. Even the elderly man from Block B, with his precise and careful strokes, had stopped his morning swims altogether. Over the course of May, it was only ever that guy and I, minding our own separate business. He'd be on the same centremost chair, reading through his paperback, while I'd float on the water, eyes closed, after a couple routine laps. Every time I took the lift down to the first floor, I'd find him there, settled beneath his parasol. This happened without fail, neither one of us saying hi to the other. Eventually I grew to rely on it: the same old pattern, the seeming order to my life. To our lives.

When May gave way to June, I found myself down at the

pool nearly every day, seeing how my school holidays had officially begun. My friends and I were the types to hang out at night, for dinner or for movies or for drinks, which meant that my afternoons were kept largely free. The guy on his deck chair had moved on to his third paperback by then, although who he'd been reading all this time, I still couldn't tell. My things had always been placed at a corner, far away from his.

There was one day, a Wednesday, when the guy had not shown up. It was the fifth of June. I placed my belongings on a deck chair, wondering where he was. I felt almost sad. I could always count on him to be there, whenever I used the pool. Now the water appeared cold, and empty. A passing breeze nipped lightly on my thighs.

I began my usual routine. I started from one end of the pool and swam, freestyle, to the other end and back. Each time I surfaced above the water I'd cast a look towards the deck chair, the centremost one, and found it just as empty and vacant as the minute before. It was strange; I wondered what the guy could be up to, spending his afternoon somewhere else. I then returned to my laps with a renewed sense of purpose and energy. I'd decided to put him out of my mind for the time being, and after I was done with my laps, my blood pumping and body brimming from all the effort, I walked over to the centre of the pool, took off my goggles, and kicked my body off from the tiled floor. I floated on the water, eyes closed, against the bright rays of the sun. I stayed there for as long as I could, first tensing my muscles and then relaxing them, one portion of my body at a time. Finally, after a while, I settled into what I felt was my freest.

Time passed; time slowed. Time didn't matter anymore. Time, in some sense, ceased to exist.

I opened my eyes. Nothing about my day seemed to have changed: the sky was still exactly the same, and my surroundings were left just as how I had remembered them. I lowered my body back down, and dunked my head into the water. I then came back up for air, grateful for the relief of cold water on my face. When I opened my eyes again, however, I noticed that one thing had changed about my surroundings: a person, seated on the centremost chair, just metres away from where I stood.

It wasn't the usual guy, though. It was a woman this time, and she seemed to be in her mid-thirties. I had never seen her before, not around the condo. But she had the most beautiful skin: it shone, golden almost, from all the sunscreen she had applied. And she seemed to have the roundest, deepest set of eyes. She raised a hand.

"Hey you," she said to me. "Great day, isn't it?"

I nodded. I had never spoken to anybody by the pool before.

"Hi," I said. "The day's great."

The woman didn't smile, not particularly, but her manner seemed inviting. She let her hand down. "It's the perfect weather for sunglasses, don't you think?"

"Yeah," I said. I squinted my eyes as I looked towards the sky.

"I can't really wear them, though," came the woman's voice. When I turned back to her, she was pointing at her nose. "I've got this really problematic bridge. It barely slopes at all, so things like spectacles and shades can't really stay on my face," she explained. "It's kind of like a disability."

"Do you wear glasses?"

"Nope."

"Well, I do," I said.

"Oh? Are your goggles prescriptive?" the woman asked.

"My eyesight's pretty bad," I said.

The woman leant forward on her chair.

"Can you see me at all, from that far away?"

I shook my head. I strained my eyes.

"Your face is kind of a blur to me."

"Come closer, then," the woman said. She beckoned me forward with her hand. "Just come to the edge of the water. You'll see what I'm talking about."

"Are you talking about your nose?"

"That's right," she said. "Come on."

I walked in the water. I walked until I could rest my arms on the edge of the pool, over the white plastic grates that covered the drain. I could see her better from there.

"Ah," I said. "No offense, but, your nose is exactly what you say it is."

"Isn't it?" the woman exclaimed. She moved her head from right to left. "Are you seeing this? Look at this. My profile makes me look like a dinosaur."

"It's not so bad."

"Come on. Have you seen *The Hours*?" The woman leant back against her chair. "My nose is kinda like Nicole's, I think. But people often talk about how she had to look ugly for the part. I don't really like that movie."

"Well," I said. "I've never even heard of it before."

The woman let out a laugh.

"Thanks," she said. "You're a good kid." She then closed her eyes before peeling one back open. "You've got a great tan, by the way."

I thanked her. "People tell me that all the time."

"I bet they do," she said. "You're quite famous, you know."

"What do you mean?"

The woman smirked. "I think everybody living here knows who you are. Tanned, broad shoulders. No hair on his head. You're the guy that's down by the pool all the time."

I shrugged. "My parents say I'm addicted."

"God, no," the woman said. "Don't think of it that way. It's good that you're so active."

"I'm not, though," I said. "I swim for a bit, but that's all. Mostly I just float on the water."

The woman smiled. "You really like doing that, don't you? Every single time I go out on the balcony I see you there, just floating away, like a starfish on the sand. It's enough to make anybody jealous."

"Jealous?"

The woman nodded. "You look so free," she said.

I thanked her again. The woman sighed.

"I'd love to be just as free as you are," she said. "But I don't have that kind of time on my hands."

"What do you do?" I asked.

"I'm a freelancer," she said. She smirked again. "I do interior design. I've only started for about a year, I think, but it seems to pay well."

"Have you always been freelancing?"

She gave me a peculiar look.

"This wasn't part of some grand plan I had, if that's what

you're asking. It's just something I happen to be good at. Plus it pays the bills." She paused. "Where do you live, by the way? Which block?"

"Block D," I said. I pointed to my left. "Twentieth floor."

"Wow," said the woman. "That's really high up. Don't you ever get scared?"

"Scared? I don't think so," I said. "I'm not afraid of heights."

The woman made an ooh-ing sound.

"That's rare," she said. "Almost everybody is afraid of heights."

There was another pause. I asked her where she lived in return. She said she lived in Block C.

"Fifth floor. With my daughter."

"How old?"

"She just turned six, two months ago. So as you can see, I've got my hands full."

"What about your husband?" I asked.

She fixed me with a stare.

"I love him," she said. "With all my heart. But I don't want to talk about him."

"I see," I said. I dipped my head in the pool and came back out again. My face had started to feel dry.

"I live with this other guy though," the woman said. "A roommate. He helps to take care of my girl."

"'This other guy'…?"

The woman smiled.

"I'm sure you've seen him around," the woman said to me. "He's been coming down to the pool as well, to read his books and stuff like that."

"I know him," I said. I felt legitimately excited at the mention. "He's always here whenever I am."

"And vice versa," the woman said. "He tried to kill himself, however. He's done it in the past, multiple times, but it never seems to work. This time it's not so bad, but he's still got to rest at home. Which is why I'm here instead of him."

I nodded. So that's where he was.

"You make it sound like you're taking turns," I said. "Like you have to be in his place or something."

The woman laughed. "I guess so, when you put it that way. I just want to be in his space for a while. Just to see what it feels like. We have very unique living arrangements, I must admit."

I nodded again.

"Why don't the two of you come down the pool at the same time? That would be nice, wouldn't it?"

"Hmm," the woman said. She puckered her lips together. "I wonder why we've never thought of that before."

A minute passed between the two of us. The woman had her eyes closed again, with her arms folded behind her head. She seemed to be having the time of her life. Overhead, a cloud passed by across the sun and then moved on, its brief shadow no longer than a moment.

"What do you do, by the way?" the woman asked. "I realise I hadn't asked."

"I'm in uni," I said to her. "Undergrad."

"What major?"

I told her. She then asked which year I was in, and I told her I was in my second. She looked at me, intently, with her small but watchful eyes.

"And do you know what you want to do, after you graduate from university?"

I thought about it.

"Truth be told," I said to her. "I don't know."

The woman smiled once more.

"I hate to break it to you, babe. But if you don't know by now, you never, ever will." She then closed her eyes again. "Take it as a blessing, though. Trust me on this." The woman added nothing more after that.

●

The guy returned on Friday, two days later; neither he nor the woman had gone down to the pool that Thursday. Why that was the case, I hadn't got a clue.

He was seated in his usual deck chair, with an open book resting on his chest. The day's paper had already been folded and set aside, on the paved floor next to his bag. He seemed to be sleeping. The parasol, fully opened as always, cast a wide shadow across his frame. I looked at him for a while, wondering if his body betrayed any signs of his last attempt. But I couldn't tell what he had done. His flatmate hadn't said anything specific about it.

After my eleventh lap, I made my way towards the centre of the pool. I looked up at the sky. The weather hadn't looked ideal that day, with only patches of clear sky amongst the gathering clouds. It was only a week later that I learnt that it was the start of the haze. I turned my head over to my right, just to get one more look at the guy, resting under the parasol, when he began to stir. He rubbed his eyes, just as his book fell off his chest. He made his way, slowly, to pick it back up. He then caught sight of me looking directly at him.

I froze in that moment: it had been the first time either one of us had established eye contact. He nodded his head, and I had nodded mine.

The guy returned to his book. I began walking over to the edge of the pool.

"Hey there," I said to him. "You've been missing for quite a while."

The guy looked up at me, in an alert kind of way. He seemed surprised that I had spoken.

"I saw your flatmate, though. Two days ago. We had a nice chat."

He said nothing in reply for about five seconds or so.

"Yeah," the guy finally said. His voice sounded strained and yet clear all the same. "Su Lin told me about it," he added.

"Su Lin?"

"That's her name," said the guy. "You didn't ask?"

I shook my head.

"She didn't ask for mine."

The guy said nothing to that. I could sense he wasn't disapproving.

"She told me why you were gone," I said to him.

The guy smirked. "Did I worry you?"

"It's not the same without you around," I said. "I like to think we're friends, on some level."

The guy kept on smirking. "So we're friends now."

I let out a laugh. "I guess so."

"Well, with that in mind—I'm sorry, then. I apologise." He shook his head. "Whatever I keep doing to myself—it's a bad habit of mine. I can't quite shake it off. If anything, Su Lin isn't worried about it at all, so you shouldn't be either."

"She isn't?"

He shook his head. "I am an oddity. Oddities aren't meant to exist. It's why I do what I do, but it's also why everything has failed, so far."

I kept quiet, for a bit.

"I'm Zhiwei, by the way. That's my name."

I waited for him to respond. The guy appeared to consider whether he ought to or not.

"I'm Kevin," he said eventually. "Kevin Lim."

"That's a pretty common name," I said. It was the first thing that came to my mind. "Sorry. That just came out."

He rolled his eyes. There was a smirk, playing at the corner of his lips.

"Your name's pretty common too," he said.

"True," I said. I smiled. "That's true."

From somewhere overhead came the screech of a chainsaw, whirring away at a high, grating pitch. Kevin raised his eyes, as though to see where it might have come from.

"You know, all this while I've been waiting to hear a bird in the trees."

I looked behind me.

"The trees?" I said. I turned back towards him. He held his gaze onto the distance. "What bird is this?" I asked. Kevin kept his gaze firmly on the sky.

"The weather's changing, isn't it."

I moved my legs in the water.

"I guess I should get out soon, then," I said. "Why don't you ever swim, by the way? The water's nice."

Kevin looked at me, with eyes that seemed almost sad. "I'd love to," he said. "But I can't. I become a different person when I do so."

I felt confused. "What do you mean?" I asked. Kevin tilted his head to the side.

"Tell me something instead," said Kevin, shifting himself to the edge of his chair. His figure, for the first time, came into full relief under the sun, and his skin turned out to be paler than I'd imagined. Kevin set his bare feet onto the ground, and placed his elbows on his knees. "Why do *you* go into the water? I wanna know."

I thought about it.

"I just like it," I said to him. "There's no particular reason."

Kevin smiled. "There's no reason to lie either, Zhiwei."

I blinked. "Well, then, I suppose—I suppose I like how the water makes me feel," I said.

"And how does it make you feel?"

"Free, I suppose," I replied, although I knew I was merely quoting Su Lin. I then reiterated my point. "Total freedom," I said to him again; "like I'm not connected to anything in the world but the water."

Kevin nodded. His hair, I realised, hadn't been tied back with a band that day. It fell in thick locks across the front of his eyes.

"Thanks for telling me," he said. "I appreciate it." He paused for a few seconds. "Su Lin actually wanted to swim that day, apparently. When she was out here on Wednesday. But you seemed to be having a great time. She didn't want to disturb you."

"Really?" I said.

"Yeah. She actually wanted to try floating on the water as well, just like how you do it."

"But?"

He smiled.

"The whole pool seemed to be yours."

I looked at him.

"You can come in, if you want. By all means. Nobody's stopping you, least of all me."

He shook his head. "It's fine," he said to me. "It's not anything that I need to do." He then retreated, back under the shade of his parasol. "I'm surprised nobody else has come down to use the pool. It's always just the two of us."

"You know about the incident, don't you? About the body in the pool?"

"Yeah," said Kevin. "It took place in April, didn't it? On the third."

"I think so," I said.

"I remember the hoo-hah," Kevin said. "The policemen, the reporters and the management, whom we never get to see. Every day there was somebody knocking on our door, asking us if we ever knew the person."

"Did you recognise him, though? You seen him around before?"

Kevin gave me a look.

"Have you?"

I shook my head. "He turned out to be this woman's brother-in-law, didn't he?"

Kevin nodded. "Huge fight, apparently. The woman's husband found out she'd been sleeping with his twin brother the whole time. Very dramatic."

"The husband—what did he do? He pushed him over the balcony?"

"He knocked him out first," Kevin said. "With a golf club.

Pow. All this took place while the wife was still at work. The balcony thing happened after his brother was unconscious."

I tried to imagine: a man swinging a golf club down on another man's head, but a head that had looked identical to his own.

"From what floor did he fall?" I asked. "I'm sure you remember."

"I do," Kevin said. He looked almost excited. "Sixteenth floor." He then pointed towards the right. "Block B." He paused. "The things we get up to, because of lust."

I looked at him.

"I haven't been with anybody in a long time," I said.

Kevin raised an eyebrow. "You didn't have to say that."

I shrugged.

"Since when?" he asked.

"Since I was…fifteen? Sec Three. It was a boy's school."

Kevin tilted his head to the side. "With whom, might I ask?"

"Not a classmate," I said. "A relief teacher. She was really young, though. She was still in uni back then."

"And who approached whom?" asked Kevin. I told him I had.

"It was the first time I'd ever wanted anything in my life," I said to him. "I'm an only child, and so my parents always gave me everything I'd ever wanted. And then here comes something I never had before. And she was so pretty. So cool. I wanted that kind of confidence for myself, I started to think. And then after that it became a kind of attraction. One day I saw her waiting for the bus: it was nearly five o' clock, and nobody else was there at the bus stop. I asked her where she was going."

"And?"

"She said she was going to the same train station as I was. And then we started talking."

"How did conversation lead to sex?" Kevin asked. He seemed genuinely interested.

"I don't actually remember," I said to him. "Not the specifics, anyway. I just asked her if I could come over to her place, I think, and then she let me. And that was how we ended up together."

Kevin shifted in his seat. He had ignored his book entirely at this point.

"How was it?" he asked.

"It was good," I said. "She really made sure that I was comfortable with everything, and I had to remind her that I was the one who wanted it more." I paused. "After that day she stopped coming to school. Her time as a relief teacher had come to an end, and I never tried to see her again after that."

Kevin asked why not. I told him I wasn't sure.

"I guess I felt I didn't need anything else anymore," I said to him. "I wonder if you know what I mean?"

Kevin simply looked at me.

"I do," he said. "But in a different way, I suppose." He paused. "Do you think you've changed a lot, since then? Like you became a different person?"

"Since the time I had sex?"

He nodded. I thought about it.

"I suppose so," I said to him. "You're still a growing person, at the age of fifteen. You haven't settled into anything just yet. Although things do start to happen to you, and that affects your growth somehow." I gave him a smile. "I guess that happens to everybody, though. So I'm not exactly answering your question."

"It's okay," said Kevin. "I understand." He put one leg over the other. "Did you love her, Zhiwei?"

"My teacher?"

"Yes," said Kevin. "Your teacher."

I could feel the water, swaying against my body, as it lapped into the drain through the grates.

"I suppose so," I said. "In the way a fifteen-year-old could love a person."

"And did she love you back?"

I looked at him. I saw Kevin looking back at me, the object of his gaze never wavering. I told him what I knew. "She said she loved me back as well." Kevin then nodded and closed his eyes. He felt around for his book and brought it back up to his chest, the pages open against his skin.

"Thank you," he said to me. "I think that's enough chat for one day." He then fell asleep, his lips parted by a small gap. You could just about see a small flash of his teeth.

•

The haze crisis began soon after that. Forest fires, burning across Indonesia, sent plumes of smoke into our skies. I could barely see anything outside the window.

For a long time, across the stretch of June and a bit into July, I hadn't returned to the pool. It just wasn't the sensible thing to do, not with all the ash drifting in the air; the situation was so bad I found it hard to even make a case against my parents' wishes. And so I had to let the pool go.

Since then, I haven't seen either Kevin or his flatmate, even after the crisis was over. It seemed like I'd never learn how it felt for them, for either one of them to finally swim in that pool. I miss him, in a way. I miss them both. And it seemed like I'd never get to tell anybody about how, after all those years, I bumped into Ms Neo again.

II

Ms Neo

Ahab and I met every Wednesday night, at the coffee shop situated at Block 146. There was a huge field of grass between the block and the train station; every time Ahab appeared at the exit, he'd wave at me, just a quick sort of gesture, and I'd wave back, all the way from our usual table. It was easy to spot one another, because of the lights that came on at night. Whenever we met, he'd have his small black backpack, worn over the shoulders with the straps tightened to the limit.

We started meeting at the coffee shop ever since the incident with the brother-in-law. It had made quite a splash, so to speak: the guy had been sleeping with his twin brother's wife, and ended up getting clubbed in the head for it. His brother then threw him off the balcony, with enough force to land him straight into the swimming pool. Ahab had sent me there to check it out, to make sure nothing nasty had been left behind after they'd taken the body away. "Who knows what could be in the water," he said to me. And that was how I found out about Kevin.

"He's living with who?"

"A mother and her child," I said. I was on the phone with Madam Lim.

"Who are they?" she asked. "What have they got to do with Kevin?"

I told her I wasn't sure. "In any case," I said, "my colleague and I will keep an eye on him, now that we know where he is."

"That's good," said Madam Lim. "Thank you for all that you've done, Ms Neo."

"Your problem is mine," I said to Madam Lim. "Managing the situation is the best that we can do."

"Hmm," she said. "You mean to say he can't exist, am I right?"

I didn't answer.

"It's all right, Ms Neo. I understand." Madam Lim paused. "You need to find a way to speak to Kevin. Of course, you can't just walk up to him."

"No. Not after what happened to Mr Haruhito."

There was a second pause.

"I recommend observation," said Madam Lim. "See what he's like now, what he does. Decide if he's safe to be approached."

"That's the plan," I said.

"Has he ever left the condo, by the way?"

"No," I replied. "Like I said: all Kevin does is spend his time by the poolside. And all he ever does is read."

"What is he reading?" she asked.

"I don't know," I said to her. "There's a face on the cover, but I can't really tell."

"All right," said Madam Lim. "It doesn't matter." For some reason or another, I felt like I wouldn't hear from her ever again. "When you do get to talk to him, could you please pass along a message from me?"

"Sure," I said. "If the opportunity arises."

"Tell him I've been to Japan," she said. "Multiple times. Tell him I've been to the bookstore, and the hotel. Tell him I understand everything now."

I frowned. "What do you understand?" I asked, but Madam Lim didn't seem to have heard my question.

"Tell him I gave birth to him," Madam Lim continued. "Tell him how hard it was for me that time, all those hours in pain. How I had given up. Tell him it's my fault he doesn't have a soul."

I bumped into Zhiwei again, on the nineteenth of June.

It'd been more than two months since Ahab and I had started frequenting the coffee shop. It's a pretty simple one, with a drinks auntie and a mee pok man and a nasi lemak stall. On one corner there is a television, tuned permanently to Channel U. Gathered beneath the TV set was the usual crowd of old men, in brown polo tees and dark pants and black leather sandals. The one with the perm always ordered the same five bottles of Tiger beer.

"Eh auntie," Ahab would say. "Kopi peng, thanks."

It had been one of those peculiar days. The sidewalks were empty, and the air smelt of dead things. Burnt things. Evening skies drenched in unnatural hues. Whoever you met passing by had a N95 mask on, strapped across their noses and mouths, so that you saw nothing but their eyes, a little vacant as they stared straight ahead. Even the five old men, seated beneath the TV, sat slumped back in their plastic chairs with their masks still on. Other than them, however, there was nobody else in that coffee shop: nobody except Ahab and myself, on Wednesday evenings.

"We'll have to be extra careful, yeah," Ahab said to me that evening. He had taken off his mask so he could drink his kopi. "Dead things floating everywhere."

He had a book with him that evening, and he'd laid it down on the table. There was nothing on the cover: it was just a blank white surface. I stared at it, wondering why that was the case.

"What is that?" I asked him. He spun the book around to show me the spine. "It's Japanese?"

"From one of Shimao's authors," he said to me. "*Sora no Nikki*."

"What's it about?"

"It's about a notebook this guy purchases, except it turns out to be a diary, written twenty years ago," he said. He flipped through the first few pages. "In the diary, the writer recounts how he had run away from home, and how he struggles to make his journey back."

"Two narratives," I said. "Your Japanese has to be really good."

Ahab made a face.

"Not bad la. I improved a lot after my trip."

"Do you like the book so far?" I asked. According to his bookmark, he was only through a third of the volume.

"It's okay. Two narratives like you said. It jumps between the present day and the diary, so that can be difficult."

"But Shimao likes it?"

Ahab nodded. "Shimao loves it."

Ahab had received the call from Mr Shimao a week before I'd learnt about Kevin's whereabouts. We still hadn't known where he was at the time, but Ahab took on the job anyway, hoping to learn more about how shirikodamas could be stolen or extracted from other people. But when he came back, he said he'd learnt nothing: he never got to meet the kappa, and this girl in their team had a plan of her own the whole time. The only thing he gained was a bad case of athlete's foot, which meant less groundwork for him when he returned and more time on the job for me. Ahab resumed charge on the twin brothers' case after he made a full recovery.

"The wife's hearing will take place in a couple of days," he said.

I nodded. Over the years I'd learnt to trust his instincts, when it came to picking which cases were worth pursuing. "How is she?" I asked.

"She's okay," said Ahab. "A bit thrown off by everything. But the haze isn't helping things."

"Why do you say that?"

"She's just staring out of the window," said Ahab. "Nothing's a better sign for crazy than that."

The wife's name was Noor. Her husband was a restaurateur, a man in his forties named Henry Tan. Harry was the name of his twin. Ahab had been keeping tabs on both husband and wife, but he'd been paying special attention to Noor, watching her from the HDB flat directly opposite her parents'. A car park stood between the two blocks.

"Her parents have been keeping their windows shut, just like everybody else," said Ahab. "But Noor keeps pulling them wide open."

A while later, we moved on to Kevin. I told him that Kevin was appearing less regularly by the pool.

"My assumption is that the haze is disrupting his usual schedule," I said to Ahab. "If the weather keeps up like this, we might find ourselves less able to predict his movements."

Ahab pursed his lips.

"What about the other guy?"

"The other guy?"

"The one who's always swimming in the pool," he said. "Is he going less often as well?"

"He hasn't appeared in two weeks," I said. "Not once. He might have stopped his routine altogether."

Ahab nodded.

"You say they might be friends, yah? You saw them speaking to one another a while back."

"Yeah," I said. "But I can't make any guesses beyond that. That was the last time the swimmer went to the pool."

Ahab leant back in his chair. He took what was left of his kopi peng and drained it.

"I wonder what they could have talked about," Ahab said. He set his cup back down. "You think the swimmer might be Kevin's next target?"

"I hope not," I said.

Ahab paused. I felt the weight of his gaze upon me.

"What's up?"

I looked at him. "To be honest, there's something about the guy…"

"What about him?"

"I don't know," I said. "He looks familiar, somehow. Like I might have met him before."

"You think?"

I nodded. "A boy I used to know."

Ahab left twenty minutes later. He put his mask back on, and made a grab for his book. "Ciao." He then made a beeline across the field of grass, straight towards the train station. It was nearing eight o' clock.

I got up, and went over to the nasi lemak stall. There was somebody else already standing in front of it, and I recognised him in that instant: it was the swimmer, the one whom Kevin had spoken to the previous Friday. The swimmer was in a white shirt and blue shorts, and a good head taller than myself. His crew cut hair was bleached in some places. I knew he was my only way into the condo.

I tapped him on the shoulder. "Do you know what's good here?" I asked.

He looked over his shoulder. We locked eyes. He appeared stumped, for some reason.

"No," the guy said. "No way."

I didn't get what was going on. "I'm just asking," I said automatically. And then I knew.

A friend had once asked me what the biggest regret in my life was. We were drinking beer, just the two of us, over the bridge at Clarke Quay. This was way before I'd met Ahab; before I got my life all sorted out, and learnt the value of cutting ties. I told my friend about the time I'd slept with a fifteen-year-old kid, some boy whose name I didn't remember. I'd slept with him because he told me he loved me. When he had said those words he looked so much like Eric.

"Do you remember Eric?" I asked my friend. She said she did.

"He was in that car accident."

"Yeah," I said. "That's right."

My friend chugged down her beer.

"You know, Irena and Daria—they both had a crush on him."

"Really?"

"We're Europeans," she said. "We love big tits on a man."

And then my friend laughed. I tried to as well, but my face hurt. We'd smoked so much weed beforehand, and we were still high. Later, my friend said: "All it takes is a single thing— just one, single thing. And then everything else will follow."

Meeting Zhiwei again was one of those things you don't plan for. People say this all the time: that things will come and go, that things are always coming and going. They enter your life and leave it, never to return. But that's not true. Things come and go, but they always come back. This is the part I have yet to learn.

The following Wednesday, Ahab and I met again, except this time he had to avoid the field. It'd been pouring wet that afternoon—the largest rainstorm we'd seen all month—and the field was left ruined and muddy. It even hailed at one point, somewhere in the west. Ahab slammed his book down on our table.

"Oh, dude," he said to me. "Dude!" He pointed to his bookmark. "Look at how far I've read. This book is amazing."

I smiled. "Tell me about it," I said.

He began.

"So the protagonist, yeah, his name is Maru, and the diarist is only known as X. And X is, like, trying to go back home to his parents, except he can't even remember the address of his old house. All X has are these rich details of his childhood home, like his bedroom and the kitchen and his parents' study, and the garden that surrounds his house. It's like a fantasy land he can't connect to reality. And so in his diary, the most he can do is record the trains he's gotten on, the strangers he's hitched rides from, as he tries to make his way back home. At one point he finds himself stuck at a bakery he remembers, and takes a different bus each day from the nearby bus stop. Day after day after day, X is led down a different route, and he does this for a whole week until he gets on the right service.

"Maru, on the other hand, is the total opposite. He's stuck in his home, and he doesn't step out of it. We learn that he is a hermit, but never why. The readers just have to accept it. All his food he gets from his parents, who feed him every day and demand nothing more from him. But Maru is traumatised, however, by this constant barking from his neighbour's dog—he can hear this constant yapping and barking through the walls, and it drives him insane, like totally loco. So much so that he starts dreaming of ways to kill it."

"Oh wow," I said.

"Uh huh, uh huh. There are these long scenes that Maru comes up with, yeah, of tying the dog up and muzzling it and feeding it bad things to make it throw up. It's horrible."

"It does sound that way."

"But then!" says Ahab, "it turns out that all of these plans were in fact the ways in which he's been torturing *himself*. He's been killing himself the whole time, in all those cruel and horrible ways he described. Maru's the 'dog', basically, in the house that he lives in. He's the metaphorical pet that his parents have been keeping and sheltering from the outside world, for the past however-many years of his life."

I felt impressed. Ahab's enthusiasm was rubbing off on me. I asked him who the author was, and whether any of her works had been translated yet. He said her name was Chiba Mari.

"She *must* have been translated," he said. "She's an award-winner and everything."

I picked up the book. I flipped through its pages; Ahab only had a few chapters left to the end. I then closed the book, and stared once more at its cover. Under the light of the coffee shop, I could spot a couple of indents on the jacket, spelling out the title of the novel.

"I know the first character," I said to Ahab. "It stands for 'sky' in Chinese." I set the book back down. Ahab smiled and nodded.

"It also stands for 'empty'," he said.

The sky was red that night, as Zhiwei drove us down the road. He looked forward, and then looked to the side. He looked forward again. His left hand moved the wheel, seemingly of its own accord.

"You're just the same," I said to him.

Zhiwei smiled.

"I'm really not," he said to me.

He turned into an alleyway. It was a small, narrow kind of road, with shophouses standing on either side. Zhiwei had to drive slowly because there were people about, people with drinks in their hands and gas masks over their faces, shouting about the apocalypse. "The world's ending," one of them shouted at our car. The guy knocked on my window. "It's the end of the world, baby," he said.

Zhiwei found a parking lot by pure luck; the streets had been packed that night.

"Can you drink at all?" I asked Zhiwei.

"Just a little," he said.

"Do you drink often?"

"Define often." He laughed. "Come on."

He took me to a bar. It was in the courtyard of a shophouse, with tall white walls surrounding the space on all sides. The red sky was nothing but a large square above us, like a section of something unreal. Zhiwei went up to the bartender and ordered two pints of Guinness.

"You like this place?" I asked. We found a small bench by a corner, placed against one of the walls. House music played from the speakers.

"I come here with my friends," he said.

I cast a look around the courtyard.

"Who are your friends?" I asked. "I want to know."

He told me. They were a group of laidback guys, guys he had known from the army and from his modules at university. One of them had found out about this place, and the lot of them had frequented it ever since.

"We're not really into clubbing," Zhiwei said. "We much prefer sitting down."

I nodded.

"So you live in a condo near Potong Pasir?"

"Yep."

"Is it nice?"

"My family moved there," he said. "Shortly afterwards."

I didn't know what he was referring to.

"After what?"

"After us," he said. "After our night together."

"Ah," I said. "Okay." I scratched at an eyebrow. "It's been a long time."

"It has, yeah," he said.

There was a pause. We drank from our pints. I asked him if he was seeing anybody at the moment. Zhiwei shook his head.

"And you?" he asked. "Are you seeing somebody right now?"

I felt warmer, all of a sudden.

"No," I said to him. "I'm not attached."

"Are you busy with work?"

"You could say that," I said.

He asked if it was teaching. I told him it wasn't.

"That was just something I did for extra cash."

"Oh," said Zhiwei. "So what are you doing now?"

I smiled.

"Something else," I said.

Zhiwei smiled back at me.

"That's a coy thing to say, Ms Neo."

I let out a laugh. He laughed as well.

"Oh god," I said. "*Ms Neo*. It sounds so different coming from you."

Zhiwei kept on smiling.

"How do I say it differently?" he asked. I looked at him. He was looking right back at me.

"I had a boyfriend once."

"You did?"

I nodded.

"His name was Eric," I said. "He was a good guy. When he found out about my plans to start relief teaching, he started calling me Ms Neo. Ms Neo, Ms Neo, can I have your permission to go to the toilet, Ms Neo? Shit like that."

Zhiwei laughed again. And then he stopped.

"He *was* a good guy?"

I blinked. "Huh?"

Zhiwei paused for a bit. "The past tense," he said. "You're using the past tense."

"Oh," I said. "I'm sorry. He's not—he's not dead, or anything."

"Okay."

"He was involved in a car accident," I said to him. "Somewhere in Kota Bahru. Several cars, and one giant truck. His sister passed away."

"What?"

I nodded.

"Eric hasn't been the same since," I said. "He's still a good guy, though. He just became different."

"Right," he said. He looked at my glass. There was barely any stout left.

"Shall I buy you another drink?"

"Excuse me?" I said to him. I nearly laughed again. "I'm the working adult here."

He shrugged. He was smiling at me again.

"I don't have to work for my money," he said. He stood up. "Hang on, all right?"

When he came back, the music had changed. It was a

slow beat: a rising sort of cadence, a chorally layered synth. Columns of sound. Some people rose from their seats and benches, and some even began to dance. They danced beneath the section of the sky, burning red above them all. Zhiwei came over, with a new pint of Guinness in his hand.

It was a big sort of hand. It was wide and smooth, with fingers twice as large as your own. It was a hand you could hold on to and then let go of, just as easily. It was a hand larger than my own.

●

Ahab came round to my place in his Honda Civic, on the twenty-eighth of June; it was two in the morning. He told me to hop in. "We're going to town," he said. "We have to hurry."

When I got in I asked him what the matter was.

"It's Noor," he said.

Ahab got onto the expressway. The roads were empty. The streetlamps, as tall as the trees, bathed the roads in an orange, unearthly light. Ahab's gaze remained focused on what lay ahead. We still had a while before we got there.

"So have you finished the book?" I asked.

"The what?"

"The Chiba Mari book," I said. "The one about the sky."

"Oh," said Ahab. "It's not about the sky, though."

"I know, I know," I said. "Last meeting you were only a few chapters from the end. Are you done with it now?"

"Yeah," he said.

"When?"

"This afternoon?"

"Wow," I said. "It's a good feeling, isn't it? Finishing a book."

"Best feeling ever," Ahab said. He kept his eyes locked forward. "You know, once I was on the train, and I saw someone finish a book right in front of my eyes. The look on the girl's face was priceless."

"That's nice," I said. I looked out of the window. "Would you recommend the book to me?"

"Sure, yeah," said Ahab. "I'd recommend it to anybody."

"But me, specifically?"

He took a quick glance at me. "Yeah," he said. "No problem. It'd probably take a while, though, for the English translation to be released. Unless you want me to spoil the story for you?"

"Are you talking about the ending?"

"Yeah," said Ahab. The car entered a tunnel. Bars of light passed over us, continuously, in a long belt over our heads.

"Probably not," I said to him. "You've spoiled me enough already."

"Have I?"

I nodded. "I don't want to know how the story ends."

We came out on Holland Road, and turned left towards Tanglin. Soon we got on to Orchard. It was the heart of town, but none of the usual lights were on. All I could see were tall trees, and even taller buildings. A soft and thick light, hovering in a soft mass, like a mist. Ahab stopped the car. There were no people on the sidewalk, save for one solitary woman, walking past Far East Plaza. She had a large T-shirt on, and barely anything else. The soles of her feet were black.

"Go talk to her," Ahab said to me. "I'll remain close by."

I got out, and closed the car door quietly behind me. It was so quiet, save for this sound in the background, like someone breathing over your ear. I stepped onto the sidewalk, and took one final look around. No other cars. No other people. I went up to Noor.

"Hi there," I said.

She didn't seem to have heard me. She turned her head to the right.

"Hey," she said. She took note of my presence, as though I had always somehow been there. "Hey, you."

Noor was moving slowly, one step forward a time.

"What are you doing out here?" I asked.

"Me?" Noor said. "I don't know. I don't know what I am doing."

"Do you know where you are?"

Noor stopped. She looked at the buildings around her. Clouded light, all around.

"Tell me where I am," she said.

"You're in Orchard."

"I am?" Noor said. "But nothing's how I remembered it."

"How do you remember it?" I asked. But Noor didn't seem to have heard my question.

"This is a dream," she said to me. "I am home. This is just a dream."

"A dream?"

She nodded.

"I am walking in my dream," she said. "I am always walking in my dreams. And I am always alone."

I looked over my shoulder. Ahab's car was only a few metres behind us.

"You're not alone," I said to Noor. "My friend and I are here to help."

Noor looked behind her as well. She smiled.

"This is a dream," she said. "I am alone. I don't need help if I'm in my dreams." She turned towards me. "Do dreamers need help?"

I looked back at her. I didn't know what to say.

"Let's keep walking, my dear." She beckoned me to follow. "Let's just keep walking."

For half an hour Noor and I walked, side by side, down the empty sidewalk of Orchard Road. We walked past Wheelock Place, past the roads on the junction; we walked past Ion and Isetan, followed by Ngee Ann City. The both of us just kept on walking, across the empty and quiet heart of the city.

I received a message on my phone. It was from Ahab. *Get her in the car*, it said.

"In the car?" Noor later asked. She turned behind once more. "Is that the one?"

"Yes," I said.

"Okay," she said. "Let's do that."

Noor and I got into the backseat of the Honda. Ahab locked the doors. He then stepped on the pedal, and started driving us back towards Bukit Merah, where Noor now lived. Noor sat by the windows and watched as the buildings went by, faster and faster and faster.

"All these trees," she said. "It's the trees that never change." She turned away from the windows.

"I know you," she said to Ahab. "I know the driver," she said to me. "Even with his mask on. He's been watching me, for quite some time. I see his face in the black windows."

"How do you know?"

She sniggered.

"He thinks I can't see him, but I can. I can always see him."

Ahab remained silent. I asked her if she knew how she had ended up in Orchard, of all places.

"Isn't it quite far from your parents'?"

"It is," said Noor. "It's just a dream, though. You fall asleep in your own bed, and then you wake up in a different place. That is what dreaming is all about." She turned back to the window. "Harry and I would go to Orchard all the time, back when we were still dating. Before we got married. It's the thing you do, if both individuals happen to be uncreative. You just meet up in town and find a place to eat."

A momentary silence settled over the car. We had just passed by Bukit Merah station.

"Don't you mean Henry?" I asked.

"What?"

"Henry," I said. "Don't you mean Henry, instead of Harry?"

A blank look passed over her eyes. She then coughed: it was a wet cough, full of phlegm. Her eyes began to water. Her clothes smelt faintly of ash.

"Ah," she said. "Of course. That's right."

I waited in the car, as Ahab guided Noor back to her parents' flat. When he came back, he patted me on the shoulder, and told me I had done a good job. I thanked him. It was almost five in the morning.

"I want to know now," I said to Ahab.

"Know what?"

"The ending," I said. "Would you tell me, please? Tell me how the story ends."

•

Madam Lim showed up at the coffee shop, unannounced, at the foot of Block 146. This took place the following Wednesday, on the third of July. There were others now, aside from the five old men, sitting at tables and eating their food. The haze crisis was nearly over.

"Good evening, Ms Neo," said Madam Lim. "It's been a while."

I took my seat. I wondered how she had learnt to find us. "Have you ordered a drink?" I asked.

"I got my coffee," she said in reply. "I took the liberty of ordering you something as well."

I asked her what she had gotten for me. She said she couldn't say; it was meant to be a surprise.

"I think you'll like it all the same," she said.

The drinks auntie came round. She gave Madam Lim a cup of kopi o po, and myself a bottle of Tiger beer.

"You're still young," Madam Lim explained. "You should drink more often."

I drank straight from the bottle. Madam Lim reached into her handbag.

"There's something I need you to give to Kevin," she said. She took it out: a notebook, bound in a simple black cover. She slid it across the table. "I'm assuming, of course, that you have yet to speak to him."

I took the notebook. It wasn't a thick sort of notebook, and it felt used, somehow—like it had gone through a lot with its owner.

"I haven't, admittedly," I said to Madam Lim. "I'm sorry."

"It's all right," she said. "That's perfectly all right." She took a sip of her kopi o po. "I know it's horrible to say this, Ms Neo, but I've slowly started to feel like myself again."

"Is that so?" I asked. Madam Lim smiled.

"We're nearly there," she said to me. She got up from her chair. Her coffee was barely touched. "All we need is one final push."

"Where are your parents?" I found myself asking. We were in Zhiwei's living room later that evening, looking towards his balcony. The view on the twentieth floor only went so far, before stopping altogether. A wall of fog remained standing between this world and the next. But the air, thankfully enough, had started to smell like air again.

He said his parents were at a wedding. "It's my mom's cousin's second son," he said to me. "It's not something I have to attend."

He brought two open bottles of beer from the kitchen.

"I told them about you, by the way."

I looked at him.

"You did?"

"Yeah," he said. "Just the more recent bit, though. I told them I was seeing an older girl."

I drank from my bottle. My second beer of the night.

"Is that what this is?" I asked.

He nodded. He drank as well.

"It is," he said.

Zhiwei and I looked at one another. He placed a hand on my cheek, and ran a thumb across the corner of my lips. I closed my eyes and felt the warmth of his palm, spread across the side of my face. When I opened my eyes again his face was just centimetres away from my own, and all I could feel was heat, the gentle brush of it, across my eyes, my nose, my cheeks. I laid a hand on his knee, and moved it upwards, across the length of his thigh.

We wrapped our arms around each other and kissed. I ran my hand over his shirt, and started undoing his buttons. He took off his glasses. He then lifted me, with both of his arms, and carried me to his bedroom. After we were done, his mouth was on my ear, his breath warm and moist on my earlobe.

"I thought I had enough," he said. "I really, really did. From back then till now, I thought my life was over."

Later that night, I woke. I glanced at the clock in Zhiwei's bedroom, mounted on the wall before us. It was nearly three in the morning. I slid out from under the covers; Zhiwei's chest rose and fell, locked in a deep, peaceful sleep. My heart was pounding.

I went out into the hallway. I made my way, quietly towards the kitchen. I switched on a light, and poured a glass of water to calm myself. As I drank I could hear sounds, vaguely, of what seemed like laughter, but didn't know where it came from. I took my glass and walked across the living room, sliding the door to the balcony open. Far below, down in the pool on the first floor, was a single white figure, floating across the surface of the water. Kevin flashed me a smile.

Come here, his smile seemed to say. I went back into the living room and grabbed my bag.

The lift arrived at the first floor. I stepped out into the cold, following the signs that led me to the pool. By the time I arrived, Kevin had lain himself across one of the deck chairs, his eyes tracking my every movement.

"Good morning," I said. I sat down beside him. He seemed to be shivering.

"Good morning, Ms Neo. Where's your friend?"

"What friend?"

"The one with the knife," he said.

"He's not here," I said. "He doesn't know I'm here." Laughter, I kept hearing; at the end of the pool was a Jacuzzi, in which a mother and child were playing. "Who are those people?" I asked. Kevin turned and looked at them, splashing about in the bubbling water.

"We live together," he said. "Although I'm sure you know that already."

I looked at him. His skin was marble white, and covered in black spots. A pair of gills flapped on the sides of his neck, sucking on the air every few seconds. Kevin continued to shiver.

"The mother is Su Lin," he explained. "Michelle's the child." He then turned away from them, and fixed me with his gaze. He seemed worried, somehow. "Don't ever breathe a word of this to anybody," he said in a whisper. "But you see, that girl…"

I nodded.

"I see it," I said.

He looked surprised.

"You do?"

I nodded again.

"Her child," I said. "The girl's soul is missing."

He fell silent. His mouth hung open, a small gap between the lips. He then closed his mouth. Kevin settled, still shivering, back into his chair.

"You do see, after all."

He turned back to the mother and child. They were laughing and screaming, at three in the morning, but nobody seemed to mind. Kevin asked if I knew why he had chosen to live with them. I told him I didn't know.

"You don't?" he said.

I shook my head.

"It's kinship, Ms Neo. Familial."

"How so?"

He paused.

"The three of us are waiting," said Kevin.

"Waiting?"

He nodded.

"We're waiting for a man," he said. "A man with a silver car. One day he'll come and pick us up. We'll see his lights, cruising down the main road."

"I see," I said, even though I didn't. I didn't know who he was talking about. I reached into my bag. "I met your mother earlier."

He didn't stir.

"You did?"

I took out the notebook.

"She wanted you to have this."

He blinked. Kevin stared at the notebook, and took it in his hands. He flipped it open, and turned the first couple of pages. It was mostly empty.

"Is this it?" he asked. He kept on flipping through the pages, right to the very end. It was all the same.

"No," I said. I placed my bag aside. "Your mother wants

you to know that she's been to Japan, many times over the past year. Even the bookstore, she says. And the hotel. She wants you to know that she understands everything now."

Kevin froze. He became absolutely still for a couple of seconds. Even his gills seemed to stop. A while passed before he finally closed the notebook: he laid it down, slowly, onto his lap.

"What else?" he said.

"She wants you to know that she gave birth to you. And that it was a hard and difficult labour." I paused. "She says that it's her fault that you don't have a soul."

Kevin blinked. He seemed confused, at first, unsure of what he was being told. And then he looked at the mother and child, playing in the Jacuzzi. And then he turned back towards me. I watched as an inexplicable calmness spread, slowly, across his features. The tension seemed to melt away, leaving behind a strange composure. He leant his head back against his chair, and then directed his gaze towards the sky.

"Is that everything?" he asked.

I told him it was. Kevin thanked me.

"You've been so helpful, Ms Neo."

He paused. He continued to look towards the sky.

"Do you know what's the first thing Su Lin taught me?"

I said I didn't know. He smiled.

"It was something she'd told her husband, Michelle's father," he added. "She said to him, 'There's only one way by which you can leave this world, and that's the way you came in.'" He licked his lips. "For the longest time, her husband couldn't figure it out. And neither could I. I knew what she said—I understood what she meant—but I didn't know how it could apply to me."

He paused again.

"I know how this all ends, Ms Neo."

"You do?"

He didn't react. He remained silent. I waited a little while longer, before choosing to speak.

"Is this remorse, Kevin? Over what you did to Mr Haruhito?"

He looked at me.

"No," he said.

"Nothing at all?"

He didn't even blink.

"Remorse and regret are different things, Ms Neo."

"Right," I said. "I understand."

He looked away. He turned back to the sky.

"I've tried all kinds of ways. All kinds of methods. All on my own. I guess I was trying to preserve some sort of dignity, doing it myself—but none of it ever seemed to work. I don't know why. But thank you, Ms Neo. I think… I think I know of a way now."

I looked at him. The sky above showed no signs of changing, and yet he kept on looking. There was a row of palm trees, standing between the outer wall and the main road. Kevin and I remained seated, unmoving, as Su Lin and her daughter continued to play.

"Do you hear that, Ms Neo?"

"Hear what?" I asked.

Kevin continued to smile. "Music," he said.

8

THE KAPPA QUARTET

SEPTEMBER 2013

KEVIN

When I close my eyes, I can hear the song of a bird, calling out towards me. It is a sweet and gentle song, like a hello one hears in the morning, when the weather is still cool and the sun half-risen. I remember hearing a bird like that, whenever I visited my father as a kid: it was hidden, in the midst of a tree standing outside his window. Sometimes I'd sit on his bed and gaze at the view, just listening to its cry.

"It's beautiful, isn't it?"

"Hmm."

My father's voice was strained. "I only hear it, whenever someone special visits me. Someone important to me."

"Oh, really?"

He smiled. "Do you know what I mean by important?"

I shook my head. I told him I didn't know.

My father grabbed the front of his gown, and wiped his

face with it.

"Something will happen," he said, "on the day that you die."

I closed my eyes.

"What is it?" I asked.

"You will meet with four important people," he said. "Four important individuals. And each one of those individuals will help you move on."

"Move on to what?"

My father shrugged. "I don't know," he said.

I've been thinking a lot about my father, lately, and what he said about the four people I would meet. It's been years since he passed away, and I had dismissed it as ramblings at the time. And yet these days, as I inch closer and closer to my own death, I find myself wondering if there is any truth to his claim.

According to my father, it runs in the family. When his grandaunt died, her four children surrounded her, each one with a hand on her body. The night before his second cousin died in her sleep, she said she'd been dreaming of lovers past: Wei Kiat, Navin, Boon, and Ah Xiang. And on the day my grandfather died, he said he had seen his wife, holding hands with his childhood friend, a man he hadn't seen in thirty-six years. Later he had a vision—a hallucinatory fit of some sort—in which he saw his older brother, dragged out of the house by a Japanese soldier. The soldier didn't shoot him: he'd just wanted to hear a man plead for his life. And then my grandfather had his stroke.

I don't know whom my father saw on the day he passed away. My mother and I were home that morning, silently watching the news. We were still waiting for the cab to come round.

●

Alvin and I went to the bookstore, earlier today. The dusk had settled over Nakameguro, over its bare trees and neat hedges—over the river itself, lying low and waiting in the canal. On the opposite side stood a block of flats, its east-facing windows and balconies thrown open to the breeze. Alvin asked if I had found the right place, and I told him that I had. It was just different now.

I looked through the windows. The café was warm, and bright, and I could see the counter, stocked with cakes and pastries on display. Placed at the back was a coffee machine, all coppery and brass in the honey light. A bell rang as the door swung open—and I could hear music, coming from inside the café. It spilled out the same way light does, in sharp swathes across the sidewalk.

Holding the door open was a waitress. She had a wide forehead, and was pleasant looking, and seemed to be about the same age as I was. A slight frown had creased her forehead as I asked, in English, if we were at the right place for the address.

"Yes," she said, haltingly. "This is café."

"Okay," I said. The word *Lisa* was printed across her nametag. I asked Lisa if this café used to be a bookstore. She bit her lip.

"I'm so sorry. I don't—I don't know…"

There was a pause. I looked at Alvin, and Alvin looked back at me. During that pause, neither Alvin nor I did anything, unsure as to what our next step should be. Lisa then asked if we would like to come in anyway. Alvin smiled, and said that we would like to. "It'll be nice," he said, with a hand on my back. "Let's do this."

Lisa brought us to a table, situated in a far corner of the café. Alvin and I took our seats. There was an empty space in the centre, in which stood a piano, a drum set and a double bass. Lisa walked away and returned with the English menu, followed by a poster of two men and two women. The four of them stood under a headline, typed out in bold: *The Kappa Quartet.*

"Playing soon," Lisa said. She placed her finger on the taller of the two men, the one holding a saxophone. She said the guy was her friend. She giggled. "This is my friend," she said again.

Fifteen minutes later, the Kappa Quartet began to play. The four members had been seated beside the piano the whole time, chatting to one another, warming up for the upcoming set; when it was time they rose and took their positions, to a smattering of applause. Lisa came back with our orders just then, placing our drinks on the table.

"My friend," said Lisa for the third time. She held the tray close to her chest. "That is my friend."

Their first song was a slow tune, soft and easy: it was an atmosphere, I realised—an ambience they sought to enhance. You could slip in and out of the music, whenever you chose to, and yet you found yourself changed by it somehow, little by little over time. It was that kind of song. When I looked over at Lisa, I saw how an unknown yet delicate quality had smoothed over her features, lending her a softness, a comfort

I had never seen in a person before. I found myself staring at her, for as long as I could, until she walked away again, off to serve another table. Her friend continued to play.

I kept my eye on her for the rest of the evening. In my head, we had entire conversations, in languages neither of us understood. When she came by again she attended to an elderly couple, seated two tables away, and the three of them murmured amongst themselves, out of respect for the players. I turned my attention to Alvin. Alvin looked the same as he had the last time; he hadn't changed at all over the past two years. Earlier he'd ordered a flat white, and said he wanted nothing else.

"I'm not hungry," he'd said to me. "I don't want to eat anything."

There was a round of applause. *Thank you*, the pianist said, speaking into a microphone. *Domo arigatou*. The café was getting full now, crowded even, as dinnertime approached its peak. According to the poster, the band would play again at nine, for their second set of the evening: *John Coltrane*, it was written on the poster. *A Love Supreme*. But the ongoing first set, it seemed to me, featured the Quartet's original compositions.

The band started their next song. First, the piano played a series of chords; the drummer then joined in, gentle on the snare; Lisa's friend, the saxophonist, remained quiet as the double bassist started to strum. His turn would come soon, undoubtedly, but for now their music reverberated, along a single, rippling, unified plane.

"Do you listen to jazz?" I asked Alvin. He said he didn't. "Do you?"

I shook my head.

"They're good though, don't you think?"

"Yeah," he said. "They're very good."

I spied one final look at Lisa. She was now at a fair distance, looking at the Kappa Quartet play, from her place behind the counter. She seemed comfortable, somehow, hiding in the shadows. And yet her face had a way of catching the light, in a way I couldn't explain. At that moment I realised that there are people out there who look like love, and then there are others for which love looks just like them. The difference was unmistakeable. Alvin asked what I was looking at, about halfway through the third song—and I said I was looking at something, but not particularly anything. He said okay.

Mr Five arrived a while later. The band had disappeared after their first set was over: they'd left their instruments and scores behind, and made a quick exit behind the counter. A burst of applause had escaped from the kitchen, just seconds before the door swung shut, and the café filled up once more with banter, with conversation, as waiters and waitresses went round to every table, placing a lighted candle on each.

A bright yellow orb flickered in every flame. At the front of the café was a large window, with a wide view of the street outside, but the scenery was barely visible at night: all I could see instead was another café, a ghostly café just like this one, with the tables arranged around a clearing in the middle. The people in that café floated above the river, amongst the branches of the trees, their smiling faces hovering over the canal. And everywhere in that window was a dark fog, pressing on all sides, framing the lovely scene. And then the bell rang—the door swung open—and the vision of that café disappeared. It was all just an illusion.

A man walked into the café. Lisa followed closely behind him. He wore an ivory-coloured three-piece suit, and a wine-coloured tie to match. Alvin and I watched as he made his way towards us, in a manner both slow and purposeful. He moved as though time hardly mattered to him at all.

"Good evening," said Mr Five, coming to a stop beside our table. "The both of you look very lost."

Alvin and I got into the backseat of his car. Mr Five had parked in the basement lot of a nearby building complex, and he had to follow the signs, pointing the way to the exit: he turned and turned, until he got us on the road. It was the same silver Lexus as before, roomy and yet somehow nondescript. Alvin said something about boxes, and Mr Five merely smiled.

"Do you have everything?" he said. "Everything you need?" He then paused: he was waiting for an answer. I took a quick glance at Alvin's bag, placed between his knees.

"We do," said Alvin. "Everything's with us."

"That is good," said Mr Five. He made a turn to the right. "Would either of you mind if I played music from the radio?"

"I don't mind," said Alvin.

"And you?"

I told him me neither. "It's your car, Mr Five," I said.

Mr Five smiled once again. He kept his eyes on the road before him. "It is my car, indeed. But tonight I am merely the driver."

Alvin and I remained quiet. The both of us knew what he

meant. With one hand still on the wheel, Mr Five reached an arm out, and slowly adjusted a dial. The music started and stopped, as he scrolled past the various stations: a split second of a pop song—a split second of a commercial—a split second of laughter, over what I would never know. Finally, he let go of the dial. Classical music started to play.

"Do you recognise this?" he asked.

There was no reply.

"It's Wagner," he said. "*Tristan und Isolde*."

A few minutes passed. The car sped down the expressway, with hardly a moment for pause. All was silent in the car, except for the music: the music rose and swelled, as the drama began to climb. Nothing seemed capable of stopping the music from growing—it surged, richer and clearer from the radio, demanding more and more from the listener, from the players, from life. I wanted to thank Mr Five, for planning the music somehow, even though I knew there was no way he could have timed it so perfectly. But the words left my mouth. According to Mr Five, what we'd heard was only just the prelude.

"The rest of the opera is five hours long," he said. "So this is only just the beginning."

I nodded. "Do you remember how we met, Mr Five?"

"I do," he said. "At the corner of a bookshop."

I smiled.

"And tonight we meet again."

Two hours later, I saw the hotel. At first I saw a small light, then a bigger light, and eventually an entire building, the Hotel Koryu, as the car coursed its way down the road, in and out of the tunnel. It stood brilliantly against the night, amidst the trees of the hillside: you could see every single one of its windows, casting light onto the roadbed. A coach bus was parked on the other side of the car park, from which a group of tourists alighted. They clambered onto the gravel, one by one, and made their way to the hotel.

In the corner of the lounge was the fireplace, burning quietly on its own. A number of guests ambled about, to and from the dining hall, the public baths. Alvin and I stood behind Mr Five as he spoke to the manager, explaining to her the situation. He then turned around.

"You have a room on the fourth floor," he said. "These are the keys that you will be needing."

Alvin took hold of them.

"Thank you," he said.

"You are welcome, Mr Alvin."

Alvin then thanked the manager, standing behind the front desk. The manager merely smiled, and bowed towards us both. Mr Five chuckled.

"A moment ago she told me a very curious thing. Apparently it is the first time my acquaintances have ever returned to this hotel."

"Really?" said Alvin.

"Yes," said Mr Five. He appeared wistful. "It has never happened before, according to her memory. Usually they leave and never come back."

There was a pause. Mr Five then turned towards me, and extended a hand.

"This will be the last time you and I will ever meet, Mr Kevin."

I took his hand. I looked straight into his eyes as I shook it. "Thank you, Mr Five."

The man smiled. He didn't let go of my hand, but instead continued to hold on to it.

"I will remember you. Always. Farewell, my friend."

Our room was a small one, with just enough space for the two of us. Alvin set his bag down beside the television, and started laying out the futon. I went over to the closet and slid open the door. There were two sets of yukatas, hanging on the rack.

"Look at this," I said, taking them out. "One for each of us."

Alvin and I changed out of our clothes, and put on the robes. They were both yellow, patterned with morning glories.

"You look nice," Alvin said. I smiled at him.

"You look nice too," I said.

The two of us stepped out of our room. We locked the door behind us. We were on the top floor of the hotel, its hallway both long and spacious. There were only rooms up here. A window stood at either end, through which you could see nothing but black. How familiar. Alvin turned towards me.

"What do you want to do?" he asked.

"Let's take our time," I said.

He smiled.

"Let's do that."

Alvin and I walked down the hallway, from one end to the next, from the fourth floor to the first. I ran my hand across the walls as we did so, over every door we passed by. I told myself to remember every touch, every sensation, every change in feeling. I told myself to take in every detail, every scene, every moment to carry over.

We were down on the first floor when Alvin said that he wanted to use the baths.

"You don't mind, do you?"

I shook my head.

"How long will you take?"

He said he wouldn't be long. "What will you do while I'm away?" he asked.

I gestured towards the resting area.

"I'll be here waiting," I said.

I stood and watched him go. The curtain swayed as he disappeared. I then turned around, and made my way towards the vending machines. There were six of them, big ones, standing in one long row. There was a sign towards my right, and I saw a woman standing there with her arms crossed.

"I can't decide," she said.

I turned back to the vending machines.

"Me too," I replied.

The woman shook her head. She was olive-skinned, with long and curly hair, which she had tied in a large bun over her head. She had large breasts, as well as wide hips, and so her yukata didn't fit her properly. I guessed she must have been part of the tour group I'd just seen, earlier from inside Mr Five's car.

"I think I'll go with coffee," she said.

"That's nice."

She turned towards me.

"And what will you have?"

I looked at the vending machine before me.

"I don't know," I said.

The woman grew silent. She then tilted her to head to the side, as she tapped her lip with a finger. "Maybe I won't go with coffee after all," she said in a soft murmur.

For the next minute or so, neither one of us said a word. And neither one of us made a move. Eventually I said, "I think I'll go with milk."

The woman grinned.

"Me too."

I popped a few coins into the vending machine, and watched as my bottle fell down with a clang. The woman followed suit, ordering a bottle from the exact same brand. The two of us then made our way towards a large sofa in the middle of the resting area, and popped open the caps. We took our first sips together.

"I'm Kevin, by the way."

"Hi, Kevin," the woman said. "Where are you from?"

"Singapore."

"Ah," she said. "My friends and I spent quite a while there, when we were younger." She paused, briefly. "My name's Ana."

"Hi, Ana."

She smiled.

"It's spelt A-N-A, in case you were wondering. There's only one N."

I asked her why. Ana shrugged.

"My parents were hippies," she said. "They actually lived in a commune, for a significant period of time. They only time my mother didn't smoke pot was when I was in her belly. After she gave birth to me, the commune collectively decided that I should be named after an artist."

"Wow."

Ana shrugged again. "Do you know Ana Mendieta?"

I shook my head.

"She died," she said. "Fell from the window of her apartment. This happened about a week before I was born."

Both of us drank again.

"What kind of art did she do?" I asked.

"She was a performance and conceptual artist," Ana replied. "She'd use dirt to make these amazing, life-like sculptures. She used blood as well, animal carcasses too. She was obsessed with that kind of thing. With mortality. With Mother Nature. She'd burn these objects made in her likeness, and then film the entire process."

"And are you an artist as well?"

She smiled, somewhat sadly.

"I'm not, I'm afraid. Sorry to disappoint. I tried to be, in the past, but I'm just not cut out for it."

"Why not?"

She laughed.

"Don't make me answer that question, young man."

"All right. It must be strange," I said, "to be named after something you're not."

Ana's smile grew sadder.

"I don't know," she said. "I don't know what they were thinking, to be honest. Naming me after someone who had just died."

There was a pause. We stared at the bottles of milk in our hands.

"I'm sorry," I said. "I didn't mean to hurt you."

Ana shook her head.

"You did nothing, young man. I've been hurt before."

There was another pause. For a moment we simply watched the television screens before us, each one tuned to a different channel. There was an animal documentary on one. On another was a news item of some sort, of a car that had crashed into a tree.

"If I told you I was going to die tonight, would you believe me?"

Ana looked at me.

"I would. But does it have to be tonight?"

"I suppose so," I said.

"Hmm. Why not wait till the dawn?" asked Ana.

"The dawn?"

"Yes," she said. "The dawn."

"But why?" I asked.

"Well, I'd hate to die in the dark," she said. "Call me strange... but I believe that whatever you see last you will continue to see, forever and always, for the rest of eternity. The last thing you do will determine how you'll spend it."

"You believe in eternity?" I asked.

She smiled again.

"Young man," she said. "Death is a clock with no hands."

Ana took another drink from her bottle. I did the same with mine.

"I've attempted suicide before," she said. "Multiple times. I tried once, when I lived in Singapore, but that didn't work. Nothing ever seems to work, no matter how carefully I plan it. I guess it's just nature's way of saying that my time has yet to come." She then stared once more at her bottle of milk, its contents now half-empty. "Do you think it's your time, Kevin?"

I nodded.

"You're my third person, today."

She looked up from her bottle.

"Your third person?"

"Yes," I said. "'On the day you die, you will come across four important individuals.' My father said that to me."

"Who was the first?"

"A waitress named Lisa."

"And the second?"

"A man with a silver Lexus."

Ana gave me a look.

"That's impressive."

I laughed.

"I suppose," I said. "It's a nice car."

Ana smile slowly returned.

"So who's your fourth?" she asked.

"My friend," I said. "He's taking his bath right now."

"I see," said Ana. "And how do you know he's your fourth?"

"He'll help me," I said. "He's the only one who can do it."

"I see," said Ana. "I believe you." She took a deep breath, and exhaled through her nose. "You will both wait, won't you? You and your Mr Four?"

"I will."

"Do you promise?"

"Yes," I said. "I promise."

Ana and I raised our bottles to our lips once more. This time we finished the remainder of our milk. We then set the bottles aside.

"Where are you from, by the way?"

She didn't answer me straightaway. She had a distant look in her eyes.

"Somewhere far away," said Ana. "Farther than you can imagine."

●

There is a smaller car park, located on the other side of the main road; a gravel path extends from a corner, leading the way down to the lake. There are no sounds here, no stirring, no rustling. No waves lapping. Alvin and I sat on the shore, watching the water, as the pebbles crunched and buckled beneath our weight.

"Thank you for doing this," I said.

Alvin maintained his silence.

"You know, I've been reading this book, and it has this face on the cover. But on the face there's a cavity, like"—I pointed to my forehead—"right here."

He didn't even nod. Alvin simply watched the water. I tried to watch it as well, but then I realised—I couldn't. There was no light.

"I killed a man once," I said.

He sniffed. "You did?"

"Yes. Though he didn't die right away."

He asked me how. I looked at my hands.

"I reached into him. Deep inside. And then I took out his soul."

Alvin said nothing more for a while. I could barely see him

in the night, huddled against his knees. All I could see was a gleam, a glimmer, the wet light in his eyes. In the darkness he asked me, softly, how it had felt back then—to hold a soul in my own hands—and I said I didn't know. I said I couldn't tell. A soul was something I could feel, but couldn't see. It was something I could hold, but would never have.

I asked him if he still remembered that dream I once had, and Alvin said yes, he did. He hadn't forgotten a thing: the pool, the floating. The silence. "That's where I shall be," I said to him. "That's where I'm going to next." Into the company of love I shall return.

•

I lower myself into the lake. Alvin asks if I am ready, and I tell him to wait. "Just wait," I say. "Just wait."

This is the part where waking turns to sleeping. The light changes. Things wane, and then brighten. I can see the water now, and how blue it has become. I see the sky too, watch it change before my eyes. I see the low stretch of cloud, spanning over my head. Surrounding me are the low-lying mountains, tinged by a wash of pale fire.

Alvin lifts my head. He wraps my neck with cling film, layering the plastic over my gills. He twines it, repeatedly, until the film is finished. It's excessive, but I don't blame him. A while passes before I begin thrashing, but he is holding me still. He's holding me still with both of his arms, and he's telling me it's okay. "It's okay," he keeps saying. "It's okay. It's okay." And then the light changes again, just one more time—and at first I see nothing; I see everything; I see nothing at all.

NOTES & ACKNOWLEDGEMENTS

The epigraph was taken from the album liner notes to John Coltrane's *A Love Supreme*.

"There is this world, and then there is another … the way by which you came, baby": Su Lin's words to Alvin were paraphrased from Akutagawa Ryunusuke's novel *Kappa*.

"… there's Bill Murray in one shot and Scarlett Johansson in the next": this is a scene from Sofia Coppola's film *Lost in Translation*.

The idea of the specialist (or "*senmon-ka*") is taken from Nisio Ishin's light novel series *Monogatari*.

The teenager's dream in Chapter 3 references Kinji Fukusaku's film *Battle Royale*.

"I saw the summer come once…I won't ever forget it", "I've only ever seen the spring once, and I would never forget it": this refrain originates from the opening line of Marjorie Barnard's short story, "The Persimmon Tree".

The poster in Perdido boasts a direct lyric from the song of the same name. The hotel Takao later mentions to Lisa is the Furusato Kanko Hotel, which filed for bankruptcy in October 2012.

The "Blue Room" is a reference to David Hare's play, *The Blue Room*.

Kitchen Town is known as "Kappa-Bashi"; while it is not known what the "Kappa" actually refers to, the street has taken advantage of the homophone, and officially adopted the mythical creature as its mascot.

The manga Ahab describes throughout Chapter 6 is "The Enigma of Amigara Fault", a one-shot collected in Ito Junji's *Gyo*.

The paperback Kevin reads in Chapter 7 (and which he later mentions in Chapter 8 to Alvin) is Oscar Kiss Maerth's *The Beginning Was the End*.

"Into the company of love I shall return": a paraphrase of the final line of Robert Creeley's poem, "For Love".

●

I would like to acknowledge and thank the following people for reading my novel, at its various stages of development: the novelists David Peace and Ian Sansom; friends from Warwick University; members of the Image-Symbol Department, in particular Tse Hao Guang and Prabu Daveraj; Amanda Lee Koe and Samuel Caleb Wee of the Sunday Snooker Girl Gang, whose detailed feedback and support I have found utterly invaluable; and of course Daryl WJ Lim, Sophia Schoepfer and Wong Yiping, the precious three who'd been there when I only had the first half of the novel written down, and needed a push to carry on with the second. I can't thank you guys enough.

Finally, I would like to thank the team at Epigram Books—to my editor (and mentor), Jason Erik Lundberg; my designer, Allan Siew; and my publisher, Edmund Wee—for putting their faith in a manuscript like *Kappa Quartet*.

ABOUT THE
AUTHOR

Daryl Qilin Yam is a co-editor of the *SingPo WriMo* anthology series, a director at Sing Lit Station, and a stageplay producer at Take Off Productions. He holds a BA (Hons) in English Literature and Creative Writing from the University of Warwick, and spent a year studying at the University of Tokyo. His prose and poetry have been published in a number of anthologies and literary journals. *Kappa Quartet* is his first novel.

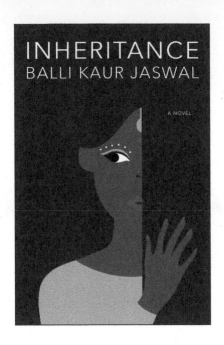

INHERITANCE BY BALLI KAUR JASWAL

- Winner of the 2014 Best Young Australian Novelist Award -

In 1971, a teenage girl briefly disappears from her house in the middle of the night, only to return a different person, causing fissures that threaten to fracture her Punjabi Sikh family. As Singapore's political and social landscapes evolve, the family must cope with shifting attitudes towards castes, youth culture, sex and gender roles, identity and belonging. *Inheritance* examines each family member's struggles to either preserve or buck tradition in the face of a changing nation.

ISBN: 978-191-2098-00-2
PUBLICATION DATE: May 2017

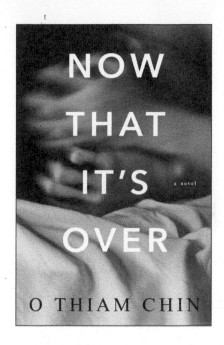

NOW THAT IT'S OVER BY O THIAM CHIN

- Winner of the 2015 Epigram Books Fiction Prize -

During the Christmas holidays in 2004, an earthquake in the Indian Ocean triggers a tsunami that devastates fourteen countries. Two couples from Singapore are vacationing in Phuket when the tsunami strikes. Alternating between the aftermath of the catastrophe and past events that led these characters to that fateful moment, *Now That It's Over* weaves a tapestry of causality and regret, and chronicles the physical and emotional wreckage wrought by natural and man-made disasters.

ISBN: 978-191-2098-69-9
PUBLICATION DATE: July 2017

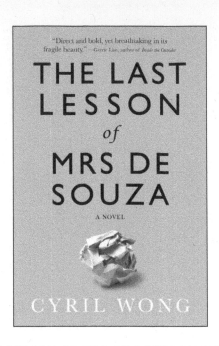

THE LAST LESSON OF MRS DE SOUZA BY CYRIL WONG

One last time and on her birthday, Rose de Souza is returning to school to give a final lesson to her classroom of secondary school boys before retiring from her long teaching career. What ensues is an unexpected confession in which she recounts the tragic and traumatic story of Amir, a student from her past who overturned the way she saw herself as a teacher, and changed her life forever.

ISBN: 978-191-2098-70-5

PUBLICATION DATE: July 2017

SUGARBREAD BY BALLI KAUR JASWAL

- Finalist for the 2015 Epigram Books Fiction Prize -

Pin must not become like her mother, but nobody will tell her why. She seeks clues in Ma's cooking and when she's not fighting other battles — being a bursary girl at an elite school and facing racial taunts from the bus uncle. Then her meddlesome grandmother moves in, installing a portrait of a watchful Sikh guru and a new set of house rules. Old secrets begin to surface, but can Pin handle the truth?

ISBN: 978-191-2098-66-8
PUBLICATION DATE: September 2017

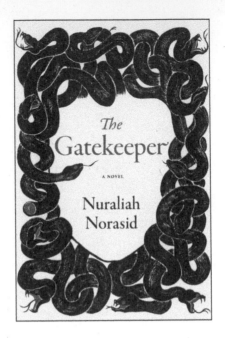

THE GATEKEEPER BY NURALIAH NORASID

- Winner of the 2016 Epigram Books Fiction Prize -

The Gatekeeper tells the story of a ten-year-old Gorgon girl named Ria, who petrifies an entire village of innocents with her gaze. Together with her sister, she flees the jungle of Manticura to the underground city of Nelroote, where society's marginalised members live. Years later, the subterranean habitat is threatened when Ria, now the gatekeeper, befriends a man from the outside.

ISBN: 978-191-2098-68-2
PUBLICATION DATE: September 2017

LET'S GIVE IT UP FOR GIMME LAO! BY SEBASTIAN SIM

- Finalist for the 2015 Epigram Books Fiction Prize -

Born on the night of the nation's independence, Gimme Lao is cheated of the honour of being Singapore's firstborn son by a vindictive nurse. This forms the first of three things Gimme never knows about himself, the second being the circumstances surrounding his parents' marriage, and the third being the profound (but often unintentional) impact he has on other people's lives. Tracing social, economic and political issues over the past 50 years, this humorous novel uses Gimme as a hapless centre to expose all of Singapore's ambitions, dirty linen and secret moments of tender humanity.

ISBN: 978-191-2098-67-5
PUBLICATION DATE: November 2017

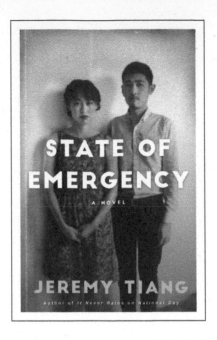

STATE OF EMERGENCY BY JEREMY TIANG

- Finalist for the 2016 Epigram Books Fiction Prize -

A woman finds herself questioned for a conspiracy she did not take part in. A son flees to London to escape from a father, wracked by betrayal. A journalist seeks to uncover the truth of the place she once called home. A young wife leaves her husband and children behind to fight for freedom in the jungles of Malaya. *State of Emergency* traces the leftist movements of Singapore and Malaysia from the 1940s to the present day, centring on a family trying to navigate the choppy political currents of the region.

ISBN: 978-191-2098-65-1
PUBLICATION DATE: November 2017